T0357143

THE LOSTING FOUNTAIN

LORA SENF

NEW YORK

UNION SQUARE & CO. and the distinctive Union Square & Co. logo are trademarks of Sterling Publishing Co., Inc.

Union Square & Co., LLC, is a subsidiary of Sterling Publishing Co., Inc.

ISBN 978-1-4549-5528-3 (hardcover)
ISBN 978-1-4549-5529-0 (paperback)
ISBN 978-1-4549-5530-6 (e-book)

Library of Congress Cataloging-in-Publication Data
Names: Senf, Lora, author.
Title: The Losting Fountain / by Lora Senf.
Description: New York : Union Square Kids, 2024. | Audience: Ages 14 and up. | Audience: Grades 10-12. | Summary: Told in alternating voices, three teens from different time periods are called to the world of the Fountain to restore balance and prevent its eldritch creatures from seeping into the real world.
Identifiers: LCCN 2024003365 (print) | LCCN 2024003366 (ebook) | ISBN 9781454955283 (hardcover) | ISBN 9781454955290 (trade paperback) | ISBN 9781454955306 (epub)
Subjects: CYAC: Fountains--Fiction. | Imaginary creatures--Fiction. | Fantasy. | Horror stories. | LCGFT: Fantasy fiction. | Horror fiction. | Novels.
Classification: LCC PZ7.1.S45 Lp 2024 (print) | LCC PZ7.1.S45 (ebook) | DDC [Fic]--dc23
LC record available at https://lccn.loc.gov/2024003365
LC ebook record available at https://lccn.loc.gov/2024003366

For information about custom editions, special sales, and premium purchases, please contact specialsales@unionsquareandco.com.

Printed in the United States of America

2 4 6 8 10 9 7 5 3 1

unionsquareandco.com

Cover design by Melissa Farris
Interior design by Rich Hazelton

Cover Images: Shutterstock.com: Deka Vision (hands); Dinkoobraz (moon, wolf); Eskova Ekaterina (centipede); ImagineerInc (mouth); Larch_tree (ink blot); Elina Li (birds); Mrs. Opossum (deer); My Stocks (claws); Sergey Pekar (landscape). Vecteezy.com: Alisa Aleksandrova (tentacles); Aliaksei Brouka (skull)
Interior images: Shutterstock.com: Dinkoobraz: 1; Elina Li: throughout; Sergey Pekar: 71
Page 339: "Nothing Gold Can Stay" by Robert Frost. Originally published in 1923.

For Jessica and Paula. You know why. I love your faces.

And for Kellie—I love and miss you always.

PART ONE

All the Losting Things 3

PART TWO

The Island 55

PART THREE

What Happened There 137

PART FOUR

The Fountain 255

EPILOGUE

Found 337

Content Warning available on page 347

PART ONE

All the Losting Things

THE fog makes it quiet and the filtered sunlight makes it strange.

With twisted trees, furtive, scuttling things and a muted palette of layered watercolor, it is an answer for some.

For others, a punishment.

Chapter One

Ember

(1913)

Ember sat a few feet from the well. Close enough to have a good view of it, but not so close she would get wet. She took off her heavy boots and socks and flexed her toes in the too-tall grass. She closed her eyes as tired limbs soaked up the bright morning sun. Temporary though it might be, a warm sort of peace filled her, and she breathed in as deep as she could, expanding her chest to offer it more room.

And she waited, but not for long.

Soft music filled her head, and Ember knew it was almost time. Her heart thrummed against her rib cage. She was excited and nervous, but also relieved.

She opened her eyes to see water spilling over the rim of the well and onto the thirsty ground. If Daddy had ever thought to ask her why the grass around the well was so green, Ember could have explained it to him. Not that he would believe her. If Ember was looking for a punishment, telling Daddy about the well would be the quickest way to get there. Daddy didn't suffer crazy.

The water poured out as it rose beyond the confines of the well. A pale, sharp-nailed hand reached over the edge. It was followed by a second hand that seemed to be holding something tightly within.

The mermaid pulled herself into the light. Her hair and skin glowed silvered ivory. Her features had an unfinished quality, and reminded Ember of stones grown smooth from a lifetime spent under the running waters of a stream. Only her eyes were sharp, wide and turquoise. They seemed to really *see* Ember. No one else did that any longer. Hank had always seen her but, of course, he was gone now.

The mermaid's forearms rested on the lip of the well. Ember had never seen the visitor's bottom half, so she was not certain *mermaid* was an accurate word, but it was the best one she had.

Ember only ever saw the mermaid when she was alone at the well, and not every time. The mermaid only began visiting after Hank died the previous spring. But the music had been with Ember much, much longer. Stringed instruments Ember could not name played strange melodies, gentle and cool. The music came and went, unheard by all but Ember, and it always swelled when days at home were especially bad. On those restless nights, her own private orchestra played her to sleep.

"Hello, I'm glad you came back. I'm never sure you will. I just wish I knew who you are. Or why you're here."

The mermaid smiled. It had taken some time for Ember to get accustomed to that smile. The visitor's teeth were pearl white and needle sharp. And the inside of her too-wide smile was very, very red indeed.

Like a fish, Ember thought. *Like a beautiful, dangerous fish.*

The mermaid did not answer. She never did. But on this day, she responded by extending her clenched right hand out toward Ember. *Take it*, her eyes said.

Ember considered the sharp teeth in the broad smile, and thought perhaps she should be afraid. Cautious, at least.

But she was neither of those things.

Ember approached the mermaid and extended her own hand, palm up. The mermaid dropped something small and hard into Ember's hand, and then grasped that same hand with surprising strength. The girl and the mermaid held hands like that for a moment, a young woman's work-worn fingers against those of a cool, soft creature. They were close enough now that Ember could smell the minerals in the water that streamed out of the mermaid's hair and over her bare shoulders.

The music in Ember's head became a symphony.

Ember looked into the mermaid's ocean-colored eyes and saw in them sadness and compassion and something else, ancient and dangerous.

But still, she was not afraid.

Later, Ember would wonder what the mermaid saw in *her* eyes, and if whatever she saw there was the thing that made the mermaid sad.

With a squeeze, the mermaid released Ember and, as quickly as she had appeared, was gone. She slipped back into the well and back to wherever she was from. The water stopped running over, returning to its proper level. The music subsided, but did not disappear.

Ember looked at the object the mermaid had given her. It was a small stone, the size of a quail's egg, deep burgundy with silver streaks running throughout. The stone was cold and damp from the mermaid's touch.

Ember had received few gifts in her life, and this was by far the most special. It was not every day one received a present from an impossible friend.

Ember sat back in the grass, turning the stone over and inspecting it from every angle. As best she could tell, it was just a rock, albeit a pretty one. She would later notice no matter how much sun fell on it, or how long she held it in her hands—and she frequently would, even in her sleep—the stone never warmed.

It was a pretty rock. And a special one. And, soon, it would be important.

Chapter Two

Sam

(1989)

By the time he was fifteen, Sam had tried every way he could think of to escape.

He had dark hair and darker eyes, and skin that would have bronzed had it seen enough sun and fresh air. As a child, Sam rarely went outside and never left the neighborhood. Venturing beyond sight of his house resulted in bad things.

Sam and his mother lived alone in their neat, white house in their neat, suburban neighborhood. Everything about the house, and those around it, was modest but well-kept. Sam and his mother had three radios in the house, one in each bedroom and one in the kitchen. There was one television, a squat, heavy box in the living room. Mother had conceded to pay for cable. Though the picture wasn't always great, and it was expensive, Mother was determined Sam would have some exposure to the people outside their home. He might be better someday, or different, and would finally be able to join the rest of the world.

Once, when Sam was eight, he traveled nearly three blocks before the sounds became unbearable. They filled his head, then his marrow, then all the small in-between spaces he could not name. The sounds teemed and festered like a blackening infection.

He was forced to return to the center of his small world—to home and to Mother.

"To keep you safe. To protect you" was the only answer Mother ever had. She would put her hands in his hair and pull him close. But the house was still his cage, and his mother his captor.

When he was ten, Sam decided again to run away. With more than a half decade of practice, Sam had developed an exhausting but reliable control over the noises in his head. The farther he wandered from home, the harder it grew to keep a grasp on that control. The noises would gather, threatening at the edges of his mind, a mounting rumble just off his private horizon. He could not silence them, but he was learning to keep them back.

Eyes closed, Sam saw himself standing in the center of a vast, colorless landscape. He pushed against the sounds. Palms out, muscles straining, Sam would hold the sounds at bay. He knew they did not relent, and they did not surrender. But, for a while, the sounds would retreat, a swell against an invisible wall, only to later regroup and return like a flood.

Ten-year-old Sam made it to the Corner Mart a quarter mile from his house. He thought Mother didn't know. Through the front windows of the convenience store, Sam saw a mousy, doughy woman behind the rust-colored counter. Sam pushed through the door. Focused on nothing but keeping his mind clear until he could beg her for help, he did not anticipate what came next.

The clerk turned to him, opened her mouth just too far, and from her throat came a dislocated-jaw scream. For a long moment, Sam stared dumbly at her rotting back molars. His trance shattered when the few customers in the store stepped into the aisles, turned to face Sam and joined in the scream.

The sounds from his head had escaped and invaded the world around him.

Sam understood even as he fled. He knew it would be the same everywhere he went, with everyone he encountered.

Mother had added barbed wire to his invisible fence.

"To keep you safe. To protect you," was all she said when he returned home. She held him as he cried. She never struck him. She didn't have to.

In his eleventh year, Sam made frequent and irregular attempts at escape. They all ended badly. And Mother was always there to hold him after. He resented her affection, detested that he needed it.

Early one spring morning when he was twelve, Sam hid in the back of a neighbor's blue pickup. A few minutes after seven, the owner kissed his wife, grabbed his keys and lunchbox, started the truck, and drove toward the building site where he operated a small crane.

The driver and his stowaway made it nearly to the bottom of the half-mile hill, the highway beyond in sight, before stopping at a red light. While stopped, Kyle Mitchell suffered an aneurysm rupture and promptly died. Later, his young wife and two blond daughters would be inconsolable.

Horns blared. Soon, commuters left their own cars in the road to investigate, to help. Sam had time enough to take in the slumped corpse in the truck's cab before he snuck away from the scene, unnoticed in the growing chaos on the suburban street.

Mother was waiting for Sam when he got home. Tears and snot ran down his face as he told her about the dead man in the truck. He might have cried for Kyle, or for his young widow and her now-fatherless daughters but, in truth, he cried at the frustration of yet another failed attempt at freedom. All his years of isolation had made Sam determined and resourceful, but having so little contact with the world had stunted his empathy—concern for others had not had opportunity to take root in him and flourish.

She held him, but he believed it was only out of habit. He knew her patience and sympathy were waning.

Sam thought he understood her always, knew that Mother's only purpose was to keep him away from something he had not yet discovered. But would.

The death of Kyle Mitchell changed Sam's approach to escape. Murder meant there was no limit to what Mother would do to keep him. So he no longer fled. Instead, he isolated. And practiced. Even as he became paler and more withdrawn, he grew stronger in the ways that mattered. One day, he knew he was strong enough. Sam walked down to the end of his block and around the corner until home was just out of view.

The sounds crept up at the edges of his mind and then bounded toward him. Sam could feel their excitement, monstrous puppies ready to greet him at the front door. As soon as they appeared, Sam sat down on his neighbors' lawn under a large pine. At the same time, he sat in the bleak landscape of his mind. Eyes closed, he crossed his legs, rested his hands in his lap and waited. He did not push back. For the first time since he was small, Sam allowed the sounds to grope him with liquid fog fingers. They were everywhere around him, like the horn of a massive ship. His head was so full there was no room left even for fear.

Sam took a deep breath and thought, *We need to talk.* For a moment, fascinated silence. The sounds came together like smoke in a vacuum. Joining to form a vague figure, they sat in front of Sam, and hummed low and steady. The shifting plasma mimicked his shape and posture. They looked back at him, or seemed to. The Sounds tilted their undulating head, curious.

The cacophony Sam had lived with all his life pulled together to form words. *Brave boy. Interesting turn,* the Sounds said. *We are listening.*

Sam spent a lot of time watching television, especially sports. Especially baseball. He saw every game of the 1987 World Series, and even though it was not terribly exciting, he didn't miss an at bat. When the

Twins managed to win in seven games, it was pretty anticlimactic. The '88 series was better, if shorter, with Hershiser helping the Dodgers upset the A's in five quick games. Sam would be long gone before the '89 series wrapped up, and the A's rallied back from their loss the year before to beat the Giants 4–0, despite the earthquake that threw everyone off for a while. Thanks to sports and sitcoms and videos on MTV, Sam could have a conversation with almost anyone who happened to visit, and they would never guess he was a shut-in.

Because Mother worked all day, Sam was homeschooled in as much as he taught himself. Fortunately for both Sam and his mother, he was smart. Brilliant, maybe. Sam was able to complete his coursework, provided by a series of homeschooling manuals and textbooks, with few mistakes and in short order. As a result, all the drop-ins by the lady from the school district went well. Her notes indicated Sam was working at or above grade level and was polite, if a bit withdrawn. Her visits always ended with a reminder Sam was eligible to participate in extracurricular activities provided by the local schools. These suggestions were met by a gracious "thank you" from Mother, who promptly threw away the fliers emblazoned with school logos as soon as their guest was out the front door.

The summer before the earthquake rocked California and the A's won the series, Sam's mother died on his sixteenth birthday.

When Sam found his mother in her bed, it was clear she was gone. Her face, smooth and plump the day before, had sunken in around her cheeks and eyes. She did not look like she was sleeping. She looked dead. If she smelled like piss, well, Sam ignored it.

On the pillow next to her were two pieces of paper and a pen. The letter didn't say everything. There was so much his mother didn't know. But it told him enough. Reading that letter broke something fragile inside Sam and something new and harder was forged in its place.

He cried a short, violent torrent of tears. He cried for his mother, and he cried for himself. Sam's love for his mother had been contaminated by the circumstances of a life neither of them understood. But somewhere deep underneath the broken shards of an unrealized childhood, he was still a boy who loved his mother as only boys can.

Sam sat with her for a time, perched on the edge of the bed. He pushed her dark brown hair back over her forehead, off her closed eyes. Her skin, now gone sallow, was dry and cool. Her hand was stiff as he held it and pale on the top, but her palms were dark where the blood had settled. He kissed her on the temple and whispered, "I love you, Mommy." It had been years since he'd called her Mommy, but it was what she called herself in the letter, and he wanted to give that small thing to her. Sam wished he'd said it last night, or any other time, when she could still hear him. The regret he felt for words said and unsaid made his bones ache.

Leaving the room, Sam avoided Mother's vanity mirror. He looked too much like her, dark eyes and hair and quick-to-tan skin. They had been a matched set, even when neither of them wanted to be. He didn't want to see himself, alone, in the mirror where her reflection had always been. Sam pulled the bedroom door closed and did not return.

Sam packed a duffel bag with what he thought he might need, and the few things he wanted. Clothes, a toothbrush, a blank journal his mother had given him, and the pen she had written the letter with. He included what cash he knew was in the house, and other mostly practical items.

He called 911 from the phone in the kitchen. His mother had a heart attack, or a stroke maybe. He was alone and needed help. While he waited on the steps outside the front door, he reread the letter. Sam creased it with care and put it in his pocket as the fire truck arrived.

Chapter Three

Miles

(Present Day)

Miles ran.

At seventeen, he wasn't as fast as some of the guys on his cross-country team, but his stamina made up for it. Miles could run longer and farther than anyone in the district. This year, he hoped, longer and farther than anyone in the state.

On a bright Saturday morning in April, Miles ran the three miles to his high school. The crisp spring air made for perfect running weather, and running was a good warm-up for the two hours of swim practice to follow. He left home earlier than necessary so he could be the first in the pool. If Miles was a strong runner, he was a stronger swimmer. He was an okay-to-good student but not great, and he hoped swimming or running or both would help him get into—and maybe help pay for—a decent university.

As he passed the wooded park halfway between home and school, Miles saw a woman standing in the trees. Her hair was matted and greasy, and the heavy coat she wore hung on her shoulders as if she had borrowed it from a much larger person. He couldn't tell if she was staring at him or through him, but despite a cold unease that urged him to run faster still, he raised a hand in greeting as he approached her.

She did not wave back, though he could feel her flat, too-dark eyes follow him as he passed.

The chill that crawled down the back of his neck was soon forgotten as he focused on the road ahead.

There was just one car parked in the school's back lot, and it belonged to Coach, which meant the door to the gym would be unlocked.

"Morning!" Miles called as he walked through the locker room. He stripped down to his swimsuit, threw his stuff into a locker, grabbed a towel off the rack, and headed toward the office in the back corner.

"Hey, Miles." Coach met Miles in the doorway of the office and handed him a large key ring. "Go open up. I'll be there soon. If you start before I get there, I don't want to know about it."

They both knew Miles wouldn't wait for Coach, or for another swimmer, before he got in the pool. It was a rule they had silently agreed to ignore long before.

Miles unlocked the heavy door to the pool and walked through without flipping on the lights. He inhaled, filling his lungs with chlorine-scented air.

The door shut behind him, leaving Miles alone in a black and windowless room.

The door had never closed behind him before.

With a certainty that froze him in place for a beat, Miles knew he was not alone.

The light switch was next to the door. Next to whoever had closed it.

Miles had only a moment to consider if it was one of the guys playing a not-very-inspired prank when the muttering started and his adrenaline spiked. Miles gently wrapped his fingers around the keys in his hand to prevent them rattling. Instinct directed him to make no sound.

The voice was low, and the man seemed to be speaking to himself. The unintelligible words a rapid string without pause. That voice was enough for Miles to know he shared the room with a madman.

Silent on bare feet, Miles took slow steps backward to make space between himself and the man at the door. The muttering became urgent gibbering, but the man seemed to stay in place. The smell of something wet and rotten and sick filled the air, and that smell scared Miles as much as anything.

For the first time in his life, he was so afraid he was trembling.

Come on, Coach. Comeoncomeoncomeon! Miles thought the words as loudly as he could.

He managed another dozen steps back. The voice grew louder and became something just short of a yell. And then the man began to move toward Miles.

Even in the lightless room, Miles knew the man was unsteady. The sounds of the stranger's feet on concrete alternated between dragging and thumping, his hard-soled shoes squelching with every step.

It was that bizarre realization, that the madman was wearing wet dress shoes, that pulled Miles out of his fright and shoved him into action.

There were about ten feet between the pool and the wall. Gambling his instincts were right, Miles dropped the towel and pushed himself against the wall. With one hand extended in front of him, he took off at a hard run toward the door. If he could get around the limping man, he might make it out before the stranger caught him and . . .

And what?

Before he could answer that question, Miles's fingers brushed the light switch. He meant to open the door, but his hands instinctively flipped the switch.

The room flooded with flickering, fluorescent light.

Miles saw many things at once.

The man was dressed in a button-down shirt that had once been white, but was now grey and stained with filth. He wore dark slacks and, as Miles suspected, black dress shoes. Everything he had on was faded and dingy and thin with age. He was gaunt, his flat eyes buried deep in their sockets. The skin on the man's face, waxy and almost as grey as his shirt, sagged off his skull as though it had once fit but no longer did.

Because he's dead, or is supposed to be. It couldn't be true, but Miles knew it was all the same.

And the man was soaking wet. Water dripped from his hair and his clothes onto the concrete. A trail of water led from the pool to the place the man had been standing behind the door. There was no shallow side to the pool; it was six feet deep from one end to the other. For reasons Miles did not have time to consider, the fully dressed should-be-dead man had taken an early-morning swim.

It was then that Miles saw the pool was cloudy and brackish, not the clear water it should have been. It smelled not of chemicals but of shallow, pooled lake water left to putrefy in the sun.

His mind wanted to focus on that, needed to focus on it. To puzzle out why the water was dark and the chlorine smell gone, replaced with something dank. But he couldn't, because the man was still gibbering loudly, and he hadn't stopped moving toward him. Not when Miles ran past him, not when the lights came on, and not now. The only change was he now seemed to be addressing Miles rather than himself.

And the man had a length of pipe in his right hand.

Miles took it all in in a single moment. It was all he had time for. The man lumbered toward him. The man's legs moved out of sync, as though he wasn't accustomed to using them to stand upright, much less walk.

Miles was out the door and had it locked behind him before the man closed half the distance between them.

"Coach!" It seemed the word still echoed when the older man burst out his office door.

"What? You okay?" Coach rushed toward Miles.

"Yeah. No. There's a man in there. All wet. And a pipe." Miles couldn't control his words.

"A man? At the pool?" Coach moved swiftly from worried to furious. He reached out to unlock the door.

The yelling from behind the locked steel door stopped. Silence sliced the air like a clean blade.

Miles grabbed the older man's wrist, and whispered, "Don't."

"If there's a guy in there, I'm damned well getting him out."

And then the silence exploded into a brittle, tremulous scream. The steel door shuddered in its frame as the man on the other side threw his body against it.

"Don't. It's one of *them*."

Coach drew in a slow breath as the color drained from his face. When he spoke, his words were slow and deliberate. "Are you sure?"

The thuds of flesh against the metal door stopped and was replaced by metal on metal. Miles understood the man was wielding the pipe he'd carried, attempting to bash his way out.

"Yeah. I'm sure."

"Call 911. I'll make sure no one comes out."

A thick, sickening thud came from directly behind the door. The thud was followed by a second. And then a third, wetter and meatier than the last.

Miles dialed 911 and told the operator that, yes, he was sure. It was one of the strangers. And he was also pretty sure the man was beating himself to death with a long metal pipe.

Chapter Four

Selah

The silo stood tall and narrow and dank. It was furnished with a concrete floor. An iron ladder stretched up the south side. Three thick beams ran across the top, meeting the walls where they began to taper to a cone. She believed it was a grain silo, years past its useful life. Now, it only housed Selah and, occasionally, the men who kept her there.

And, sometimes, the girl.

Selah rested on the center beam, exhausted from beating her wings bloody against the walls of her prison. She had never been more mothlike, a moth in an overturned vase.

Dressed in a filthy mauve tunic and leggings, Selah had the appearance of a fine-boned girl of sixteen. Her ebony hair, normally tied tight at her nape, hung loose and tangled down her back. After a lifetime of bathing in silvered water, her pale skin shone pearl grey in the silo's ever-present shadows. Her wings, always so agile and quick, ached. Heavy and dull on her back, Selah thought they wouldn't carry her for long nor very far.

She was dangerous in her own way, but the men did not know that yet. All Selah had shown them was a frightened, trapped creature. The girl saw past the panic. The girl saw something more in Selah. She had to. Selah was counting on it.

Despite the men's assumptions, Selah was not an angel. She knew much of Heaven, but it was not her home. Selah was a refugee of the

Fountain. She had fled the island it stood on, and all its promises and threats, to follow a trail she had not been certain would lead her anywhere but alone.

But here, at the end of the trail, in this forlorn and forsaken place, Selah had found something miraculous in the girl. A cool light. At least Selah believed her to be a cool light. She could not be sure unless she got closer, and if she were wrong, it would be done.

Selah had meant to fall from the Fountain's grace, but she did not mean to be caught. Falling and freedom were supposed to be one and the same.

The winged young woman woke from a half sleep, one in which she dreamed of moldering and unsought things, to the sound of men's voices. She peered down from above the beams, her movements mimicking the shifting shadows. She did not want the men to know she was awake, much less that she was aware enough to study them.

Selah thought they must be brothers. They had the same hard eyes and square jaws, but the older was small and wiry where the younger was tall and broad.

"She looks tired," said the older of the two men. In her days in the silo, Selah had learned he was called Paul.

"She looks dead," said Joe, the younger man.

"She's not dead, stupid. She's still up there, isn't she?"

"Maybe. Still . . . She still looks dead to me. Or like she's dyin'."

"Not sure angels can die," said Paul. He reached up for his brother's shoulder. Another kind of man would have done it to calm and support them both. Selah believed that for Paul, it was a small gesture of control.

The two men talked on while the girl stood silent in the doorway of the silo, forgotten by the men, watching and listening as the evening light faded. Selah had not forgotten her, not for a moment, but as the men never called the girl by name, Selah did not know it.

THE island is at the center of a lake, one not much larger than a large pond, sometimes not much smaller than a small sea.

The Fountain is at the center of the island.

The Fountain is everywhere. And nowhere at all.

Chapter Five

Ember

The year after she lost her brother and gained a mermaid, the year she turned fourteen, Ember became invisible.

No one had ever told Ember about the opposite of love not being hate, but indifference. She knew it to be true, though. She knew it very well. Being ignored stung just a bit at first. Over time, and with enough repetition, it struck like a closed fist.

There was a time Daddy used his fists. That was before her older brother, Hank, died. Now, all the fight had gone out of Daddy. All that was left was apathy and meanness.

And Mama wasn't there anymore. She made meals, kept the house neat as a pin, and sent Ember to school with clean clothes, but that was all. While she did all those chores, and countless other thankless tasks, Ember's mother was gone. Not for lack of trying, Ember's daddy hadn't been able to beat the light out of Mama's eyes. It took losing her oldest child to land the final blow. After Hank, Mama shriveled up like a leftover party balloon in the summertime. Now she shuffled along the ground, deflated. Used up.

And after Hank, Ember lost the rest of the world at the same time she lost her family.

The few friends she once had drifted away, and if they were glad for some distance between themselves and Ember's sad life, they may not have even realized it. They let her go, just the same. Daddy wouldn't allow her to run around with them anyway, and she certainly couldn't invite anyone to the house. Ember figured she was as alone as any fourteen-year-old in the world.

The loss of Hank hurt like a jagged piece of steel in soft skin, twisted in and scratching bone. Being left and being alone hurt in a different sort of way, deep and dense.

After Hank, it didn't take long for Ember to make a decision. Choosing to be unseen was vastly preferable to being ignored, forgotten, and abandoned. Having experienced all three, Ember decided to become invisible. She found she was quite good at it. It took little time for her chestnut hair and green eyes and tall frame and strong shoulders and soft voice and huge, huge heart to fade into the crowds and corners of the spaces she moved through.

Being alone meant Ember had plenty of time to think, and she spent most of her time thinking about the maybe-angel in the silo. She wondered where the angel had come from and why she was there. Ember didn't understand why the angel, if that's what she was, didn't just magic herself out of the decrepit metal building. She didn't understand why God didn't reach down and help her. Help them both.

Mostly, she worried about what Daddy and Uncle Joe were going to do to the angel when they got their hands on her. And they would catch her. Given enough time, Daddy would get bored. Or frustrated. Or the meanness in him would win out. *That* filled her with a thimble full of boldness. It wasn't much, but maybe it would be enough.

Ember was not about to let an angel, or a whatever, be killed on her watch. She knew she had to do something. She also knew impossible things did not happen to girls like her, much less two impossible things at the same time. Which meant the mermaid and the angel had something to do with each other.

And since the mermaid never answered her questions, Ember would have to ask the angel instead.

Ember listened as the house put itself to bed for the night. She listened to the winding-down sounds of Daddy, Mama, and Uncle Joe. She heard Daddy get one last drink in the kitchen before shuffling up the stairs to sleep it off. She heard Mama run a bath. She heard Joe's truck-engine snores through the wall separating her bedroom from the one that once belonged to Hank.

When enough time had passed, and the house itself groaned and settled with sleeping noises, Ember picked up the schoolbag from the foot of her bed and crept out her window.

Once outside, she inhaled until she no longer could. Ember was glad to be in the open of the night, and out from under the heavy shroud that blanketed the farmhouse, pressing down so every morning Ember woke to a little less air in the rooms.

The silo wasn't far from the house, and Ember covered the distance in just a few minutes, careful of the ruts and divots that might trip a stranger. She had grown up on this land, knew it well enough to forgo the lamp she carried. When she reached the silo door, Ember hesitated, all at once recognizing her hand-tingling, shallow-breathed fear for what it was. Ember didn't know if the angel in the silo was something to be afraid of, but she suspected that was probably right.

Heart beating hard, Ember unlocked the silo door and slipped in. Not wanting to risk being seen—the thought of being found by Daddy frightened her more than whatever was waiting for her in the shadows—she closed it behind her before turning on the lamp. For just a few seconds, she and the angel were in perfect darkness together. That was all the time it took for the winged woman to make her way to the ground. Her movement too fast and entirely silent. Ember fumbled with the lantern, and when yellow lamplight illuminated the room, the maybe-angel sat on the floor perhaps five feet away from her.

Up close, the winged woman was clearly a winged girl. She was pale and grey with silver eyes that were a little too wide for any regular girl. She wrapped her lavender wings around herself like an oversized shawl. They looked like velvet, almost dusty. The wings were not ethereal. They were heavy, and somehow formidable, and *real*. And, because they were real, they *were* dusty from the girl's days in the silo. The dark patches Ember had taken for dappled spots were, upon closer examination, a mix of contusions and dried blood. Ember fought the desire to reach out and stroke those injured, miraculous wings.

"You're not an angel," Ember said, feeling a mixture of disappointment and relief.

"Oh, no. Not an angel at all." Her voice was small, but not thin. It filled the emptiness in the silo, but did not echo. Ember thought she would be able to hear that voice from any distance, would forever know it anywhere. Ember was relieved that, unlike the mermaid, the not-an-angel would answer her questions.

"Are you a fairy?"

"Hm. No. But closer, I suppose."

"What's your name?"

"Selah."

"Selah." Ember tried it out. It was soft like wings, like an echoless voice. "I'm November. But Ember is easier." Ember reached into her backpack and found a jug of water and an apple butter sandwich wrapped in wax paper. She held them out to Selah.

The almost-fairy smiled. "Ember, I am so glad to know you."

They did not talk again until half the water and the apple butter sandwich were gone.

Chapter Six

Sam

Sam's life was not easy in the days after his mother died, but it wasn't a Charles Dickens novel, either.

In his way, Sam missed his mother. And after Mother died, the Sounds went away because he made them. Sam was surprised to find he missed them, too. The missing felt like sadness, but it also felt like weakness. And the unwelcome weakness brought with it a low and thrumming anger.

With no one close enough—by distance or relationship—to take him in, he stayed in a children's home on the outskirts of the town where he and his mother had lived. The other kids seemed to already know one another, and he didn't bother trying to fit in.

Sam's father was located and notified in less than two days. He could have been found sooner; Sam knew where his father lived, but claimed ignorance when asked. As far as Sam was concerned, being with his father would be worse than being alone.

He sat on the steps outside the home, rereading his mother's letter as he waited for his father to arrive. When the flashy, midnight blue car pulled up the long drive, Sam folded the letter and tucked it back into his journal. It was not a mistake Sam's mother did not mention his father in the pages she had written. Sam's father was not a participant in this part of Sam's life any more than he had been in the rest of it.

Dennis had a long history of being rather disinterested in his son. He left Sam's mother when Sam was small. After that, when she began to build walls and create barriers between the boy and his father, Dennis simply let it happen. Birthday and Christmas cards were written by his second wife, who held no animosity toward Sam. Mother always said Juliette was well aware she had broken Sam's home and not the other way around.

Despite the rage, liquid and venomous, he felt while being embraced, Sam allowed himself to be hugged and consoled. "I'm sorry, kid. I am so sorry about your mom. I know how close you guys were."

As far as Sam was concerned, Dennis didn't know anything about anything.

"Thanks, Dennis. Can we go?"

Sam's father gave him a look that was both dismissive and exasperated. Dennis quickly rearranged his face into something kinder, but Sam had already seen the truth.

After papers were signed, and insipid words were said regarding Sam's bright future and how very lucky he was to have his father, they began the three-hour drive to Dennis and Juliette's condo. After a few weak attempts at conversation, Dennis conceded defeat, and they spent most of the ride in silence.

Juliette greeted them at the door. "Sam! Sammy?"

"Sam, please." He was glad she was uncomfortable.

"Yes, of course! Sam, then. You are so handsome. Do people tell you how much you look like your father? All the time, I bet they do!"

"People I know don't know what my father looks like." Sam was a little proud to feel much of the air leave the room.

"Well, *Sam*, I know it has been an awful few days, and you must be so tired. And, *Sam*, I am just so sorry about your mom." Sam thought if

Juliette kept enunciating his name that way, just to make sure he knew she was calling him Sam and not Sammy, he would lose his mind.

"Okay. Where am I sleeping?"

"The guest room. Well, now it's your room! Of course we'll have to redecorate. Is that really all you brought with you?" She gestured painted fingers toward his duffel bag. "Guess we'll have to take you shopping, too. You'll need clothes and shoes and, well, we'll figure it out."

"Sam," called Dennis from the kitchen. "What's for dinner tonight, kid? You choose!"

Sam chose to go to his room.

He yanked the door closed behind him and had no doubt Dennis and Juliette would give him all the space he wanted. He took off his shoes and crawled onto the overly decorated queen-sized bed, pushing aside floral pillows and precisely folded throws. He sat in the center of the bed with his legs crossed. His eyes closed, hands in his lap.

Sam sat in the bleak landscape in his mind and waited.

The Sounds did come, sullen and unhappy to have been sent away. They sat across from him, rippling like smoke in a draft just below the surface. *We have missed you. Is it time for you to come home? We think it is time now. There is no one left to take care of you. No one who cares for you. We will take care of you. Come home.*

Sam sat with those words, turning them over, and found he wasn't entirely sure what *home* meant. It was, he supposed, the place in the world you most belonged. If that was right, he'd never really had one. He believed now that his mother had tried, had done everything she knew to do, but the two of them had been too distrustful of each other, too wary. The little white house had never been his home. The promise of belonging *somewhere* tugged at a tender thread Sam didn't know was there, and the tug was strong and insistent.

If home—belonging, finally—was what the Sounds were promising, Sam thought there was little here to keep him from finding out if they were right. And if they weren't, if they were lying to him, Sam would find a way to make sure it didn't happen again.

How do I get there?

The Sounds told him what he needed to know. The plan was simple and entirely unfeasible. Sam had no choice but to believe it would work.

Sam did not unpack his bag that night. He wouldn't be staying long.

Chapter Seven

Miles

It took hours for Miles to get home from the high school. Between the police and his mom, Miles was certain he'd never answered as many questions as he had after locking the stranger in the pool room.

And so many of the same questions, asked over and over again.

"Yes, the door was locked from the outside when I got there."

"No, he never said anything that made any sense."

"No, I've never seen him before."

"Yes, it seemed like he knew me."

"Yes, there was a weird lady in the woods. Maybe I shouldn't have told you that."

"Yes, I think he was one of them. Her, too. Probably."

The first news van pulled into the parking lot as Miles and his mom drove away. The stranger—very bloody and very dead—had been taken out of the school on a stretcher hours before. Everyone would know soon enough. One of them had been found in the area. Maybe two. The town would panic like people all over the country had been for weeks.

No one connected the attacks at first. No one saw the murders as linked, random and unprovoked as they were.

But then the commonalities began to surface. The randomness itself was a commonality. The fact the strangers could not be identified.

The fact they were almost universally incoherent. And, as early DNA results trickled out to—and through—the media, the confusion grew exponentially. Samples from the strangers, or from their bodies, were mapped against databases. When the strangers themselves couldn't be identified, relatives were sought. And the results only led to more questions. If these people were who the tests showed them to be, they should be much older. Or long dead.

It was another hour before Miles finished telling his dad the story and answering all his questions. Miles was in a hurry but couldn't show it. He knew Simon and Gabby would be in his bedroom waiting for him. If today was the day his parents found out about the winged kids who had been visiting him for most of his life, he did not expect it would go over well. His parents were distraught enough as it was.

Finally free, Miles took the stairs two at a time as he escaped to his room. His parents were both on their phones, and Miles knew family and friends would keep them busy retelling the story and answering questions. He had some time.

Miles opened his bedroom door and closed it quickly as he slipped through.

Simon and Gabby were perched on his bed, waiting for him. There was no mistaking the two were siblings. Their hair was the same dark copper color, and their wings the same green-brown. Simon looked to be about nine, and Gabby close to sixteen. Though Miles was not actually sure how old they really were, as Simon and Gabby had not aged in the decade he'd known them.

"Hey, guys. I figured you'd already know what happened."

"Yes. And we must make decisions." Gabby's voice was low and firm. She shared her brother's huge, grey eyes spaced almost too far apart on her narrow face. Miles was struck, as often happened, by how beautiful Gabby was. Beautiful or not, Miles's reverence was that of a younger brother. Gabby had been a surrogate big sister all his life, and even though they now looked to be about the same age, that dynamic had not changed at all. While Simon radiated youth, his sister had always been the authority amongst them.

Simon couldn't wait for his sister to explain. He bounced rhythmically, eager and impatient. "You are coming with us!"

Miles furrowed his brow, pulled his hands through his white-blond hair. "Going with you? But I thought you said after Ava—"

Gabby interrupted. "Things have changed. We can no longer protect you here. The . . . people . . . arriving in your *when* are appearing more often. They are circling you, and I do not believe that is a coincidence. Miles, I think they are here for you. And the longer you stay, the closer they will get."

The idea that the undead people were showing up—*killing* people—because of him made Miles's veins icy and his knees weak. It was fear, yes, but also an unexpected rush of shame and guilt.

"But why—" Miles was interrupted before he could finish asking.

"I do not know why. Not for sure. But we cannot wait to figure it out. The strangers, as you call them, have been . . . something else . . . for a very long time. Only here in your *when* do they have the appearance of the people they were before. And make no mistake, there is nothing good or moral left of the humans they once were."

"What *is* left, then?" Miles thought he had some idea.

"Only the worst, basest parts of them. Only the parts of them that would make them effective and efficient killers. They are always hungry and not particular about what they fill their stomachs with."

This Miles understood, and it was repulsive. "So they're cannibals?"

"If you like."

Miles laughed despite himself. "I *don't* like."

Gabby gave him a withering look she reserved for when he and Simon were being intentionally obtuse. "The longer you are here, the longer the people close to you are in danger. And others." Gabby paused as if unsure how to continue. "These strangers are just the beginning."

Miles looked to Simon who shook his head and wouldn't meet his eyes. He couldn't imagine how things could possibly get worse than murderous not-dead people coming out of the water. "And that means what exactly?"

Gabby squinted as though she were looking for the right words. "Imagine a small, freshwater pond full of plants and fish and all manner of living things."

"Okay."

"Now imagine it is quite close to an ocean, salty and full of much different life. What would happen if that ocean . . . overflowed . . . into the pond?"

Miles thought it was obvious. "The water in the pond would rise. I guess there would be a flood."

"Yes, but more. Little that lives in fresh water can survive in the brine of the sea. The salt water would overtake the fresh, killing what was healthy before. Your strangers can only arrive because there are holes forming in the boundaries between our worlds. Those holes let through a water different than salt or fresh—a water that will poison yours. There is so much more than you can imagine—oceans that dwarf what you know. But not just the water. The beasts that live in it are deadlier and hungrier than your worst creatures—"

Hands sweaty and blood cold, Miles interrupted. "Floods, poisoned water. Monsters. It's like the apocalypse."

"Not *like* an apocalypse. In a very short time, it would be the end of your world. For now, the breaks in the boundaries are small and few. In time . . . I do not know."

"So the world could end because of *me*?" It was absurd. Miles had been dropped into a movie, the sort where a regular guy was faced with becoming a hero and saving the world. He didn't like those kinds of movies and certainly didn't feel like a hero.

"Perhaps."

It was not the answer Miles wanted. He looked again to Simon, who only nodded. The boy's face was serious and pity filled his eyes.

Miles had never had a panic attack before, but he wondered if that was about to change. His heart raced and there was a ringing in his ears. "So what do I *do*?"

"For now, you leave. With you gone, there will be nothing for the strangers to come looking for. No reason to further make holes in the borders." Gabby's words were sure, but there was something in her eyes that told Miles she was more hopeful than certain.

"Are you sure I'll even be allowed?"

Gabby paused and then, "Your birth mother was welcomed once, and we believe you will be as well. Given the circumstances."

It would mean leaving his parents without explanation. If Gabby was right, there wasn't *time* for him to explain it to them—he needed to put quick distance between himself and his family—between himself and the world—and he doubted his parents or the police or anyone else would believe him if he did try to explain. And even if they *did* believe any part of it, he knew his loving, protective parents wouldn't turn their only child's safety over to two winged kids from a place that sounded made-up.

Despite the apprehension and dread that ran through him, Miles did not argue. There was no point. Miles trusted Gabby as much as anyone in his life. If Gabby was directing him to do the one thing she'd never allowed—go with them to the Fountain—she had to believe what she was telling him.

And, of course, Miles had another reason. One that, if he were being honest with himself, was just as important, if only to him. Miles wanted to see the place where his birth mother had spent so much of her time. The place where she had chosen to die rather than stay with him and live.

"When?" His voice shook a little and he hoped Gabby and Simon didn't notice.

"Tonight."

SOMETIMES there are boats, and sometimes bridges, and then it nearly bustles.
Sometimes no one visits for a long, long time.

Chapter Eight

Selah

Selah and Ember sat on the cold silo floor. Each considered the other in silence. Selah wondered at the name of the girl. An ember was a hot thing, it burned red from its core. A funny name for the girl with such a cool light. And there was something else, but Selah could not quite name it.

Ember broke the quiet with a flood of questions. "Please. Will you tell me? What you are? Where you came from? Why you are in our old silo? Why don't you leave? Why can't you leave? You have to leave. You. Have. To leave."

Selah raised her hand, meaning to quiet the girl. At the raised hand, Ember flinched back, turning her face away. The girl caught herself, the movement so slight it might have gone unnoticed.

Selah missed little and took note, adding it to the growing list of what she knew about the girl. Perhaps she had flinched at the sight of Selah's hand, much longer and sharper-nailed than she might have realized. But Selah thought not. She thought that in the girl's grey world, a raised hand was often followed by pain.

Selah pushed back her dark hair, looked beyond the walls of the silo, and began to tell a story.

"There is a place lost things go when they want to be found. All kinds of things. Anything at all. Sometimes animals. From time to time, people. All lost, all wanting to belong again. All the losting things wanting to go back home. The place is a fountain of sorts. Not a fountain in a city park. Perhaps like a spring. No men built it, but it is not natural, either." Selah spoke cautiously, thoughtfully. She had never tried to explain the Fountain before. She found the task difficult.

"The losting things?" Ember asked. "Things that are lost?"

"Yes. But no. Some things are lost and forgotten. Some things are lost and remembered, missed maybe. And then, there are some things that are lost and sought. Sought until they are found. Lost and sought, both, sometimes for years. Sometimes for a lifetime. Those are the losting things."

"Losting things. Losting people." There was a sadness in Ember's voice. "So they go to the Losting Fountain because they hope to be found?"

The question made Selah smile wide. "Yes, if you like, a Losting Fountain. I have never heard it called a name. I think yours is a good one.

"Consider it, Ember. If lost things go to the Fountain to be sought, seekers, too, must go to the Fountain to find what they are missing. Sometimes, seekers get to the Losting Fountain on their own. Sometimes, they need help getting there. And sometimes, the seekers are greedy and desire more than they need. My job is to help find seekers who need what is lost, and to . . . dissuade . . . seekers who only want."

"What," asked Ember, "happens to the things that aren't . . . sought?"

"They wait."

"And what about the animals?"

"They wait as well. The island takes care of them. It has acquired a lovely menagerie."

"And what about the people, the people who aren't sought?"

Instead of looking away from Ember, Selah looked into her. There were, of course, people both losting and sought. But there were also many people who others gladly lost and never bothered to look for.

Ember's world was all the better for many of them being gone. The Fountain and the island were important, but they were not, perhaps, the most important parts of *Selah's* world. There were other places, with other functions. It was, Selah thought, too much to explain in the time they had. And, in its way, too awful. She made a decision then: "For another time, Ember."

Ember reached into her bag, dug into the corners. When she withdrew her hand, she brought with it a small, deep-red stone. She held it out to Selah who, eyes wide and mind racing, took it from her.

Selah clutched the stone in her hand. Even this small fragment sang to her. She did not need to inspect it. Selah knew exactly what it was and where it was from. She was at a loss as to how it had found its way into the hands of a lonely farm girl.

"Where did you get this?"

The girl hesitated, then said, "A mermaid? At least, I think she is. A mermaid, I mean. She visits me sometimes. In our well."

Selah watched Ember closely as she spoke and saw nothing but truth in the girl's eyes. It was troubling news. Selah was aware of another *when* in which the borders between the Fountain and standing water on the other side had become porous. Creatures that should not pass through were, and it was causing chaos on both sides. But that *when* was more than a century after Ember's. That it was happening in *this* now meant the threat was far worse than she had suspected. Perhaps worse than even the Philosophers, the most learned of all those on the island, even knew.

"And this mermaid, what does she say to you?"

"Nothing. Not ever. But when she comes, the music comes with her. I don't know how to explain it . . ."

"You need not explain. This stone, it is part of something much larger. Something I know well."

"Do you . . . do you want it?"

Selah did. Very much.

"No. It was given to you, and now it is yours. But promise me you will be careful with it. You'll keep it with you."

Ember nodded. "I promise."

Selah held the stone tight in her long fingers for a second more before handing it back to the girl.

When Selah left the island, she did not plan to return. But Ember, and her coolest light, and her horrible people, changed that. Selah would have to go back. Now that she knew about Ember's mermaid, she had to go back as soon as she could. Against all rules and traditions, Selah had left without permission. But she hoped they would welcome her home when they met the girl and heard the news she had to share.

Having left the Fountain without being sent, without a duty, had stripped most of Selah's power. Now she had Ember, and by association she had a little piece of the Fountain, and she would grow stronger for them and because of them. More than anything, she longed to be rid of the silo. She could leave now, tonight, but that would mean leaving the girl behind. And Ember needed to leave as desperately as Selah. So she would wait a few more hours, and they would go together.

Selah and Ember made a plan.

Chapter Nine

Ember

When Selah made her decision, Ember made one of her own.

"You have to leave."

"Yes."

"And you are going back? To your island and to the Losting Fountain?"

A pause. "I will try."

"I'm going with you." Ember was surprised at the authority in her own voice. She expected argument to meet her announcement.

"Yes. You have to. I cannot go back without you. And, besides, this is a horrible place. And your people are horrible people."

Ember nodded in agreement, surprised at how easy it was to acknowledge the secret she'd hidden so long, but then a sinking feeling rushed through her. There was good reason for her to hide.

"They'll look for me. Come after me." Images of Daddy and Uncle Joe hunting her like an animal flooded her mind and turned her stomach. *And why does this winged girl need me to go back with her? Who is stopping her from going home? What did she do?* In one heartbeat, Ember found herself drowning in fears and questions and uncertainties when moments before she had felt so sure. But moments ago she had also been certain Selah would tell her no and leave her behind. Why wouldn't Selah abandon her? Everyone else had.

"No. No, I don't think they will." Selah glanced toward the open backpack.

Ember handed the last sandwich to Selah, sat quietly while her mind screamed, and allowed the starved girl to eat. With so much waiting to be discussed, the silence between the girls was thick, but it was not uncomfortable.

Although Selah assured her everything she needed would be at the Fountain, and the trip there would be a short one, Ember could not see leaving home without at least a change of underclothes and a hairbrush. But, in truth, the thing that kept Ember there one more night was that she needed to say some sort of a goodbye to Mama.

Despite the coldness and hostility and apathy the woman had shown her for as long as she could remember, despite the fact Mama let Daddy get just as mean as he wanted to, Ember loved her. She wished she didn't. Had, in fact, prayed for release from the burden of her one-sided affection. But it was for nothing. Ember loved her mother so much that every small scowl and indifference flayed her open a little more. She needed to tell her, for what might be the last time, that no matter how much she detested her daughter, Ember loved her anyway.

She spent the rest of that night, and early into the next morning, packing and unpacking her schoolbag and thinking through the simple plan. Thinking through the words she would say to her mother.

Ember would leave her house after Daddy, Mama, and Uncle Joe were asleep. Ember would go to the silo. The girls would leave the silo. Ember would find a way to say her words to her mother. The girls would go to the Fountain. And then . . .

Ember didn't know what came next, but she trusted Selah. Or she wanted to trust Selah. At least, she trusted Selah more than she did her own people. That was enough.

As the sun peeked over the neighboring farmhouses, Ember finally slept.

She woke to Daddy hollering from the kitchen. "Lazy girl! Hey, worthless girl! Nova! Get up!" Ember sat up, blinked hard. Still in yesterday's clothes, but she knew Daddy wouldn't notice.

"Coming, Daddy!" Hearing her father's mood in his voice, Ember moved as fast as she could. She took the red stone from under her pillow and put it in her right sock. It made an uncomfortable but reassuring lump against her ankle.

Ember's father stood in the middle of the kitchen. His jaw was tight, and he was very still except his hands, which clenched and unclenched like the beating of a heart. Ember recognized this dangerous version of her father and knew to keep her distance as best she could.

Uncle Joe and her mother sat at the table. Joe ate while her mother stared at her still-full cup of coffee.

"Nova, eat something if you're quick. We're going to go get that damned thing out of the silo. You're gonna help. The only way up to it is the ladder, and I don't think it'll hold me or Joe. Once we got it, I'll decide what we're gonna do about it."

Uncle Joe looked up from his breakfast and grinned through his eggs. "Oh, it ain't an *it*. It's a *her*."

Ember was frozen. She had nowhere to go, no next step, and no plan for this.

Then Ember's mother caught them all off guard.

"Joe, Paul." Mama spoke with a calm authority Ember had never heard from her. It reminded her of her own sure voice the night before, like her mother had settled her mind on something and wouldn't be deterred. "I don't know what you've got in that silo. It's got nothing to do with me. But after everything, you have to do *this* for me." Her face, usually slack and without emotion, was taut—the muscles beneath the skin rigid. It scared Ember. "If it's like you say, if that's an angel in there, then she could have saved my Hank. She didn't. I don't care why. If that's an angel in there, you don't hurt her. You kill her. You kill her for not saving my boy." Mama was done. She never looked up from her cup. She did not address her daughter.

Ember's father made a gruff, throaty noise in acknowledgment. He committed to nothing, but Ember could see the wheels turning behind his eyes. "Joe, Nova. Up. Now." He was ready to begin whatever would come next.

Ember trailed the men as they crossed the deep yard, her hands held down at her sides, gripped so tight her knuckles were white. She stayed a few steps behind, certain they would read what must be written on her face. She could not plan, couldn't even think. There was no way to warn her new friend without making it so much worse for both of them. Tears of fear and frustration leaked from the corners of her eyes. Ember wiped them away before anyone noticed.

When they reached the silo door, Paul paused for a moment before entering. Ember watched as her father ignored a voice, so soft it might have been in their heads. "Turn around. Turn around and go back home to your breakfast. This can stop right now."

Not one to be told what to do, Ember's daddy opened the silo door.

THE Fountain requires tending.

And feeding.

Sometimes, lost things want to be found.

Sometimes, lost things make their way to the Fountain.

Chapter Ten

Selah

Selah crouched on the center beam in the silo, waiting. She was so much better now, and stronger. And her hearing was remarkable.

When Paul opened the door, bright morning sunlight filled the bottom of the silo. At the top, Selah remained wrapped in dim shadows. Here they were, all together again. The winged thing, two men, and the girl.

Ember's father grabbed Ember by the upper arm with his mean hands. He snatched her through the door, shoving her in front of him. "Go get her."

Selah spoke in her quiet loud way. "Paul, you can stop this now. Turn around. Go back to your wife and to your breakfast. There is nothing for you here. Go back and try to be a good man."

Selah could see panic rising in Ember, could hear it in the girl's voice. "Daddy? I can't. How can I? How do I even get her? She's as big as me and it's so high . . . and . . . but Hank . . ."

"Ember, come up the ladder and fetch me."

Ember, now compelled by both her father and by Selah, did as she was told. She climbed the ladder, cautious and wary at first, with more confidence as it proved equal to her weight. Her father had been right, it would not have held a grown man, but Ember was smaller and the ladder was sure enough. When she reached the top, her steps were steady, and she was no longer trembling.

Selah defied all the usual rules of gravity and crawled along the wall of the silo like a housefly until she was face-to-face with Ember.

The men below them were yelling, cursing both Selah and Ember in turn.

Selah ignored them but Ember's eyes kept glancing down to her father and uncle. Selah's kind fingers took Ember's chin and turned her face so they were eye to eye.

"Can you hold on? For just a minute? Are you strong enough?"

"Yes."

Selah wrapped the fingers of her left hand over Ember's right one, held it. "Be strong, then. And look if you must, but do not if you cannot." She let go and was no longer at Ember's side.

And then there was the winged girl, unnaturally quick, on the floor of the silo directly behind Paul.

"Let us go, Paul. Let us leave and this is over."

"I mean to have those wings." He pivoted in a slow arc to face her, his fists clenching and releasing to the beat of his heart. Too little, too late.

Selah reached up, too fast for the man to flinch, and placed her hands on the sides of his face. Her fingers pressed his temples, cautious at first, and then with more insistence. Paul slumped but did not fall. For a moment, Selah saw, tasted, the dark and bitter chaos inside him. She could smell the fear and the hate and the green-black rage. It was awful, then it was gone. Paul swayed like a sapling when she released him, but he stood.

Selah turned to Joe. He charged, but she was quicker. In one swift movement she had him. Selah held the big man by the temples. Joe's feet dangled inches off the floor as she rose into the air.

Selah saw something more than chaos and rage in Joe, something nastier. At his core he was toxic and deformed. She saw just how terrible this place would get for her Ember. Selah gagged and pressed harder than she had to. While Paul remained standing, Selah released Joe, and he crumpled into a heap on the ground.

Silence filled the silo. The encounter had taken less than a minute.

Selah opened her wings, lavender grey on the outside but jeweled lilac within. She flew up to the girl on the ladder and, so much stronger now, brought her down.

They left the silo.

They left Paul standing, swaying, empty, with his brother collapsed and still at his feet.

Chapter Eleven

Sam

Sam walked out the front door. He was not particularly careful, nor was he quiet. He didn't care who heard him, who he might wake. No one would try very hard to stop him from going.

He didn't have anyone to say goodbye to.

Chapter Twelve

Miles

Miles snuck out his bedroom window, careful and quiet. He did not want to wake his parents. If his mom cried—or worse—his dad, Miles wasn't sure he'd be able to go through with it.

His body remembered all his childhood tricks, hard won with late-night bumps and bruises, and he made his way from the second floor to the ground as quick as he could.

"Love you guys," he whispered, looking up at the dark window of their bedroom. And he did. A lot. Which is why his eyes were stinging as he turned and started toward the empty street.

Miles traveled light, and, aside from his parents, the one thing he regretted leaving behind was his phone. Gabby assured him it wouldn't work on the island. More importantly, she reminded him time was going to be different, and he might not want to know what was happening back home. Nor how quickly the time in his world would pass while he was away.

Chapter Thirteen

Ember

"I have to go see Mama," Ember said. "One more time. Just in case. Please." With the men gone, so was the urgency. All that stood between them and the Fountain was her soft, aching heart.

"I know." Selah did not argue. "We can go to her."

At the door of the farmhouse, Ember felt more than ever like a stranger. She ran her hand through her hair and over her now-filthy dress. She almost knocked but caught herself in the last possible moment. Ember hesitated to cross the threshold. For all the awful there, it had been home. And all at once it was not. The change was dizzying.

She opened the door.

"Mama?" Ember called from the doorway. "Mama, I've come to say goodbye. And there is someone with me. I . . . I don't want to scare you."

Ember's mother walked out of the kitchen and into the front room, dishtowel in hand. She looked from Ember to Selah and backed away, stopping when she ran into the china cabinet. Her face was horrified, disgusted. Her tone low and dangerous. "Nova, what did you do? What did you bring into my house?"

Ember walked into the dim room, knees threatening to buckle under the weight of what she was about to say and the permanence of the words. "Mama, I'm leaving. I love you, and I'm leaving."

"Where is your father? And your uncle?" Mama looked at Selah. "What did you do to them?"

"Mama, I love you. And I'm leaving . . ."

"Quiet, Nova. Shut your mouth. You, *thing*, what did you do to my husband?"

Not even an acknowledgment from her mother, much less a profession of her own love. Certainly no pleading with her only living child to *please stay*.

Selah spoke to Ember's mother in a sad, soft voice. "Ruth, this life could have been so different. It could have made you anything at all, and it chose to make you a mother. A mother to a soft, gentle boy and to a strong, kind girl. You were blessed. But you squandered it all."

Ember held her breath and hoped for something, some spark from her mother. Some fight, for Hank, or for Ember, or even for herself. Some hint of love.

Her mother clutched the kitchen towel and gaped like a caught fish. There was no fight and no love for her daughter or anyone else.

Ember saw that Selah saw it, too, all the apathy and the emptiness.

Selah spat out her next words with a cruelty Ember had not heard her use before, not even with Daddy and Joe. "Hank killed himself because you were not there. Even as a small child, Paul saw something in the boy he did not understand, something that frightened him. He spent years killing that part of your son, until Hank grew tired and finished it for him. You watched. You may have loved your son, but you watched."

Mama's eyes burned bright. Not with pain at Selah's words, but with hatred for her. Perhaps for them both.

Selah and Ember's mother were so focused on each other, Ember was sure if she were bleeding or even dying, neither of them would notice. In her fourteen years, she had had enough of meanness for a lifetime and, in this moment, when she had hoped for just a bit of love, couldn't stand another cruelty.

"Enough. Please, enough." Ember could not hear any more. She couldn't watch Selah destroy what little was left of her mother.

Selah turned toward her as though she had forgotten Ember, surprised and maybe ashamed. She was almost finished. "Your husband will never hit you again, but he may not do much else, either. The other one might be dead. Ember, come now. It is time."

Ember looked at her mother for the last time. Tears ran down the girl's face. "Mama? *Mama*." One last chance, then. One last bit of hope Ember's mother would reach out to her, tell her to stay. That she loved her and needed her and was so, so sorry.

The woman's eyes were hot and dry. She ignored her daughter, or did not hear her at all.

Nothing. It was the nothing that broke Ember's heart for a final time. Ember felt it happen, a fissure deep and permanent.

As she stood, shattered and weeping, her mother spoke instead to Selah. "Tell me. The truth, thing. Could you have saved my boy?"

Selah shook her head. "No. No, but you could have. Many times." She wrapped the sobbing girl in a soft wing and walked her out the door of the farmhouse into the bright light of a new day.

PART TWO

The Island

THE Fountain has rules.

The Fountain is patient.

The Fountain is kind to those who need it and cruel to those who cheat it.

The Fountain collects lost things, and the Fountain collects stories.

Sometimes the Fountain creates stories of its own.

While there are as many ways to reach the Fountain as there are stories, every story begins the very same way.

Once upon a time . . .

Chapter Fourteen

Selah

As the girls passed the silo, Selah looked through the still-open door. Paul stood where she had left him, motes shifting in the sunlight that cut through the shadows and illuminated his blank face. There was nothing left of him that mattered, Selah was sure. Joe was at his feet, dead.

Holding Ember close, strong wing wrapped around slumped shoulder, Selah pulled her wing up a bit higher around Ember's face, protecting her from the sight.

They made their way across the deep farmyard to the fields beyond. The girls walked on, reached the edge of the fields that seemed to disappoint Ember's father every season.

"Why are we here?" Ember's voice was flat.

"We are going to the Fountain."

"In Daddy's . . . in the wheat fields?"

"For now."

Ember would later have many more questions, but in the moment she seemed void of curiosity. The day had knocked it out of her. The girls crested a low hill, and it was then Ember saw what waited for them in the gold and green pasture.

"Is that a *lake*?" Hints of awe crept into Ember's voice.

"A small one, yes."

"And in the lake . . ."

"My island. And on the island, the Fountain."

"When did it get here? The lake, the . . . all of it? Did it follow you? Has it been here all this time?" Selah understood the questions. It would seem, after all, unlikely a lake had appeared in the middle of a struggling wheat field and no one had mentioned it. Not that they would have mentioned it to her, but Ember certainly would have overheard talk of it.

"I am sure it just arrived. To meet you, here. I hoped it would."

"You hoped it would? You *hoped* it would? Selah, you didn't know it was here? You *hoped* it was? But what if it wasn't here? What would we have done?" Anxiety took root and grew in Ember.

"It *is* here. We are here. It means you are welcomed. That is enough for now."

Ember stared off at the new horizon. Selah saw she was troubled again by the words. "You said *I* am welcomed, not *we* are welcomed. Are you? Welcomed, I mean?"

Selah considered before answering. "The island will welcome me. The Fountain, I do not know. I hope . . . I believe it will because you are with me."

Ember shook her head, impatient now. "But, why? Why does the Fountain care about me? What did I do? What does it want from me? None of this makes any sense, and you keep saying words but you aren't telling me anything. You don't *say* anything. None of it makes any sense and I am so, so tired of no one talking to me." Her voice rose until she yelled, the sound carrying well across the field.

"I will explain it all. I promise. The Fountain is many things, but it will not abide doubt. You must believe me, trust me, if we are to cross the lake. There will be time for explanations."

Ember sat down hard and heavy in the dry wheat. She winced as the stalks poked her back and arms through her thin dress sleeves. "No. No, that isn't good enough. You have to tell me something. You have to give me more than more promises. And you know what? I don't think you'll make me go if I don't want to. I don't think you can."

Selah sat next to the livid girl, close but not touching. She was glad to see the anger. Ember deserved to be angry. "You are right, I cannot. I will persuade you if I can. I will plead with you if I must. But I cannot force you. I would not even if I could. I want the choice to be yours. Do you believe that? Do you believe me?"

After a time, Ember nodded but questions remained in her eyes.

That was fine, good even. The girl should have questions. And the answers would come.

Selah crouched in front of Ember and was surprised to find herself thinking of the girl as *a friend.* Perhaps it was a friendship, or would grow to be. She took both Ember's hands in her own and rested her wingtips on the girl's shoulders.

"The Fountain is not good. Nor is it evil. The Fountain is powerful, and it is carefully, precisely balanced. It is a place for the losting, yes, but that is true because it is a middle place." Selah looked for the right words. "A border. A boundary. A dam between your world and another. And there are cracks in the dam."

"Cracks?" Ember asked.

"Yes, I'm afraid so." *Very afraid, in fact.* The thought of all those creatures escaping in all those *whens* was the stuff of nightmares. As if the island's own fireside tales, whispered to each generation of hatchlings to thrill and scare and teach, had been granted life.

Selah shuddered, wanting for Ember to understand. In fact, she *had* to understand. This was the crux and consequence of it all. "You see . . ." She tried to think how to say it. "A chosen group tends to the Fountain, sees to that balance. It is the Jury, in consult with a select few, who decides what the Fountain returns and what it takes away. Who is rewarded, and who is punished. But the Jury has become . . . unreliable. And there is fear on the island."

Selah shifted uneasily. It had to be said, if Ember was to trust her.

She steeled her resolve. "There is something coming to the island, or maybe it is there already. Something that will destroy the precarious balance of the Fountain. But I believe you can help keep the scales from tipping. I left the island in search of a way to save my home. And in doing so, I found you. And now I am choosing to return, to protect my home from whatever is about to come. And I'm hoping that you will come and help us."

Ember spent a long moment in silence. "Am I in danger if I go?"

"Yes."

"Am I going to die?"

"I hope not. I, and many others, will do all we can to protect you."

"Are you going to die?"

"I might." *Probably, yes, I will die.*

"How? How do we make it right?"

A pause. "I do not know. But if we don't try, there will be vast and permanent consequences. We will either restore the balance or watch as the dams that separate our two worlds and all our *whens*"—here she swallowed—"fall."

Ember lowered her voice to a whisper. "What happens then?"

Selah closed her eyes and imagined it. "A flood of brutality and disease and death that would end it all."

Chapter Fifteen

Ember

Ember was not scared. She was terrified. And so very sad.

She wanted to turn back and run through the fields, across the farmyard, and through the door of her house. She wanted to find her mother, apologize to her even now. Tell her she would never leave again, would never ask her for anything. And maybe, someday, Mama would grow to tolerate her. Even need her.

Except.

Except, when Ember looked in just a little deeper, she saw she did not want any of that. She didn't want to be ignored and tolerated and resented. She didn't want to live in a house that was so full of the anger and fear her father created, and the awful sadness that was Hank all around them.

Hank had been the spot of warmth in her life. His face freckled and dimpled, he would smile at her while looking in her eyes, put his hands on her shoulders as they talked. Hank would touch her hair when he sat down to join her at breakfast. He would kiss her cheek good night. Hank told her stories, listened to her talk about anything at all. Hank was the one person who saw Ember. So, when he hanged himself in the silo, Ember became invisible. Not hated, but unloved. There was no one left to see her.

Ember was angry for a long time, at Hank and her parents and the awful waste and her loneliness. Angry at not being seen. And then the sadness poured in, poured over her. And then she resigned herself to being sad forever, and to always being invisible. The thought of never being seen again became powerful. And, without fanfare, Ember began to think about the silo. The silo, and its high center beam, began to look reasonable, possible, inevitable.

When Selah came to the silo, she turned it from the gallows to a prison. Then, as she perched on that tainted center beam and waited, she turned it into a place of patience. When she sat with Ember and told her stories, made her plans, it became a place of promise. And when Selah refused to let Daddy and Uncle Joe hurt her, hurt *them*, any longer, the silo became a place of liberation.

So, in truth, Ember did not want to return home. She wanted to follow Selah. She wanted to cross the lake and walk on the island. She wanted to touch the water of the Fountain. She wanted to help if she could.

She wanted to matter, needed to be a part of something.

Ember reached down to touch the lump in her sock where she had hidden the mermaid rock away. Despite having been close to her skin for hours, it was still cool. She slipped it into the pocket of her dress where it would be easier for her to reach and hold.

When Selah rose from the place where the girls sat in the field, she looked into Ember's eyes and held out her hand. Ember took it and stood.

With that, a question asked, and a question answered.

Together, the girls walked toward the lake and to what would be waiting for them on the other side.

Chapter Sixteen

Sam

The first leg of Sam's journey was a short one. It took only minutes for him to reach the lake.

Protected from view by a tall fence with green privacy slats, the pool sat in the west corner of the condominium complex. It was an uninspired rectangle, surrounded by pebble-studded concrete and lined with white plastic Adirondack chairs. Sam, duffel bag over his shoulder, would appear to anyone watching like a restless teenage boy sneaking out for a late-night swim.

Just one resident saw Sam as he walked to the pool, and after the boy disappeared and questions were being asked, would note the late hour and the cool conditions. "I didn't think much of it," the woman told police. "You know kids, especially boys that age. They don't let much keep them out of the water if they want to go for a swim. Besides, commercials were almost over, so I had to get back to my show."

Sam wasn't interested in a swim. In fact, he didn't know how. Sam was simply following the minimal, absurd directions given to him by the Sounds. *Go to the pool,* they told him. *Go to the pool and you will find the Fountain.*

The Fountain was all that mattered now. It was all Sam had left. He would get there, and he would find out what he was, why he was. He would find out why his mother had to die and if he had killed her.

Though, Sam thought he had. While the idea threatened to bring him to his knees, it was an idea he could live with. If there was a bigger reason, a purpose for what Sam was, he could forgive himself the death of his mother. And, maybe, he would find the place he belonged. The idea of *home* had burrowed into him and was growing roots.

At the pool gate, Sam stopped. He was certain someone was watching him. He turned to look at the windows that surrounded him, stretching up three stories. Few were lit, and those were illuminated by the flickering light of television. Most everyone was asleep. Even the sole witness to his escape had turned back to her own screen. There was no one, but the pressure of eyes upon him remained.

There was nothing for Sam to do but continue.

He threw the latch on the side of the gate. The door swung in and Sam stepped onto a beach at the edge of a small lake. The moon, the same one that lit Sam's walk across the condominium courtyard, now shone in the black, placid water.

It was his single opportunity, the one fleeting instant Sam almost quit. He considered, for that fierce second, turning around and going back through the gate behind him. He would walk back up the stairs to Dennis and Juliette's condo. If they were waiting for him, which they almost certainly would not be, he would say he'd gone for a walk. He would go to bed. He would redecorate his room, start all over at a new school—a *real* school—and try to live a regular life.

But there was nothing regular about Sam, and there was no home for him here.

Instead, he took another step forward. Then another. When Sam glanced back over his shoulder, the gate and the fence and the complex were gone. Only empty beach stretched on behind him. So much beach, it would eventually become a desert.

The decision was made for him.

Chapter Seventeen

Miles

The trio set off on foot. Simon assured Miles the walk would be short and the Fountain nearby.

As they walked, the route became familiar, and Miles became lost in memories of the place.

It was, of course, at the playground where Miles and Simon met, where they became friends, Miles the only one at the park able to see the other boy for what he was. To see those wings. Soon Gabby started coming to the park with Simon. Miles remembered the first time he saw Gabby, and she, him. It was nearly a decade prior, and she towered over him then. She had leaned low and taken his chin in her hand, turning his face first one way then the other. "You are right," she'd said to Simon. "He looks very much like her."

After that day, Miles saw Simon and Gabby often. At the park and then, not long after, they began visiting him at night after his parents tucked him in. Miles would let them in his second-story window while reminding them to *hush*. On those nights, he and Simon would fall asleep as Gabby told them stories—stories about the Fountain, about what happened there, and about Miles's birth mother, Ava.

The winged siblings were always gone when Miles woke in the morning.

As the years passed, Miles would beg Gabby to take him there, to the Fountain, like Ava.

Gabby always refused. "In the end, the Fountain was not good for Ava, and I worry it would not be good for you. Besides, your mother is here. You need not look for another."

Miles wasn't looking for another mother, the one who kissed his forehead and shared inside jokes with him and taught him to drive was the only one he wanted. But he thought maybe if he went to the Fountain, saw the places and met the people Ava saw and met, he might understand more about her. And he might learn why she had disappeared all those years ago, leaving her sister to raise the nephew who would become her son.

So deep in thought was Miles, he didn't feel the eyes following him from the trees at the edge of the park.

"It is here—look!" Simon pulled at Miles's hand, and pulled him out of his head and into the night as they approached the fence that served as a border between the playground and the rest of the world.

Inside the chain-link fence, where swing sets and park benches and picnic tables belonged, there was a lake. And an island within.

And surely, deeper, the Fountain.

ONCE upon a time, a long time ago . . .

MARSHALL was often late for important things. He blamed the pocket watch he carried. The finish was worn thin, and it kept terrible time. Marshall intended to have it cleaned and serviced, but there never seemed to be enough money. For the price of servicing the old watch, Marshall could buy a new one. If the watch had not once belonged to his grandfather, that is just what Marshall would have done.

Except now, Marshall did not have a watch at all. Marshall had lost his grandfather's pocket watch.

When he left school in tenth grade to find work and a way to help his family, he had taken very little with him. The few clothes he had, a good pair of boots, and his grandfather's watch. The watch was the one thing Marshall had that mattered, and it was gone.

He turned the room he rented upside down. He searched the factory floor. He looked on the streets he walked every day. He asked people he passed. Nothing. It was good and gone.

Marshall did not have an easy life. He worked hard for others, had little for himself, and spent much of his time alone. For all that, Marshall had a warmth and a light and a happiness that glowed in him. That light meant his hard life was a good one. And his grandfather's pocket watch was the sole special thing he owned. When Marshall lost the watch, his light flickered. The longer it was lost, the more the light dimmed.

One evening after his shift, Marshall wandered. He was not ready to return to his lonely room, but he had nowhere else to go. As night fell, he decided to cross through the big park on the north side of town. Marshall took the footpath through a thick grove of trees, and froze when he broke through to the clearing beyond.

The park was a good size, but it was not large enough for a lake. Yet, here Marshall was in the park, and before him was, indeed, a lake. And in the center of the lake, a small and densely treed island. Marshall looked around, turning a full circle, hoping to find someone who could confirm what he was seeing. There was no one. Marshall was alone with the lake and the island.

As curious as he had ever been, Marshall started at a brisk pace toward the shoreline. When he arrived at the water, he bent and reached out to touch it. Needing proof. Instead of water, Marshall's fingers met dry earth. The shoreline stretched into the water below his fingers, toward the island. Marshall reached out as far as his arms and balance would allow. The land stretched out below him.

Marshall stepped back and the shoreline retreated to its previous position. Hands deep in his pockets, he rocked back on his heels and considered. Then Marshall walked toward the shoreline and stepped beyond it. On to dry land. Another step, and the shore again fell underfoot. As Marshall walked toward the island, a land bridge formed beneath his feet.

At the rocky edge of the island, Marshall looked back for the first time. The bridge remained, just wide enough for one sure-footed young man, but solid. Before him, a rough trail stretched into the interior of the island. Marshall followed it, through trees and brambles and grasping branches. As darkness grew all around, Marshall found he could hear movement in the wild beyond the path. Slight, quick movements and larger, intentional ones. Too far now to turn back, Marshall walked faster.

When the path opened up to a broad, clear place, the light improved. Before Marshall was an enormous spring, or a fountain. It was the size of a banquet hall and backed up against a steep, rocky cliff. Luminous water cascaded down the cliff from an unseen stream, feeding the fountain below. At the base of the waterfall, flat rocks met the surface of the fountain. In the dying light, something glowed on the rocks. Something small and round. And familiar.

Marshall was certain beyond any doubt the glowing golden circle was his watch.

Now far past any previous sense of disbelief, Marshall sat down at the edge of the water and removed his shoes and socks. He rolled his trousers to the knee and waded into the water. It was cool and still. The rocks beneath his feet were smooth and even. The water never reached the rolled hem of his pants. The journey to the waterfall and flat stones was an easy one, and rewarding. There, in the gentle spray of the falls, was his grandfather's watch.

Marshall returned across the land bridge and arrived at the park almost without incident. From time to time, he caught movement in the water at the edge of his vision, something huge and deep in the lake. The creatures were not ominous and he was not afraid.

Later, Marshall would consider the hows and whys of the situation. He would mull it over, but would never arrive at a satisfying answer. It became the great mystery, and great tale, of his life. He would tell it many times to many people. Decades later his children would repeat it fondly, disbelieving, to their own children.

Marshall never found the fountain again, or the island, or even the lake. And Marshall never did have his watch fixed. Besides, after its time at the fountain, his grandfather's tarnished old pocket watch kept time perfectly.

Chapter Eighteen

Sam

Sam walked to the edge of the beach where the water lapped the shore. The sand was pristine, and his were the only footprints. The island waited for him. It was close, but out of reach for the boy who could not swim. A quarter of a mile does not look like much in the day-to-day world, when it is wrapped in the neat, red oval of a high school track it seems no distance at all. On a night-dark lake, with the moon reflecting on every ripple and peak, a fourth of a mile between one shoreline and the next is very far indeed.

Sam scanned the beach for something, anything to help him cross the lake. There was no boat, nor raft. He could see no bridge. He was not going to be able to do this. The newly made promise of home was drifting through his fingers like smoke. This was the end of it. The idea was maddening.

Sam addressed the voices, knew they would be listening. *What is this? You said it would be simple. You said you would help.*

We said it would be simple; we did not promise easy. And we cannot help you. You will be allowed, but you will not be assisted. You are a smart boy, Sam. You will figure it out.

Sam clenched his fists rhythmically. The Sounds may not have made promises, but they had misled him. He wanted to yell at them, to say something cutting. But he did neither. Sam needed what little assistance they might give him more than he needed to vent his anger.

He scanned the beach again with more care this time as his initial panic subsided. It was then he saw it, what he had missed before. In the moonlight, the driftwood was the same color as the sand it rested in. As Sam approached it, he saw it was massive. He believed it would support him, provide a way to cross the lake. It was too narrow for Sam to balance upon, but he would be able to hold on. And it would provide a perch for his duffel bag, and for his mother's letter within.

Sam set his bag safely on the beach out of the reach of the lapping water. He began the task of dragging the driftwood into the lake. The wood was heavy, and the sand worked against him as he made slow progress. When he reached the water, Sam was sweating even though the evening was cool. He removed his shoes and clothes, adding them to the contents of the duffel bag. The bag he placed in the center of the widest, flattest part of the driftwood. It was the best he could do. He slowly, cautiously, coaxed the log into the waiting lake. As it became buoyant, the job became easier.

Deeper now, Sam could feel himself relying more and more on the wood. As his feet struggled to make contact with the bottom of the lake, Sam fought a fresh wave of panic. He gripped the driftwood with desperate fingers, thrashed and floundered, remembering almost too late it carried his bag and Mother's letter.

Sam closed his eyes and breathed until the rattling in his lungs stopped, until his body ceased trembling. He allowed himself to float, to trust the water and his makeshift life preserver. The water was warmer than the air above, and soon it became difficult for Sam to tell where the water ended and his flesh began.

When Sam opened his eyes, he was calmer, but he was also drifting off course. He began to twist his body cautiously, and to kick. In time, Sam understood how to move in the direction he desired. It was hard work. He required periodic breaks, but paid for those by losing ground and floating off farther from his destination.

It was at the midpoint in his journey Sam realized he was not alone in the lake. There were regular, massive swells in the water beneath him. Sam's curiosity shifted to terror when he understood something, some *thing* was causing the water to move. His body became aware of the colossal, unseen creatures sharing the lake with him.

When something thick and rubbery pressed up against Sam's foot, he began to scream. He would be pulled in, would drown or would be eaten by whatever beasts lived in this place.

Sam, we will not permit anything to harm you. They want to, but we will not allow it. Keep swimming, Sam. Ignore their curiosity. The Sounds did not reassure Sam's raging heart, but they helped him to focus. He may die tonight, but he would not offer himself up to death. Sam continued kicking, making up for the distance lost in the gentle current.

What lived in the lake continued reaching out to Sam, taunting him.

Once, his leg was wrapped in an enormous tentacle. The creature it belonged to tugged sharply, and for a moment Sam was drowning, all but the hand grasping the driftwood submerged in the lake. The tentacle released him before he could try to kick it off.

As he drew nearer to the island, Sam felt sharp fingers dig into his calf. He glimpsed a pale figure, almost human but for its too-long limbs, in the water just below him. It was the only other time he screamed. The scream seemed to drive the almost-person away.

The journey took hours. Two, maybe three. When he reached the island, he pulled himself up onto a large rock, dragging his duffel bag with him.

As he sat, breathing heavily and unevenly, something unseen eased the piece of driftwood away from the island. Then it was jerked into the lake and was gone.

Small, fragile pieces of Sam's sanity had been chipped away during his time in the lake. He could hear them *clink, clink* at the bottom of a deep, dry well.

Naked, cold, and bone-tired, Sam thought about going back to the lake to rinse away the blood, thick and black in the moonlight, running down his calf. But he could not tolerate a return to the water, so let the blood dry and cake instead.

Sam sat on the rock until his breathing became more even. When he was sure he could stand, he dressed in his jeans and grey-and-red ringer T-shirt, secured his bag over his shoulder, and began his journey to the center of the island.

The Sounds were gone now. He did not understand why he had been invited and then abandoned. It left him frustrated and angry but also afraid.

He hoped they would change their minds.

He hoped they would hurry.

On his own, Sam did not know to look for the direct and easy path that would lead him to the Fountain. Instead, he walked into the tree line of the forest. It closed around him, and the shore was silent again.

Chapter Nineteen

Miles

Miles found his stomach high in his chest, making it hard to breathe. His heart raced as he took in the lake and the island in the distance. "This . . . has this always been here? Have I just not been able to see it?"

"Not at all." Gabby looked out across the water. "It arrived here about the time we did, maybe shortly before. And it chooses who can see it."

"How long will it stay?"

Simon raised his wings in a dramatic *Who knows?* shrug. "As long as it wants. And it wants you, so it will stay until you go to it."

"How do we get out there?" Miles narrowed his eyes at the island. "It's kind of a long way for a night swim."

"I do not think you will have to swim," Simon replied. "We cannot know until we get down to the shore. Then, the lake will tell us." The winged boy began to walk, almost skip, toward the shoreline. Miles hurried after, and Gabby followed.

When they reached the shore, there was nothing but silence to greet them. All the night creatures—those that belonged there and the one watching from the trees who did not—were quiet, waiting to see what would happen next.

The wait was short.

The bridge rose out of the lake with a roar of so much water displaced at once. It spanned the quarter mile from shore to shore in a gentle arc. At its apex, the bridge stood four stories above the surface of the lake. It was woven tightly, made from all the trees and vines and growing things waiting for them on the island.

Simon smiled. "I have not seen this one before."

"I have." Gabby was thoughtful, quiet as ever. "This is how the island greeted Ava. Every time she would visit, it was the same. The Fountain recognizes you, Miles."

A flame of hope sparked in Miles's chest, and he didn't know it had been missing until it ignited. If the Fountain recognized him, and *greeted* him, maybe it might also share its secrets. He might truly find out why Ava had made the decision she had.

They walked in single file. First Gabby, then Miles, and lastly Simon. The bridge was strong and felt solid underfoot. The material so green and alive there was a spongy quality to every step. Miles was struck by the beauty of it, the complexity and the simplicity. He plucked a leaf off the handrail, smelled it to confirm what he already knew—it was alive.

For so much of his life, Gabby and Simon had shared tales of this place with Miles. And now, here he was, on a bridge the island built for *him*. Looking over the side of the bridge and into the water, Miles could see the lake was full of life. He had no names for them, but enormous creatures turned circles and figure eights in the water. The lake had to be very, very deep as Miles could see just the vaguest outlines and silhouettes in the moonlight.

"Are they dangerous?" Miles asked Gabby, who walked ahead.

"Oh, yes. Quite."

Miles stopped walking as a hand surfaced in the lake. Nearly hidden under the bridge, he would have missed it had he not been looking down.

"Someone's down there!" Miles's first instinct was to jump in and attempt to rescue the drowning person. And he would have, had Gabby not reached out and grabbed his upper arm. Her long-fingered grip was a vice, painful.

"Not someone. Not anymore."

Miles watched as another hand broke the surface, and then another. And then a half dozen more. Some of the hands extended upward, on arms far longer than they should have been. Arms six, eight, ten feet long, with too many joints. They bent weirdly, *wrong*.

The hands reached for the trio on the bridge. Even the longest was yards too short, but it did not deter them. As Miles watched, one hand on a seven-foot arm clawed at another, longer, appendage. It left open, bleeding gashes. Like sharks, the creatures hidden beneath the surface began to frenzy as blood ran into the water. Soon, Miles and his friends were forgotten as the not-people in the lake turned upon one another. The water churned and frothed pink in the moonlight as unseen monsters savaged one another over a few drops of blood.

"What the hell?" Miles didn't need to elaborate. The idea of those vicious and long-limbed mutants in fishing ponds and swimming holes in his town made him shudder. *It can't happen*, Miles thought. *I won't let it. Somehow.*

There came an answer of sorts. A low, unintelligible answer from someone making their way onto the bridge behind them. As the figure struggled toward the trio, a piece of the bridge collapsed behind it. And then another. The bridge crumbled with every footstep the figure took, and Miles could see whoever it was wasn't going to make it. They would plunge into the lake below, and into the hands and the hungry *zombies*—Miles thought—they belonged to.

Miles took off at a run toward the stranger. As he closed in, the figure fell through a hole that had not been there seconds before. Simon screamed for Miles to stop, but he kept going, stopping just short of the now severed edge.

Two hands held on to that edge, a person dangling twenty feet above the surface of the lake. Miles thought about the crazed monsters attacking one another in the water, grasped one of the wrists and began to pull. The skin covering the bones of the wrist felt too loose, and far too cold.

When Miles paused, long enough to really listen to what the unseen stranger was saying, he realized he'd made a mistake.

The hand still holding the bridge let go, and latched onto Miles's arm. He was forced down onto his knees to keep from going over the edge headfirst. The stranger pulled herself up and Miles was face-to-face with the woman from the woods. She still wore her oversized coat and, this close, reeked of bloated things rotting at the edge of a stagnant body of water. She regarded Miles with flat, empty eyes and gibbered through a broken-toothed grin.

Miles had been mistaken about something else. The bridge had not broken, it had decayed. The twisted living things that made up the bridge had turned rotten and black at the stranger's touch. *Like,* Miles thought, *it would rather die than let her cross over to the island.*

Panic made Miles's limbs numb and his breath shallow. He slipped forward on the bridge and toward the woman and the water.

The woman let go of Miles with one hand and swiped at his face. The force of it almost dragged him over the edge, and might have, had Simon not grabbed both his shoulders and pulled back hard. The woman still gripped Miles's forearm, nails digging into his flesh.

As Simon pulled Miles toward relative safety, Gabby flew toward the stranger. She carried something thin and sharp, something that caught the moonlight as she lunged midair. Gibbering changed to furious wails as the air filled with the scent of rancid blood.

Gabby lunged again and with it came the thick sounds of a blade cutting through flesh.

The woman lost her grip on Miles's arm and then there was a splash.

Then the sound of the creatures in the lake killing one another over their new prize.

Then nothing.

Gabby landed on the new edge of the bridge. She tucked the blade away in the folds of her tunic, but not before Miles could see it was now black with blood in the white light of the moon.

Gabby lifted Miles's arm to inspect it. There were deep scratches where the stranger had held on, but otherwise he was whole.

"What the *hell*?" Miles repeated as he backed away from the newly created precipice.

Gabby helped Miles stand. "We should move off the water. You will be safe on the island. And I will explain as best I can."

Simon looked toward the mainland. "None of this is right."

Faster now, and with more purpose, the trio made their way down the bridge.

Shaken as he was, Miles was still in awe. *This was Ava's island,* he thought. Nearing the shore, and even with such limited light, he was taken by how deeply green and alive the forest was. The trees were so dense as to appear impenetrable. Miles caught glimpses of movement throughout the canopy. He would remember to ask Gabby and Simon what sorts of things lived in the forest and played at night. He hoped to see some of them before he left for home.

Simon was the last to step off the bridge. As he walked onto shore, there was a massive shifting sound.

What remained of the bridge sank into the lake behind them. In moments, the water was still. There was no evidence it had ever been there.

Chapter Twenty

Ember

As the girls made their way across the field to the waiting lake, Selah was the first to break the silence between them.

"There are . . . animals that live in the lake. Many are much bigger than they have any right to be, much bigger than a lake should allow. You will see that is often the way. The Fountain has little regard for physics."

Ember shaded her green eyes against the bright sun and peered out toward the lake. She could, indeed, see movement in the water. An irregular but frequent surfacing and diving. Creatures large enough to displace the water and create wide rings as they disturbed the surface. She had never been to an ocean but these, surely, were meant for much deeper and wider places than even a vast lake.

"What lives in the lake is dumb and dangerous, made of nothing but appetite," Selah said. "If the island, and the Fountain, are threatened, the leviathan are the first line of defense. They may menace you, us, when we cross, but they will not harm you. They act only by permission of the Jury, and the Jury will be very interested to meet you."

"The hungry things in the lake, do they eat *people*?" Ember asked, suspecting she already knew the answer.

Selah shrugged. "I suppose they might. Sometimes. They have to eat something."

When the girls reached the shore, they were still alone. Ember sat in the sand, knees to her chin, farm-strong arms wrapped around them, and looked out toward the island. A breeze tugged at her loose hair, and Ember closed her eyes. She had never been to the beach, any beach, even on a small lake. Ember felt something calm and cool and centered rising up inside her, through her stomach and her shoulders and into her throat. Behind her eyes. She felt powerful and at peace. She did not want to open her eyes, didn't want it to go away.

Ember didn't notice when her friend sat beside her.

"You can feel it," Selah said. "The island, the Fountain. Not everyone can feel it, and not everyone feels it the same way. For you, it is very good. I think the island will do well for you, and you for it."

"Thank you for bringing me here." It was a whisper.

When Ember opened her eyes again, Selah was at the edge of the shore, standing in the wet sand and looking out toward the water, to the island or beyond it. A question pulled at the back of Ember's mind, but she lost the threads when something caught her attention. Someone had been there before them.

There were many sets of footprints in the sand. They were scattered where the fields met the sand, but narrowed to a single location at the waterline. A small group of people had been recently on the shore. They had gone to the water to . . . what? A boat was the most logical answer.

Ember spotted an additional lone set of prints. She followed the footprints with her eyes, saw they stopped at a place a few yards from the water. There, something had been dragged into the lake. It looked like it had been big and heavy. Ember had no idea what to make of it. She found it unnerved her. She walked toward them, sweat gathering on her brow despite the breeze coming off the water.

Ember called out to Selah, "Who was here?"

"I am not certain. We will find out soon enough."

From the island came an enormous sound. It was an earthquake, an avalanche, a rockslide. It was something else entirely, but it filled the air and made Ember's heart lurch in her ribs.

As she watched, a small, rocky section from the edge of the island broke off, separated from the rest. Bits of island crumpled, fell into the lake. The piece of land moved straight and sure toward them, swift and almost soundless in the water.

Ember found herself backing up farther on the beach. She did not understand what was happening or what was to come next, but she knew she didn't want to be in the path of the rapidly approaching piece of the island.

"Ember, come back down. This is . . . this is unusual. The island always provides a way to help those cross who are welcomed. I have never seen the island come to welcome someone itself. The Fountain is anxious to have you. That is good for us, but it worries me as well."

As the rogue bit of island approached, Ember saw it was larger than she first thought, a rough square perhaps ten feet across. It came to rest against the beach with a soft *thump*, rising six feet above it. Ember was looking for a way for them to climb up the sheer wall until she saw that had been planned for. The section of island that was sent to meet them had a low, stone staircase. They would not have to risk even getting their feet wet in order to climb the bit of land and rock.

The girls took the stairs with careful feet. At the top, there was a wide, flat place in the center where they could stand. The strange barge did not return as quickly as it had come.

Lake-scented breeze twisted knots in her long hair as Ember took in the scene. Now, on the water rather than looking out toward it, Ember's perspective changed. Or the lake itself changed. She wasn't sure which. It had grown enormous, a seemingly infinite body of water that stretched to the horizons on either side. And the shore they had just departed lay far, far behind them. Other than their own wake, there was little movement on the surface.

In the distance, on either side of them, spouts of water erupted. At first a few, and then tens, dozens. "*Whales?* Selah, are there *whales* in the lake?"

"Not whales. Leviathan. But they, too, seem to welcome you. This day is proving full of surprises."

The island drew near, or they drew nearer to it. It was then Ember saw what her friend already knew. Someone was waiting for them on the shore. As the distance shortened, Ember saw a woman. She had dark skin and her hair was short, almost shorn. Her hands were clasped in front of her, giant blue-grey wings spread out behind. Petite but impressive and, Ember thought, important.

Their piece of rock met the island with a deep, soft *thud.*

Selah ran toward the woman. When she reached her, they embraced. Selah rested her head on the woman's shoulder for a brief moment, the gesture confirmed for Ember how very tired her friend must be. Watching the two filled her with a sad sort of longing. No one since Hank had held her with anything approaching love, and she was overtaken with a fresh wave of missing him.

When Selah turned and faced Ember, her face was stern, belied by a small grin that tugged at the corners of her mouth. It was the first time Ember had seen her wear such an expression.

"Ember, this is Alma. She is a Philosopher, and she probably should not be here."

"Thank you. I will worry about myself," Alma said. Her sterling eyes smiled. "Ember, I am so pleased to meet you. Come, girls, we have much to discuss."

ONCE upon a time, quite some time ago . . .

HARVEY was not a bad kid; he just did not always choose to do the right thing. And it was not as though he ever hurt anyone. Sometimes, people just got hurt.

That Saturday, the cards had not been kind to Harvey. He was out of chips, out of scotch, and just about out of luck. Poker was not always Harvey's game on a good night, and this had not been a good night. When none of the guys would spot him to get back in the game or buy him another glass, Harvey rose from the table on unsteady legs, bowed almost too low for his condition, and thanked the room with a sweep of his arm and a tip of his hat.

"Gooood night, gentlemen. Enjoy my money." The other men were glad to see him go. He was too young to be there at all, but they were amused by him and liked taking what cash he brought to the table.

Outside the club, across the street near the park, was a bench. Harvey, unsteady and exhausted, stumbled over to rest a bit. He needed to give his head time to clear before he figured out how he was getting home. The last thing he needed was his mother catching him drinking again.

When he woke, slumped and drooling, the night had gone from cool to cold and a young woman sat at the other end of the bench. She had the reddest hair Harvey had ever seen and huge wide-set eyes. She was a knockout. And, it appeared she had wings. She was at the moment using them to shield her small frame from the cold, earliest morning air.

The wings retracted. "You have lost your way, Harvey." That voice. After the din in the club, it sounded like music. And like she was speaking right in his ear.

"I'm good." He straightened up and adjusted his hat. Harvey's head was full of bees and molasses.

"Harvey, you have lost your way. I can take you to a place where you can find it again. A place to make you forget about the cards and the drink. A chance to get back on your right path. There is a life waiting for you, a life where you might do important things. I can take you to a place where you can get all that."

Overwhelmed with drink and strangeness, Harvey closed his eyes for the briefest moment. When he opened them, she was there next to him, almost touching. No one was that quick or that quiet. She reached up and pressed her cool fingers against his temples. And then the thick buzzing was gone, as if it had never been there. Harvey looked into her weird grey eyes for the first time. He could not read what was there.

"Harvey, I am not going to plead with you. Would you like me to take you to get well? Your way is not lost, but only misplaced. It is waiting for you."

"Honey, after that magic trick I would follow you to the moon."

Walking to the moon would have made more sense than the trip Harvey and the girl took.

There had never been a lake in the field behind the old high school. Of this, Harvey was certain. For starters, he had gone to that school until the school asked him not to come back, and he had spent time in that field doing the sort of business he would not have told the fairy girl about. More important than that, the field simply was not big enough for a lake. Yet here a lake was, complete with an overgrown island right in the middle.

"The hell . . . ?" The girl did not turn to look at Harvey again until they reached the edge of the lake and the small rowboat that rested

on the shore. She pushed the boat into the water and climbed in with practiced ease. Harvey was not as graceful.

The boat pulled away from the shore without assistance, and moved without sound toward the island. Harvey leaned over as far as he dared, looking into the water. The surface was black glass cut with silver moonlight, but below it roiled. In the dark, Harvey could not see the things churning in the depth, and they did not so much as sway the boat, but he knew they were there nonetheless. Even unseen, they were terrifying. Harvey stayed planted in his seat for the remainder of the short trip.

At the edge of the rocky island, the boat came to a gentle stop at the foot of a low stone staircase. The girl stepped out and reached in to help Harvey. He was surprised at the strength in her long hand when she took his. She did not immediately pull him up. Instead, she looked at him, almost through him.

"You have lost your way. That is what the Fountain has for you, your way. You will know it. Nothing else is yours. Nothing at all. If you choose to take what is not yours, it will not end well for you. Do you understand?"

Harvey thought he understood. "Do not take anything that isn't mine. And I'll know what's mine."

The girl nodded and they started down a narrow trail that ran deep into the darkest woods Harvey had ever been in. He tried to ignore the sounds of movement, and the chittering he heard all around, doing his best to focus on the fairy girl in front of him. When the path opened up, the light improved and so did the view. The spring before them was the size of a fountain in a city park. The water was luminous, the cascade that fed it glowed a subtle silver.

Propped up against the far side of the fountain, a few yards away, was a large roll of paper. The edges were yellowed and creased. One corner was torn. He knew it at once.

"Dad's map. But it was lost, lost with everything else."

The map of the world once hung in his father's study. Harvey spent untold childhood hours learning its geography, planning his future. Then the money was gone and the house was taken, and there was no study, and no map.

He was here for the map, then. Harvey saw the fairy girl watching him. She gave him a nod so slight he almost missed it.

Harvey stood at the edge of the fountain and looked into it. It was shallow and clear, smooth on the bottom like poured concrete. And it was littered with treasure. There were coins, both gold and silver. Not nickels and dimes, but real coins. Old coins. Gold and silver enough to fill his pockets and his hat, and his socks and his shoes. It was money enough to keep him in girls and games and drink for the rest of his life. He turned in a harried circle. There was no one but the fairy girl to see him. Or stop him.

"Only what is yours, Harvey. Nothing else. It will not end. I will not plead with you."

Harvey heard that voice so clearly, but listening and understanding and even wanting to understand are different things. He heard her, but he also heard the siren song of all that money, and it was so much louder than her words. There was just so much of it. He could load the boat back on shore, and there would still be treasure for the next guy. And the next. Harvey began to sort out how he would get back, next time without the girl, to get the rest. He unbuttoned his cuffs, rolled up his sleeves as he thought.

Harvey knelt at the fountain, reached in with his right hand. He pulled back in disgust. The water, clear as it was, was hot and thick. Not to be deterred, Harvey reached back in and grasped at the nearest coins. The water reached only his forearm as his fingers brushed gold.

The red-haired fairy girl turned away.

Something strong and slick grasped Harvey's wrist. He had time to register one enormous, sightless eye before he was pulled deep into the fountain. The water boiled, then calmed again.

After a long silence, the girl said to everyone, "I am sorry. I believed he could find his way."

She walked soundlessly into the midnight forest, wings sagging and head low, carrying the map with her.

Chapter Twenty-One

Ember

Alma offered a hand to Selah, who took it at once.

Ember took an involuntary half step back, unsure of her place. Alma reached out to her, took her arm. Ember wanted to both lean into and pull away from the contact, but she allowed it.

The three walked along the shoreline, away from the low stone stairs and toward whatever would come next. The lake to their right was placid, blue sky and clouds reflected there. To their left, the trees created a wall around the interior of the island. They were the tallest Ember had ever seen, some species she thought she could name while others were entirely foreign. The air was rich, complicated with the sharp breeze off the water and the living, green scent of the forest.

"It is good you are home," Alma said. "And I think you need not worry about the reception you will receive. Everyone is quite preoccupied with our new visitors." Alma turned to Ember. "No, not you, Ember, but I think they will be very interested in you as well."

In a brief silence between them, Ember heard birds shouting and whispering and singing to one another from deeper in the woods. Like the trees themselves, some of the calls were familiar while others were new to her.

"The Jury's boy arrived last night. He was alone. He *swam*. Well, he floated, but can you imagine?" Alma grimaced. "What an awful trip that must have been. The Jury is having second thoughts, or is toying with the child. I am not certain, and there has been no reasoning with her of late. In fact, it seems no one has seen the Jury in over a day."

Ember thought to ask about this Jury and the boy who swam, but Alma didn't take much of a breath between sentences as she relayed everything Selah had missed.

"And Ava's boy is here. Gabrielle and Simon brought him, of course." Alma looked over at her friend, watching for a reaction.

Selah stopped walking. With a furrowed brow she turned to Alma. "Ava's boy is here?"

"Yes."

"And the Jury's pet. And Ember. And the Jury is *missing*? Alma, what does it mean?"

Alma sighed. "Don't call him a pet. It makes you sound like Magdalene. I think it means we have much to do, and much to explain to Ember. What have you told her?"

"Very little."

"Then we should start now. Talk as we walk. Ember, how much do you know about our Selah? What has she shared?"

Ember glanced at her not-angel, who nodded for her to answer. "I know she stopped my daddy from hurting us, and probably killed my uncle Joe. But Daddy and Joe were going to kill her, I'm sure. And maybe me, too. I know she saved me and brought me here. I think . . . I *know* she is my friend."

At the word *killed,* Alma looked at Selah with hard eyes, but said nothing until Ember finished. "Then you have a good start, Ember. You know she is brave, and you know she is your friend. Let me fill in some of the finer points.

"Like most of us, Selah was born in the Hatchery. She became one of the best keepers of little ones I can recall. In many ways, the Hatchery is Selah's home. Selah, would you agree?" Alma did not wait for

Selah to respond. "I think it is fitting we start there. Besides, it is on the way more or less. Would you like to see it?"

"Yes, I would, Miss Alma." Ember wanted to see it all. She knew little about the island she now walked on except it was beautiful, and so entirely different from anywhere she had ever known.

Alma smiled at the girl's manners, allowed her the formality. "But there is something I need you to try to understand about the island, and the places on it. Do you recall how the island appeared in a place it was not before, in a place it did not belong? Of course you do, it was just this morning."

Ember watched Alma hungrily, wanting this information very much.

"The island appears when and where it is needed, and when and where it chooses. The island may be in many places at once, and in many *whens* at once. What you think of as the past, or even the future, does not matter as much here. All those from different *whens* are simply *now* when they are here. You do not have to understand fully. That is the role of the Philosophers, and we still debate it from time to time. What I ask is that you try to accept what I am telling you. Can you do that?"

Ember was thoughtful. She wanted to give Alma an honest answer, but found the words were jumbled when she tried to put them together. "I believe in God even though I've never seen him. I believe in gravity even though I can't explain it. I believe Selah took all the bad out of Daddy and Joe, and it turns out there wasn't anything else in there, even though I don't understand how. I believe what you're telling me. I saw a lake show up in a wheat field this morning. It is more proof than I have about God, and I still pray at night."

Alma rewarded Ember with a smile and a squeeze of her hand. "Selah, your friend is a wonder. Thank you, child, for believing. May I continue?" Ember nodded, so Alma did.

"Those of us born here are tasked with tending the Fountain, and caring for one another. While the Fountain is the center of the island, its fulcrum and its epicenter, the Hatchery is the island's heart. To each generation past, and each to come, it is home."

They crossed through the edge of the forest, and Ember found herself at the top of a steep valley. At its base was an enormous wooden structure.

The Hatchery was the largest building Ember had ever seen. Had it not been nestled in a valley, the Hatchery would be impossible to miss even from a great distance.

Wide-eyed, Ember looked from Selah to Alma, and back again at the building. "Can we go in? May *I* go in?"

In answer, Selah took her by the elbow and led her down the slope to the immense front door.

The Hatchery had far too humble a name. It was built from enormous boards of golden wood. The giant front doors, three times Ember's height, were warm to the touch. A deep, covered porch spanned the front, and wrapped around one side of the building. The entire structure felt as if it had been soaking in the sun since the day it was constructed.

Inside, it was a cathedral of vaulted wooden ceilings and simple, sweeping, elegant lines. One entered the great room, the heart of the Hatchery, directly through the front doors. There was no ornamentation, only the bright, clear light through the building's many windows. Light crossed light and shadows played, emphasizing the quiet magic of the place. The air was sweet and warm and still.

Trees grew from the earthen floor. Some reached almost to the ceiling, making them very old. And hanging from the ceiling, from the trees, on the walls and even resting on the dirt floor were dozens of soft bundles. Some were attached firmly to branches and trunks, others dangled by a thin thread and twisted in the soft breezes allowed by the windows.

"Chrysalis or cocoons?" Ember remembered reading about them in a school book with dense text and pen-and-ink illustrations.

"Cocoons. Chrysalis are of butterflies. Moths come from cocoons."

Each cocoon was no smaller than a skein of yarn. Most were much larger.

"Are you a kind of moth, then?" Ember found she was whispering. The place seemed to require it.

Selah lifted her lavender wings in a shrug. "Of a sort. You once asked if I was a fairy, and I suppose that is right in a way as well. I do not know we will agree on one word."

"It doesn't matter. This is the most beautiful place I have ever been. You were born here? And Alma?"

"Yes. Most are of the Hatchery. A few are of the wild, but they are the exception. A rare few are brought to the island from your world. Even those are brought to the Nursery."

The notion babies might be carried here from her world brought to mind images of fairies and changelings from storybooks, but Ember didn't want to offend Alma and Selah by suggesting it. Instead, she asked, "The Nursery?"

"When the little ones hatch, we take them to the Nursery. Let us see it next?"

"Please." It was clear to Ember that Selah loved this place.

They walked through the Hatchery toward an almost-regular-sized door in the back of the great room. It was, Ember saw, a bit wider than she was accustomed to. *To let their wings pass*, she thought. Through it was a smaller, less brightly lit space. White curtains hung over the open windows, allowing soft light to enter. Baskets and cradles made from what looked like the same stuff as the cocoons, hung from the high ceilings. They rocked gently. Soft music filled the room. The air itself seemed to breathe in and out, in and out. If Ember still questioned her decision to come here, it was answered in that moment. The music filling the room was the same music she'd been hearing since she was a small child. The same music she heard when the mermaid would visit.

A number of winged young women, and one grey-winged young man, sat in rocking chairs scattered about the room. They held infants or small children, comforting them to sleep. One Hatchery keeper lifted her hand in greeting. She smiled at them, and then returned her attention to her tiny ward.

Selah walked to the nearest basket and reached in. She picked up what slept in there with practiced hands. The baby boy was tiny and dark, with the same blue-grey wings as Alma. But the baby's wings looked downy, and softer than those of the adults. They were wrapped around him tightly so he was swaddled in them. Selah brought him to her chest, and he relaxed into her.

Selah's eyes hardened as she turned them away from the baby and toward Ember. She spoke in a voice soft enough to keep from disturbing the child, but with a firmness that underpinned her words. "The Hatchery is the only place on the island that matters. Everything else can burn as far as I am concerned, but we protect this place to the very end."

Ember nodded, and a silence fell amongst the three of them. She was embarrassed to ask the next question, but had to. "Selah, can I hold him? I'll be so careful . . ."

"Of course. They are like human babies in most ways. Fragile, but so much stronger than they look." Selah handed the boy to Ember, whose hands shook only a little as she took him in her arms. He was so light, and smelled of the sweet, green air of the forest. His wings were silken canvas in her hands. Ember rested her chin on his thick, black hair and closed her eyes. Breathed him in.

"I've never held one before."

"Of course you have never. You only just arrived. Or . . . you mean you have never held a baby before." Alma struggled to hide her surprise. She looked at Selah, who nodded her head in confirmation. Ember had caught the exchange but ignored it. There had been little softness in her life, and she didn't want to ruin this perfect moment by thinking about it, much less discussing it.

"His name is Imre. It means strength. He struggled at first, but has grown strong." Alma spoke in Ember's ear, wrapped her wing around Ember's shoulder.

"Is he yours?"

"He is the island's. I will help care for him and teach him when he is old enough. I teach many of the island's children. But most of the care is done by the Hatchery keepers. It does not matter what their kind, or if they are wild, or even if they are brought to the island from elsewhere—from your *where*. The Hatchery keepers care for all of them the same."

"They don't have mothers?" The idea brought tears to Ember's eyes. All her life she had tried to be a daughter to a mother who wouldn't have her. She wondered if these babies forever kept unnamed, hollow spaces where a mama should have been.

"In his own time, Imre will bind himself more tightly to one of the keepers than to the others. They will be bonded, be close throughout their lives. That keeper will be his mother or his father in all the ways that matter. Imre will be here in the Nursery for many years, they will have time together to become family."

"For years . . . right. Time is different here."

"Yes," Alma agreed. "Very good. Time is different here than what you are accustomed to. It is much slower, more elegant. When we watch your lives, it is like watching bamboo grow. We can almost hear you age. Here, there is more. More time. More space between the moments. Sometimes, when one first arrives at the island, time can be unreliable. Short hours for some, long moments for others, but always braided together eventually. We all end up on the same timeline, the same clock."

"Will time be the same for me on the island? Slower?"

"Eventually, the time you and I share here is the same."

Ember handed Imre to Selah, and remembered something from earlier in the morning. "Selah, you were a Hatchery keeper? And then you went to the Fountain? Why? This place is so perfect. And the babies . . ."

"I was not good at it. I found something at which I was better." Selah's words were clipped, and her wings were drawn tight against her back.

"That is not true. Do not build your friendship on lies." Alma was gentle but firm. "Ember, I will tell you what Selah perhaps cannot. Selah was a wonderful Hatchery keeper. Maybe that is because she was raised by Beatrix, who was a marvelous keeper before she became the Jury. The children adored Selah, and she them. Selah was still new to the role when she began to form her first bond with a little one. Mara was too small, and not healthy. Her wings were stunted, and she would not feed as she needed to. But Selah could not see any of it. She was devoted to the child. When Mara died, Selah left the Hatchery." Alma told the story plainly, but with sympathy. She stroked Selah's wing as she spoke.

Ember recalled Selah's anger at her own mother. She understood it better now. She wanted to speak, but there was nothing right to say.

Selah broke the silence. She handed Imre to Alma and said, "There is something else I would like to show you. Something I think you will enjoy very much."

Chapter Twenty-Two

Sam

Sam had no idea where he was. The not knowing was filling him with hot stones of dread and panic. The stones weighed his feet down and made each step harder than the last.

He had been lost for hours. There was little variation in the forest, and he was unable to mark his progress. Sam knew he could be headed toward the Fountain. Or toward a cliff. Or he could be walking in aimless circles.

He had made a grave error. In his excitement to finally be on the island, in his desperation to reach the Fountain, Sam had rushed into the forest with no understanding of the lay of the land, and with no plan. In hindsight, he should have kept to the edge of the island and followed the shore. Then, maybe, he would have a better idea of where to go. He might at least have a sense of how big the island was, of its shape.

He was hungry. He was thirsty and had little water in his bag. He was hot. The island was humid in a way Sam had never experienced before. The later the morning grew, the heavier the air became. He found it difficult to breathe, to think. Sam sat on a fallen log and looked around for something, for anything, that might tell him where he was.

Sam was angry with himself for being so stupid and so rash. But, he was angrier still at the Sounds. They had abandoned him, left him alone to wander without direction.

Where are you? Why are you doing this? Sam spoke the words in the grey landscape of his mind.

And then, aloud. "Where are you? This isn't fair! All my life you've been in my head. All my life, you've asked me to come. To come *here*, to follow *you*! Well, I made it. And where the hell are you? I'm here. For the Fountain, for you. For whatever this is I'm supposed to be doing."

Silence. Sam closed his eyes. No one came to meet him in the barren grey.

"Fine. Fine! I'm finished. Done. I don't want you in my head! I'm going to find my way out, and I'm going to get the hell off your island. I got here without you, and I'll leave without you. I'm done."

Sam stood, slung his duffel bag over his shoulder. He took two steps, three. He paused as he felt something change, a shift in the air and beneath his feet. Then the ground opened up and swallowed him.

It took no time at all to heal itself.

Sam woke to nothing. It was black, perfect and unblemished darkness.

He hurt all over, but the back of his head was the worst, throbbing from where he'd slammed it into the hard-packed earth. It felt like he had hit *everything* in his fall. Sam gingerly touched the back of his head. There was a lump growing there, but no blood that he could feel.

He began reaching out in the coarse, wet earth for his bag. Even the air was damp, and tasted of minerals and rot. His movements were slow and deliberate, knowing if he rushed, he would grow frantic. If he grew frantic, he would die here.

Wherever here was.

Sooner than he dared hope, Sam's hands found the canvas bag. He pulled it toward him and clutched it to his chest. Grateful tears slipped from his closed eyes. When his breathing steadied, Sam found the bag's zipper. He opened it, careful not to turn it over, making sure nothing fell out. He felt around the bag until he found what he was looking for, a high-power flashlight Dennis and Juliette had given him the previous Christmas. Arrived by mail, of course. *The perfect gift for the kid who never leaves his house*, he thought at the time. Now, it was a lifeline.

Sam found the switch and, mercifully, the flashlight responded.

Cavern was too grand a word for where Sam was, and the word *cave* implied an entrance and an exit.

Sam was in a hole in the ground.

Above him, tree roots created webbing that held the dirt ceiling in place. It was short enough he could reach up and touch some of the lowest hanging roots with his fingertips. He saw no tunnels, no burrows, nothing to indicate what had created this hole the size of a small bedroom.

As Sam played the flashlight around the hollow space, he found he was not alone. In the walls, the ceiling, the floor, were the kinds of insects and crawling things that thrived in dark, wet places. Pale, moist, and mostly blind, some pulled away from his light, others took no notice. They were repulsive and they were everywhere. There would be no avoiding contact with them.

Sam sat where he stood, could feel the ground squirming under his weight. After the heat of the morning, he was cold, shivering. He wrapped his arms around his bag and considered the situation.

The flashlight flickered.

Or Sam imagined it did.

Clink went another little piece of sanity down the deep, deep well.

Chapter Twenty-Three

Miles

"I would prefer we did not waste time tonight. There is no reason we cannot reach the Fountain before sunrise." Gabby was eager to move.

"Yeah. Okay. But what *happened* back there?" Miles stared out at the lake. There was no sign of the bridge, nor the playground they had departed just a few minutes earlier. There was nothing but rippling water, tatted into lace by the bright moon, stretching out beyond.

"We will talk as we go. I thought you were safe on the bridge, but you were not. And now I do not know if you are safe near the lake, either." Gabby began walking toward the forest.

Miles took one last look at the water. If the now-ruined bridge was his way back, he wondered how he would manage to get home.

Simon pulled at Miles's arm. "We need to follow her. To stay together."

"If we're not safe at the lake, are we safe in there?" Miles gestured toward the woods. They no longer looked quite as inviting, and he was less eager to meet what might live there than he had been a few minutes earlier considering what lived in the lake.

"We are safest with her," said Simon.

Miles watched as Gabby crossed the edge of the shore and slipped into the forest, disappearing into the dense growth. When he followed between two massive trees, a narrow path that had been invisible from the outside wound through the forest.

It was darker than on the shore, and Miles could now hear rustling in the black on either side. Looking up was dizzying, and what stars he could see above the treetops were ice bright in the indigo sky. Morning was coming, but not fast enough for Miles. He hurried to catch up to Gabby with Simon following close behind.

"The . . . whatever in the lake. The hands. And those arms . . ." Miles prompted.

"They are your strangers. The remnants of people. People who came to the Fountain with the intent to abuse, or steal, or destroy. Each of them was judged, and they were punished. The Fountain took them, and when the Fountain takes you, you change. The most fundamental elements, the core, survives and becomes . . . something else. The cores of those people were rotten, so they became rotten things. Mean, hungry, wrathful. There is nothing left but the bad. And the bad is then used to protect the Fountain, and to punish the next who come to take advantage. It is the circle of things."

"Their core? Are you talking about their souls?"

"If you wish."

Miles grabbed Gabby's arm and turned her toward him. "You've always told me Ava died in the Fountain, drowned herself in it. Does that mean part of her is still in there?" He gestured behind him, toward the lake.

Gabby paused. Then, "Yes. I think so. Somewhere. And I believe she may be the reason for the unrest in the water. And why I brought you."

Miles narrowed his eyes at Gabby, trying to make sense of what she was telling him. "Why would you think that?"

"Because the things that are escaping the water seem to be looking for you. And, today, two of them found you."

Miles's mind whirled. He tried to braid the threads together, but there were some he could not catch hold of. "How is she controlling the zombies in the lake? I thought you said only the Jury was in charge around here?"

Gabby nodded. "Yes. But the Jury is missing."

"You think Ava, what, kidnapped her?"

Gabby did not directly answer. "I think Ava wants you back. Wants you to come home."

"This isn't my home. I've never even been here!"

Simon answered in a bewildered voice. "Miles, is none of this familiar? You have been here. Many times. Ava brought you often, when you were very young."

Chapter Twenty-Four

Selah

At the top of the valley, a narrow trail took them from the Hatchery and into the forest. Once inside the trees, the day's bright sun was broken by limbs and leaves and vines high overhead. It was cooler, if more humid, than on the shore. Birds of all colors and sizes played in the forest. They were not afraid of the trio, and were often underfoot darting and hopping from one place to the next.

Alma shooed a group of what might have been sparrows, had sparrows ever been made in the brightest shade of orange. The little birds squawked indignantly and scurried away. "When Selah left the Hatchery, it was a sad time. For her, for the little ones, for all of us. But we understood. Losing Mara was terrible, more so as Mara was her first bond. Selah was aimless for a short while, and grew bored, I think. Selah, would that be accurate?"

Selah made a small, disinterested noise in confirmation. She had been bored, yes, and also heartsick and ashamed. She wanted to discuss none of it, so she let Alma carry on knowing, if allowed, the woman could talk for hours and Selah herself would have to say little.

"Selah set out to be a Fountain keeper. It is a role normally assigned, but Selah was determined to prove herself. And she did. She became adept at locating seekers out in the world, those attached to losting things. She was talented at persuasion, and few of her seekers broke any of the Fountain's rules. Seekers and losting things were reunited under

Selah's watch. There are many, many keepers of the Fountain, and Selah was beginning to stand out among them. This carried on until—"

Selah, expecting Alma would gloss over what was important to this part of the story, interrupted. "Until I began to question my role. I became unsure if I was serving the Fountain only to sometimes harm the seekers. Beatrix—the Jury—became unreliable, unpredictable. Her justice of late has not felt like justice at all. And the scales are not balanced as they should be. The Jury began to revel in darkness. So I went in search of a light."

"So you left. And ended up in our *silo*?" Ember's tone said this made little sense to her.

"I followed a bright line, and it led me to you." Selah paused. "I am sorry."

Ember stopped, grabbed Selah by the arm, and turned her so they could face one another. "No! Why? You saved yourself, saved me, brought me here. Why are you sorry?"

Selah was surprised by Ember's boldness, but glad to see it. Boldness would serve her well. She averted her gaze from the girl's earnest eyes. "I am sorry I did not try to do more for your mother. I was angry, and tired, and wanted to get you out of that place. Away from her and all the awful. I do not know what I could have done, what was left to save. But I am sorry I did not try."

Ember did not respond, did not seem to know what to say. So she said nothing, and wrapped her arms around Selah. They stood that way for a moment. Each of them, for their own reasons, not accustomed to holding, or to being held.

Alma broke the silence. "Girls, we have almost reached the Library."

Of course Selah knew that. Alma was trying to move them along. She was helping Ember to understand, and that was important, but there were other matters to be addressed. Selah looked forward to getting Alma by herself so they could speak without reserve.

They began to walk, perhaps a bit faster now, allowing comfortable silence to linger among them once again.

Chapter Twenty-Five

Ember

The Library dwarfed the Hatchery, although it was built in the same simple, clean style. The boards it was built from seemed impossibly wide and long. Ember touched the sun-warmed wood and wondered what kind of tree provided logs big enough for the lumber.

There, in the brightness, at the entrance of the Library, Ember realized just how hot the day would be.

"Is it always warm like this?"

Selah nodded. "Yes, hot and humid. The trees like it. So do the little ones, and the menagerie. It is better at night. But do not fret, as you will grow accustomed to it. Soon we will get you some different clothes, and they too will help."

As Ember had no time to change her clothes the morning her father dragged her to the silo—*that was just this morning,* she reminded herself—she wore the same heavy dress and boots she left the farm in, and had been wearing them for two days. Despite being filthy, Selah's soft pants and top looked comfortable in comparison, appropriate for the heat.

Ember turned her attention back to the Library. "Why is there such a huge library on the island? Why so many books here?"

Selah smiled. "It is not that kind of a library, Ember. There are books here, but many other things as well. Come, it will be easier to show you."

As big as the Library was on the outside, it was somehow even greater within. For a moment, the trick of walking into a building bigger on the inside than the outside made Ember unsteady on her feet. She could not see the far end of the building. She had no sense of where it stopped, or if it did.

Against the walls were shelves, rows and rows and rows and rows of them. At first, what they held made little sense to Ember. There were books, but there were also dolls. And shoes. And, there, a wedding dress. Ember saw a fountain pen, a brass horn, a photograph of two boys with an older man in a hat, and a cookie cutter shaped like an autumn leaf. She saw other things, sleek machines made of metal and materials she could not name.

There were many notebooks that must have been journals or diaries. There were reading glasses, and a stethoscope. And so much paper. Sometimes piles of it, enough to make a manuscript. Sometimes, single sheets of paper, or tattered envelopes. On one shelf, a mesh bag of what looked like tulip bulbs.

Anything, everything was here.

Near the center of the front of the room was the first of many cabinets, each with hundreds of small drawers. Ember opened one and found a tiny ring with a dark blue stone. She thought it was the kind of ring some parents gave to babies when they were born. Another drawer held an engagement ring. Another, a class ring. Ornate, expensive rings and costume jewelry with paste diamonds. Many, many wedding bands. Each drawer had a tiny label with a name and a date.

Ember opened *A. Helm, January 7, 1796* and found a copper ring turned green with time. "Selah, there is so much here. Is it every lost thing? Every lost thing ever?"

"No. Remember many lost things are simply lost. They stay where they stay, or go where they go. These are all the losting things waiting to be found. When a seeker reaches the Fountain, or when one is brought there, the losting thing goes to the Fountain, too. This, the Library, is where they wait." Selah was quiet, considered her words. "Ember, the Library is important, but, if we have to choose, we protect the Hatchery."

It was the second time she said it, and that worried Ember. She understood the importance of the Hatchery, but she could not imagine what there was on the island to protect it from.

For everything Ember learned, new questions followed. *I'm missing something that matters*, she thought. She couldn't shake the notion. Despite the island's beauty, there must be some lurking danger here, too. She could feel it in Selah's words and in her bones. There was more to this island than anyone was telling her.

What matters. That was it.

"But, why these things? Why do they matter? And why do you"—Ember looked from Selah to Alma and back again—"why do you *care*?"

Selah looked to Alma, handing the job of answering off to her.

Alma gazed up toward the soaring beams of the Library as though she were searching for the words she needed. Finally, "These losting things matter because in their being lost, something changes—goes wrong—for their seekers. Small things or large at first, but the losing of the thing starts a chain reaction of events that end badly. Sometimes badly for just one person. Sometimes catastrophic. By bringing them back together, we hope their path is put straight and lives are made right."

This made some sense to Ember. When she lost Hank—and that had been no small losing—everything that followed soured, turned like milk in the August sun. If she could have him back, well, nothing would be the same. So she could easily imagine how one event, as big as a brother's suicide or as small as the loss of a ring, could shape the days and years to follow.

"I understand," Ember said.

Alma regarded her with thoughtful eyes. “I think you do.”

“But why do *you* care? You’re here, away from all the awfulness. What difference does it make to any of you?” And another question occurred to her, it was something Selah had said at the lake before they crossed. “And why punish the greedy and the . . . the wicked? Why is that your job?”

Alma paused longer this time before answering and when she did, Ember was not satisfied.

“The simple answer is we were born to care. It is our purpose as much as we are able to understand. But purpose is a tricky thing, is it not? Like humans, we can only presume our purpose based upon the paths we can imagine paved before us and our intuition. For most of us, the island and the Fountain are a calling and a life’s work. But you must understand the Fountain and the losting and the seeking, as important as they are, are part of a much greater whole. And trivial by comparison.”

“And what is it—this larger . . . design?” Ember hardly understood what she was asking, much less how to ask it.

Alma shook her head. This line of questioning was over. “In time, if you stay with us, you may understand. You may even believe. But, for most of us, it is as you spoke of God. Few of us have evidence, most of us have only the stories told to us and our faith.”

Ember had been dismissed often enough to recognize it when it happened, even if Alma did it with kindness.

Ember had endless questions left, and she found one she thought might be answered. “Who keeps track of all these things?” She was overwhelmed with the sheer mass of it all.

Alma smiled. “The Librarians, of course. It is a good job for those who like order. There was a girl once, a girl who used to visit often. She would have been an excellent Librarian.”

“Ava.” Selah nodded her agreement.

Chapter Twenty-Six

Sam

Sam sat, once again clutching his bag in the bug-infested hole. He slept in short bursts interrupted by bouts of blinding anxiety. He would wake, open his eyes to nothing at all, and spend a terrible moment remembering where he was, that he was going to die in a pit.

He closed his eyes again, began reciting his mother's letter in his head. He could almost hear her saying the words.

No, not her, but someone.

Someone was reading his mother's letter aloud in his head.

Sammy, it was you.

It was always you, Sammy.

You had all the power always.

You just didn't have any control.

I know you didn't mean to.

I hate that you have to know.

It was a bad approximation of his mother's voice, and at the end, they weren't even trying for accuracy. It was the Sounds, performing a mean, half-hearted impression of Sam's dead mother.

Sam opened his eyes, saw the Sounds sitting across from him, their head cocked, expectant. Like nothing had happened. Like they hadn't abandoned him. Like nothing had changed.

But something *had* changed.

The Sounds were no longer collected fog in human form in the bleak landscape of his mind.

Now, somehow, the figure sitting cross-legged before him was made of pale and crawling things. Beetles and worms and insects with too many legs clung to one another grotesquely, writhing against a force Sam could not see. When the figure shifted, or cocked its head, some were crushed while others—the lucky few—fell to the dirt floor and scuttled to safety.

Sam slid back in the dirt until his shoulders touched the wall behind him and there was nowhere left to go. He put as much distance between himself and the Sounds as he could manage.

The figure had no mouth and no eyes. No face at all, just a mass of tiny monsters shaped in the approximation of a head. He managed to hold in a scream, but only just. If the figure had looked at him—or worse, smiled—he was sure he'd start screaming and never stop.

Despite the repulsive form, the voice was the same. It was the Sounds still and, he was sure, they had taken this form to frighten him. There was no other explanation.

It worked. Sam was afraid.

He did his best not to give them the satisfaction of showing his fear because, despite the fear, Sam was angry. That was something he could use, and he held on to it as hard as he could. He was angry at the Sounds for disappearing, for mocking his dead mother, for having the gall to come back at all. He felt like a small, injured animal being toyed with by a feral cat, and it pissed him off.

As irate as he was with the Sounds, he was far angrier with himself, furious, at the gratitude and relief he felt at seeing them. Even in their current state.

Why are you still down here? Are you not cold? Bored?

Sam thought they were taunting him, then realized they were whining.

We are bored. Tired of waiting.

Sam spoke aloud, all at once too overwhelmed to argue. "I'm here because I am. You were gone. I was lost. The ground . . . ate me and now I'm in this hole and there's no way to get out. *That's* why I'm here."

Of course there is a way to be free. Sam, you are smart. You will figure it out.

"Stop it. Stop using my mother's words."

You are very good at killing, Sam. A spider tumbled from the place where the Sounds' mouth should have been. They casually lowered a hand and crushed it before it could skitter away.

Sam grimaced at the easy cruelty of it, both the killing and the words. He was stung, stunned. "Not on purpose." The words were a whisper and a prayer.

Sam, but you can. If you have to. Do you remember the bunny, Sam?

Sam's heart dropped to his sour stomach and made him want to vomit. Shame and fear and *remembering* crawled through him like termites come to eat away at what was left of him.

"No. Sort of." He grasped his head, shook it. "Why are you asking about *that*?"

We will tell you a story, Sam. To help explain. It will not take long.

And so the Sounds did. They told a story about Sam and a bunny, but also about Sam's mother . . .

If Sam's mother had more time, there was so much she would have shared with him. There are things she would have tried to explain, and apologies she would have attempted. Because she ran out of time, she was never able to explain the bunny to Sam. The bunny wasn't the whole story, not by a long shot. It was, however, the first time Sam really scared his mother. Later, she would often remind herself of the bunny when questioning her own actions. She remembered the bunny to justify scaring, and scarring, her only son.

Yes, the bunny is where she would have started.

The summer Sam was five, his mother brought home the little creature. Sam was a shy boy, and lonely, in need of something to be close to other than Mother. The bunny was a small grey-brown thing with big, dark watery eyes. She was restless, and gentle, and Sam loved her at once. He named her Baby, which was a perfectly reasonable name for a little boy to give a little bunny. Baby had a pen outside with straw and food and water enough to keep her content.

One night, as summer was becoming fall, Mother brought the bunny inside. Mother worried the coming cold snap would be too much for Baby. Tucked in a cage with an old bath towel for bedding, Baby prepared to spend a comfortable night on the kitchen floor. With both Sam and Baby tucked in, Mother sat at the kitchen table later than usual sipping tea and watching Baby nestle down in her cage.

Mother was preparing to rinse her cup and shut off the lights when she heard Sam, awake again in his room.

Believing his mother was asleep in her own bed, Sam stood by his cracked bedroom door, trying to coax Baby into his room. He couldn't see the bunny in the kitchen, but knew she was there.

"Baby? Baby . . ." the little boy stage-whispered. "Wanna sleep in my bed? Come here, good bunny . . ." Baby perked her ears a bit but, being a bunny and not a puppy or even a cat, made no effort to escape her cage and go to Sam. Sam, being just five, didn't consider Baby might need help escaping.

After a few minutes of coaxing, Sam became frustrated, then furious, turned on a dime as only small children can. "Baby? Baby!" Angrier and louder this time. "Come here, bad bunny! Don't be a bad bunny or you! Will be! In trouble!"

Baby froze in her cage and died.

Mother knew Baby was dead even as it happened. There was no mistaking death, even in such a small and quiet creature. She approached the cage to be sure. Mother opened the door and lifted Baby's head a bit with her fingertips. It was too loose on its neck, too quick to fall again when, repelled, she dropped it. Still, to be certain, she pressed her fingers on its fragile side. Nothing. There was nothing at all.

Mother was not at all sure what she was going to do, when Sam called again, this time his voice was gentle. The kind boy regretted having yelled at his pet.

"Baby . . . Baby . . . come here, good bunny! Come see me?" Baby's nose twitched, she stretched to a standing position, and she looked up at Mother, as alive as she'd been less than a minute before. Mother stared at the tiny miracle, the tiny horror. She turned to her son's room as his mood began to darken again.

"Baby? Baby . . ." The bunny cowered back in the corner of her cage, terrified of something she couldn't possibly understand. Mother felt the same way.

"Sam," called Mother, "let me bring Baby to you for a good-night kiss. How will that be?" She hoped the fear she felt was well hidden. "I'll bring her right in."

"Yes, Mommy! Please, Mommy!" Bright, now. The little boy placated.

Mother opened the cage and reached in for Baby. For the first time, it nipped at her. Baby was fast and drew blood on Mother's left ring finger. And for the first time in their shared lives, she was afraid to upset her small son, so Mother was undeterred. She pulled the animal from her cage. Baby kicked with her back claws, and Mother felt the mean little nails on her chest and upper abdomen. She stood and cradled the terrified rabbit, whispering soft nonsense to her. The bunny calmed, or was in shock, Mother had no way to know.

Mother carried Baby toward Sam's room, the bunny's nose buried in the dazed woman's collarbone. As they crossed the threshold, Mother felt something hot and wet run down the front of her. As they approached the small child, Baby's bladder had let loose.

The room was dim, with just a night-light for illumination. Sam didn't notice the sharp smell, nor did he seem to register the tremor Baby had acquired. As Mother leaned over, he sat up and kissed Baby squarely between the ears. Mother leaned a bit farther and kissed Sam squarely between the eyes, trying to still the quavering in her limbs and voice.

"Good night, Sammy. I love you."

"Good night, Mommy. I love you, too." Sam rolled over and closed his eyes.

Mother carried Baby back to her cage. With the door latched, the animal did not move from where she was placed. Mother stared at the bunny for a long while, then back toward her child's bedroom.

Exhausted now, Mother went upstairs to change out of her urine-soaked clothes and take a too-hot shower. She didn't sleep much that night.

Baby lived with Mother and Sam another two weeks. The bunny spent most of her days in a semi-catatonic stupor, broken up by episodes of unpredictable scratching and biting. One night, as Sam slept, Mother took Baby to the wooded area behind the elementary school and let her go. Mother wished Baby luck, although she had little hope for a long and happy bunny life.

When Mother later told Sam that Baby had died, she was technically telling the truth.

Sam sat in the squirming dirt of the hole, head on his knees, a choking sob caught in the back of his throat. He did not lift it when he asked, "Why did you tell me that?"

To explain. Stories are for explaining. And because you need to know you can. You might take a life to save yourself, someday. Today, perhaps.

"I don't want to kill anything. And even if I did, what would I kill? The bugs?"

Maybe, for practice.

Sam found, with what felt like festering insanity, he wanted to try. The Sounds had cracked Sam open, the places he'd tried to seal, and the darkness inside him began to leak out. He hated the things crawling in what he had come to think of as *his* hole. Hated their paleness and their pointlessness. He lifted his head and stared hard at a cluster that squirmed on the wall opposite him. He hated the way they moved to nowhere, over and over again. He hated—

And they fell. The whole horrible cluster of them fell to the ground, dead and still.

Sam was shocked. Petrified.

Excited.

Interesting turn. Strong boy. Do it again.

And he did. He stared, and hated, and they died. He killed them one at a time, he killed them in groups. He was careful not to stand under the ones he killed after the first time he was rained on, a shower of little corpses in his hair and down the back of his shirt.

Try touching them. It will be better.

And he did. And this time, they did not just die. They burned. Brightly, completely, until nothing was left. The hole stank of gunpowder and burned insects. And he felt his power.

You can kill your way out of this. When you are done, find the Fountain.

Sammy, it was you.

It was always you, Sammy.

You had all the power always.

You are smart. You will figure it out.

The words of his mother. His dead mother. The one who contained him like a caged bunny. Who didn't love him—he didn't believe it for a second—but feared him. Who caged him to protect others. Who broke him to try to protect herself, so much good that did.

"Shut up shut up shut up!" Sam screamed and his voice was absorbed by the soft, dirt walls of the hole. "Stop. Using. My mother's. Words. You are useless and I hate you and will you *please* shut the hell up!" The rage and frustration that had been building in Sam released like a blown gasket.

What insects he had not already killed dropped dead to the floor of the hole, including those that had looked like a smallish person moments before. Now they were nothing but a still and scattered pile.

Silence.

Sam knew the Sounds were gone. Alone, again, he looked at what he had done by the light of his father's Christmas gift. The hundreds and thousands of tiny murders. It was exhilarating and shameful.

Sam thought through the situation with renewed interest, with hope. How was he to kill his way out of a place where nothing lived? It was a riddle to be solved.

Sam paced the hole, touching the walls, the floor, the tree roots above.

The tree roots.

The tightly woven roots were thick and strong, too heavy to cut with a knife even if he had thought to bring one. It was the roots that kept the soil above from collapsing. If the roots were not there, the whole earthen roof would likely cave in.

If Sam could kill a thousand bugs, he thought he could burn a tree. Not knowing what was above him, there was a real risk of injury when the roof collapsed. But he knew this was the way. It had to be.

Sam grasped one of the thickest, lowest hanging roots. He hoped it belonged to a very large tree. He focused all his frustration, all his loneliness, all his thoughts of Mother, all his hate on the tree root in his hand. When it happened, it happened all at once.

The root grew branding-iron hot and then was gone. There was a sizzling *whoosh* as all the roots attached to the tree were incinerated. Although he could not see it, Sam knew the same was happening to the tree above ground. There was a shifting, and then a sagging as the roof of the hole began to give way. Tiny pockets of daylight appeared. Sam grabbed another root, focused until it burned. This one created an opening big enough to see out of. Sam's eyes, grown accustomed to the dark, burned and watered. He squinted to see nothing but blue sky and treetops, and it was gorgeous. Air poured into the hole, warm and fresh and alive.

One more tree, and the opening caved in, became a doorway. There was a short series of crashes as neighboring trees were displaced, falling onto the forest floor. Sam grabbed his duffel bag, hoisted himself up some of the surviving roots, and pulled himself out.

He was covered in dirt and small carcasses. He smelled of dead, burned things. And he was free.

Sam had killed his way out of a hole in the ground.

It seemed the Sounds were not as worthless as he'd grown to believe.

Sam sat, laughing on the forest floor. He was in no better shape than he had been before, when the island tried to eat him. Tried to contain him like his mother. No better off save two important exceptions. Sam now knew how to mark his way. He also knew he could defend himself if he must.

Sam picked a direction, began walking.

He thought his mother might be proud.

Clink.

Chapter Twenty-Seven

Miles

The sky was lightening from indigo to melon and fuchsia and plum. Miles tried to take everything in at once—the rich smell of the air, the sky, the massive trees and the dirt and rocks and roots under his feet. He paid attention to all of it, searching for a leaf or a cloud that would trigger a long-buried memory. He believed Simon, who he had never known to tell anything but the truth. He had been here before and often because Ava had brought him. But there was nothing about any of it that felt familiar. Maybe he had just been too young.

A series of loud crashes broke both the quiet of the early morning and Miles's introspection. It was the sound of massive trees falling into one another and then to the ground. Their tone was strange, echoes of an echo. Great night birds, unseen until then, lit from the trees and into the air.

Simon looked down the path. "Gabby, that wasn't now, was it? That was ago."

"Yes, that was ago. The *whens* are aligning already. We must keep moving." For the first time since their trip began, Miles saw hesitation in Gabby's eyes.

"Miles, Ava is buried here on the island. Simon and I will take you there on our way to the Fountain."

Miles shook his head. "But I thought you said she was still in the Fountain."

"Only a part of her; the rest died as bodies do when they drown. That part of her, the dead part, was taken from the water. We have a small cemetery. She is there. We take care of it. Of her."

They left the path as the sun began to break through the branches above, lighting the forest.

The cemetery wasn't what Miles anticipated. There were no manicured acres and no bouquets left to rot on the ground. No concrete slabs marked the graves. Instead, around a small clearing, trees stood at each plot. Rather, all who were buried there had been buried under a tree.

On each tree was a plaque.

The plaques were at varying heights, depending upon when they were placed. As the trees grew, the plaques rose into the air with them. It was a slow and natural process toward the heavens. Most of the plaques were high up in the trees, their verdigris making them difficult to spot in the leaves and shadows.

"I love this place." Simon's hushed tone was respectful.

"Here." Gabby stood before a tree much smaller than most of those surrounding it. The trio gathered around.

Miles stood with his arms wrapped tight across his chest. The plaque was bronze and just lightly patinated. It was oval, the size of a generous platter. In the center, in flourished engraving, it read *Our Ava*.

Miles reached up and touched it, expecting the tarnish to leave his fingers green. His hand came away clean, but when he reached up to wipe his eyes, the scent of the metal lingered on them. It smelled of blood and ozone.

Miles was angry at Ava, but that didn't negate the persistent love he had for her. The anger was hot and bright and close to the surface, but the love was something that was in his bones. It was a part of him.

"Thank you." Miles spoke to no one in particular. "Thank you for taking care of her."

"Miles, we loved her. This was her home." Gabby clearly intended her words to console him.

Instead of comfort, Miles felt the sting of hurt tainted with jealousy, and in that moment love was forgotten. *I should have been enough. Home should have been where I was.*

When he spoke, Miles's voice was low and certain. He knew Ava couldn't hear him, but he said words he hoped would hurt her. "I'd like to go to the Fountain now. If Ava is looking for me—if that will put things right—let her come find me. But she can't have me. I won't give her that. She made her choice. I'll do whatever else I can to help make sure my *when* is safe—that it's still there at all. And then I want to go home. To my home. With my parents."

What he didn't say: *To the people who love me, who chose me, who didn't abandon me.*

A shriek rang out in the quiet.

Short as it was, the sound was visceral and made of agony. Something had been gravely injured not far from them. Without hesitation, Simon rushed out of the small cemetery clearing and into the trees beyond. So it was Simon who saw it before the rest of them. He stopped just before the path, staring up.

When Miles reached Simon, he knew from the boy's colorless face it would be bad.

A small stag, or what remained of it, was hanging heavy in the lower branches of a tree. Much of its midsection was gone. Fur and flesh and ropey organs hung in ragged, red drapes. Miles thought it was—had been—young, not yet the beautiful beast it might have become. Blood pooled on the ground beneath the poor creature and the smell of its torn guts filled the air around them. The stag took a final, shuddering breath. For the first time in his life, Miles bore witness to a death.

He choked back a wave of nausea.

There was a rustling in the undergrowth on the far side of the path as something moved swiftly away. Miles could not see what was there, just that it was large and low to the ground and moved like a predator.

"What was that?" Miles asked in a low whisper.

"Nothing that belongs here," Gabby replied. She pulled her blade from its sheath hidden in her tunic. It was the length of a large kitchen knife, but thinner, and wickedly sharp.

Tears ran from Simon's bright eyes, still pinned on the fresh carcass. "Help me get it down. We cannot leave it like that."

Miles moved to aid Simon as much for the hurting boy as for the dead animal, but Gabby stopped them both. "It stays until Gideon can see it. He, or another Groundskeeper. They will be able to tell us what did this. We stay on the path until we reach the Fountain. We go now, and we do not detour again."

ONCE upon a time, for many, many years . . .

JAMES loved Susan with his entire heart, and Susan loved James. They married quite young—too young, many said—and she died soon after. They had no children, and James was alone. It was all very tragic.

James would visit the cemetery often. Sometimes he brought flowers, but he always brought a book. He would sit and read to Susan as he had done during their courtship and too-brief marriage. He read to her mostly poetry, some short stories, and the occasional letter from one of their old school friends.

James missed Susan very much. He missed her so that he was unable to do much besides miss her. It made his days long and lonely. But he was so young, having that year turned nineteen. There was so much life ahead of him, but the thought of living it made him tired.

One day as James arrived at the graveyard, he found something amiss. There, where the green lawn and rows of stones like baby teeth should have been, was a beach. Beyond the beach, a lake. And right in the middle of that lake, an island. A handsome stone bridge spanned the divide between each shore. It was wide and looked strong and sound. It also looked generations old. James was fascinated and, having nothing better to do that day, put his book of poetry in his coat pocket and strolled across the bridge to the other side of the lake.

When he reached the island, James spied a footpath leading into a densely treed forest. He took it and, before long and without incident, he found himself at a lovely fountain fed by a cascading waterfall. Sitting on a stone bench near the fountain was a woman almost as beautiful as his Susan. She had silver-blond hair and a remarkable set of dappled ivory moth wings. She smiled at James in a way that made him wonder if she was also very sad.

"James, you are not dead, you know." She had the most wonderful, rich, quiet voice.

"Oh, yes, I know. But my wife is, and I'm lost without her."

"Losing yourself is a terrible thing, dear James. What is it you want?"

"I want my Susan back."

"That is something even the Fountain cannot give you."

"Well, then I wish she were not in a neat row in a tidy field with strangers. I wish I could read her poetry in a beautiful, wild place. I would like it if I could imagine her resting somewhere as beautiful as she was."

"If you could do that, read her poetry in a beautiful place, would you be able to find yourself again? To live your life?"

"I would still be sad but, yes, I think so."

"Follow me, darling James." Darling James had been Susan's name for him. He was sure the winged lady knew this.

So James followed the flaxen woman into the woods like a fairy tale. They came to a place where the trees opened up into a grove within the forest. The trees here let in more light and the sun played in the leaves and on the ground below them. Some of the trees had plaques. Some plaques were high in the branches and others much lower. The fairy took James' hand and showed him a plaque near the edge of the grove. It was polished silver and as big as a dinner plate. It read James's Beautiful Susan. *Near the tree was a low grey stone bench, much like those he had seen at the fountain.*

James looked at the fairy with wonder. "Is she . . . here?"

"She is. Susan is resting just below the tree. And that is your bench. You may come here to read to her anytime you wish. Will this place do, James? Will this place help you live a good life, and find yourself again?"

"It is the prettiest place I have ever been. It will do just fine. May I sit and read for a while?"

The fairy surprised James with a kiss on his forehead. "You are a good man. Stay here as long as you like." And she left him alone with Susan and the sunlight and his book.

So he did stay for a while, until the sun grew too weak to read by. And after that day he came back often, crossing the wide stone bridge from the shore to the island no one else could seem to see. He always came with a book to read.

James lived a good life. He went to university and found a career he enjoyed. He never married again, but he found countless ways to be happy and grateful. One day he simply disappeared. He was very old and few people missed him. Those who did assumed a distant family member had made the necessary arrangements for the kind old man.

But they were wrong.

There is a tree next to Susan's, their roots now intertwined. It has someone resting beneath it. The big silver plaque reads Susan's Darling James.

Sometimes a woman with flaxen hair and ivory wings sits on the low grey stone bench and reads them poetry in the speckled sunlight.

Chapter Twenty-Eight

Sam

The exhilaration that came with escaping the hole carried Sam on for a short time, but the hot, wet air and sense of aimlessness soon beat it out of him like a lead pipe.

He considered his options.

He could, of course, keep wandering as he had been.

It occurred to Sam he could climb a tree, a tall one, to get a better view of the island. He dismissed the idea almost as he had it. After a life spent mostly indoors and having recently fallen into a hole, he was in no condition to scale a tree, especially with a duffel bag in tow.

He thought about looking for the Sounds, asking for their help. But Sam's trust in the Sounds was eroding. They had provided no assistance in crossing the lake, and were cryptic when helping him escape the hole. What gave Sam the most pause was their attempt to frighten him by building themselves out of bugs. That, and the pleasure they took in his killing all the crawling things. It had been gross, unpleasant work, and the Sounds were gleeful as he went about it.

Looking deeper, Sam knew he had enjoyed it as well. He had taken too much amusement in destroying the bugs in the hole, had become frenzied with it. He would not lose control like that again.

But it was very, very good to know that he could. If he needed to.

When Sam discovered a slender, clear stream, two problems were solved at once. Sam no longer had to meander as he now had a landmark to follow, and he no longer had to conserve the single thermos of water in his bag. The stream had to be going somewhere, and was coming from somewhere. He drank from it deeply as he thought. It was cold and clean and tasted of minerals. He would follow the stream, go against its flow, and see where it might lead him. It was a plan.

By the time Sam realized he was being followed, his pursuer was within striking distance.

Feeling a gaze on his back, Sam froze. He turned before making a decision, unsure of what he would do with whoever, or whatever, was behind him.

A mutt, no longer a puppy but not yet fully grown, stood twenty feet behind him. At some point he had emerged from the forest, so quiet Sam did not hear him.

"Hey, dog, you scared me."

Its cocked head and wagging tail made Sam smile—both at the dog and his own fearful reaction. It was a welcome sight, something familiar and happy to see him.

"I should be following *you*. Maybe you'll take me where I need to go."

The young dog was curious, but it did not lead him. It kept a safe distance behind Sam as they continued up the stream. They walked that way for a while, almost but not quite together, but not for long. The young dog hadn't strayed far from home after all.

At a small clearing, a group of animals rested in the sun, a few drinking from the stream. Sam could see they were mostly dogs, but there was also what he thought might be a wolf, and a coyote. There were a few puppies that looked like they could have come from any combination of them, wild or domestic.

The animals were uninterested in Sam—they did not approach and did not threaten. His traveling companion bounded toward them, rejoining his pack.

Only the coyote was wary. She tensed, pulled away from the group. She began circling Sam, her path as wide as the trees would allow, working to place herself behind him.

As she circled, she also drew nearer. Sam was sure she was positioning herself for an attack. His heart began to drum. He wiped his palms absentmindedly on his filthy shirt, reached for some plan of action that was not forthcoming.

"Go! Get back!" Sam's voice wavered.

The coyote continued approaching, not deterred. She veered off one way, then the other, never releasing Sam's eyes from her own.

When she lunged, Sam reacted.

She was as easy to kill as the squirming things in the hole. She dropped to the ground hard. Gone.

Sam was frozen. The rest of the pack broke away from the stream, their high-pitched yelping a volley of sound that followed them into the trees where they ran and disappeared.

The coyote looked smaller in death. She was, in fact, smaller than many of the dogs in the pack she had traveled with. Sam closed the distance between them and knelt by her. She was lean, and her ears huge. Close now, he saw she was not the brown he had assumed. He could see the red and black and grey and white in her fur. Her vacant, fixed eyes were pale gold. She was handsome and sharp, and dead.

I'm sorry. I am sorry I did this.

Sam rested his hand on her still warm chest, yanked it off as she began to twitch erratically. She had been dead. Of that, Sam had no question. He had looked into her eyes as the light went out of them.

Now, now she moved jerkily, a marionette being pulled by an unskilled handler. She twitched and shuddered and turned her head in Sam's direction. He could see her eyes were pools of pain and nothing else. She tried to stand, spasmed and collapsed, tried again. Pink drool poured from her mouth as the coyote bit down on her own tongue, drawing blood.

He reached out once more, touched her upper back, thinking of the bunny, and his mother, and only wanting it to stop.

It had to stop.

The fur under his hands grew impossibly hot, burned. In a moment, not even two, she was gone. There was a brief, bright pyre. And then, nothing. The few ashes that remained were caught in the breeze before they could reach the ground.

Clink.

Sam wondered then if he should have allowed the island to eat him.

It had realized he was a threat long before he did. Now he understood he had brought something terrible to this place, but he was too far along to stop.

He would keep going. He would find the Fountain, the Fountain and the voices had been whispering to him about his entire damned life, and then . . .

And then, what?

Chapter Twenty-Nine

Ember

Inside the Library was cool and still and dry. So different from the island outside the doors, where plants and creatures were busy with the business of being alive in the sun.

"Yes, Ava would have made an excellent Librarian. The child loved order, for all to be in its place. It was a quality that both helped and harmed her." Alma paused, running her fingers over an ornate hand mirror. "Her son is different, easy and resilient. I think Ava would be so pleased to see how . . . healthy he is."

"Who was Ava?" Ember was curious about the would-be Librarian and her son. As she asked the question, she turned a doll over in her hands. It was a soft thing with yellow yarn hair, a doll she would have liked very much when she was a little girl.

"Ava was a regular visitor to the Fountain," Selah answered. "In many ways, it was her home. She did not fare well in the world. She was fragile and particular, lovely, too. Kind and bright. I enjoyed her company. I think we all did."

"Yes," Alma continued. "Ava was special. As she grew older, she spent more and more time on the island. It was good for her. Or so we believed. We indulged her because we were so fond of her. It was a mistake, and it was selfish."

Ember turned her attention away from the doll and to Alma. Something in the woman's tone said this was not going to have a happy ending. Ember had had enough of sadness for one lifetime and was sorry she'd asked the question that led to Ava's story.

"Over time we became concerned. Ava would speak of hating the world, her world. She became convinced she did not belong there, with her family. She came to believe nothing mattered but the island and the Fountain.

"We were torn as to what to do for her. In the end, the decision was made to turn her away from the island. We believed she needed to reconnect with her world, and with her people. She was devastated, screamed we were taking her home from her."

"You made her leave?" Ember let the doll hang limply in a clenched hand, resentful and sad for the woman she would never meet. And worried. If they had made Ava leave, someone who had grown up with and on the island, what would that mean for her? Would they force her out as well? "But this *was* her home, wasn't it?"

Alma sighed. "It was. And, in hindsight, we made the wrong decision. Ava belonged here and should have been allowed to stay. We encouraged her to love this place, to belong to it and it to her, and then we stripped it away from her. It will always be one of my greatest failings."

Selah shook her head. "Not yours alone. It was agreed upon. But it was cruel. And it broke her."

Alma picked up a hand mirror from a table full of them. She looked into it and away from the girls. "We kept track of her, of course. And, more than once, intervened when events in her life were going especially badly. We owed her that much. If she was aware of our involvement, she never showed it.

"When she became pregnant, we hoped her life would improve. Her sister and her sister's husband took Ava in. She lived with them during the pregnancy and after the child was born. Ava loved the child, Miles, but never took to being a mother. She was easily frustrated by him, and by her inability to make him happy. She did not understand it was the way with all babies, so she took it as a failure. Even when Ava was present, her sister did most of the work of raising Miles from early on.

"She pleaded with us, wanted to bring Miles to the island, for him to know it and for us to know him. So, we allowed it."

"Another mistake." Selah's voice was clipped. "Our attempt at reconciliation."

Alma did not argue. "It was, and it compounded the problems we had created. Ava returned with the boy more and more often. She wanted young Miles raised on the island, in the Nursery. She wanted this to be his only home. We pushed back, told her to allow the boy a chance to have his family. To know his own world . . ." Alma trailed off, staring at something Ember could not see.

Selah finished the story. "The next time we saw her, she was floating in the Fountain. She was gone. It was Beatrix—the Jury—who found Ava. It was very bad for Beatrix, I think. She began to change after that day."

Ember grew wide-eyed. "How . . . but what about her son?"

Alma tried to smile through wet eyes. "Miles? He is being raised by his aunt and uncle. They have been good parents to him."

"And he is here now? As is the Jury's boy?" Selah brought the conversation full circle.

"Yes, that is where I was going with this story, was it not?"

When the peace in the forest was interrupted by the sound of falling trees, Alma's face registered no alarm. "And that, I believe, is the Jury's boy. The island is slowing him down, but he will reach the Fountain soon. I would like to be there when he does, when the *whens* align."

Alma put a hand on Ember's shoulder. "Ember, let us get you a change of clothes, shall we? And something to eat. And then we will make our way to the Fountain. And hope it is finished there and then."

They were soon at a building much smaller than the two they visited earlier in the day. Inside, it was dim and smelled of cedar. Like the

Library, it was lined with shelves. Unlike the Library, the shelves held an organized selection of goods.

Selah walked the rows, searching with practiced eyes. She selected what looked like simple, white undergarments and handed them to Ember. She moved on, and then stopped at shelves piled with neatly folded, pale fabrics. "It is an outpost of the commissary. What the island does not provide, we make. We have skilled sewers, excellent bakers, shoemakers, apothecaries . . ." Selah trailed off as she found what she was looking for. "These will fit you. Choose a color you like."

"Are they like yours?" Ember asked with a note of hope in her voice. Selah's clothes were simple and so unlike anything Ember had ever seen a girl or woman wear. A fitted tunic over footless stockings of the same fabric.

Selah glanced down at her own mauve garments and nodded.

Ember's eyes fell on a mossy green pile. She took them behind a screen and changed from Mama's old dress and her wool socks and heavy boots into the new, lighter garments. She slipped the burgundy stone from the pocket of her dress to the deeper pocket of the tunic.

There was no mirror, but Ember knew the new clothing fit her well, save the long slits in the back made for allowing wings. The slits in the fabric left her feeling both free and exposed. She often spent days without thinking about the map of scars that ran across her back, but she also rarely had to look at them. She of course never displayed them. In these garments, there would be no hiding. She found herself embarrassed to step out from behind the screen dressed so strangely, but when she emerged, Alma nodded, approving.

"Much better." Shoes were next, soft and without ties or straps. As Selah changed out of her own filthy garments, Alma pulled Ember's chestnut hair up with a long band, wrapped it with deft fingers. Ember felt cleaner, more appropriate. Other than her conspicuous lack of wings, she looked as though she belonged on the island with her new companions. "These are magic."

There was a smile in Alma's voice. "Not magic, but they are good. They will keep you cool, dry quickly, and are durable. When you need new ones, you can get them here, leave the old ones to be laundered . . ."

Alma, finished with Ember's hair, stood quiet behind the girl for a moment. With cautious fingertips, Alma touched Ember's upper back, her scars. She traced them gently. "What happened here?"

Ember was ready for the question but her face burned. The scars were nasty and she was ashamed of them. "I've always had them."

"What caused them?"

"I . . . I don't know," she said.

My father, she thought.

"But I know they're ugly."

"Not ugly at all," said Alma. "They are a part of your story, nothing more. I am sorry you had to go through whatever it was at such a young age."

"I don't remember any of it." Ember didn't know what else to say. She was glad to be turned away from Alma as her face stung red and hot.

Alma and Selah shared a look, but Selah saved them from more awkward conversation when, from across the building, she asked, "Ember, you are hungry, yes?"

She was starving. "Very."

Selah brought her what looked like a piece of cornbread wrapped in rough ivory fabric. It tasted of honey and cream, eggs and almonds. It was dense and a little sweet. The piece was small, but Ember was satisfied when she finished it.

"It is filling, and is good for you. It is a staple. I have tried to make it, but mine always falls apart."

"Like the bread Mama made . . . makes," Ember corrected herself. *Mama isn't dead, just alone.* "Mine never turns out right."

"Girls, we can talk about our baking woes on the way to the Fountain." Alma handed them each a ceramic bottle of water.

"Or you can tell us about the Jury's boy?" Selah prodded.

"Yes, that is more important, is it not?"

They walked out of the outpost, and into the forest. Soon they came to a stream, and began to follow it. "All the water on the island comes from the Fountain," Alma explained as they walked. "Find a stream, follow it, and you will eventually reach it."

Ember thought about this. "Does that mean the lake comes from the Fountain as well?"

"You are astute. Yes, the Fountain feeds the streams and the streams feed the lake. And where the water in the Fountain comes from, that is an ongoing debate . . ."

Selah sighed dramatically. "The boy, Alma. Please. You Philosophers are easily distracted by your own ideas."

"The boy. He is called Sam. He was born to a human mother and father. His ties to the Fountain are unclear. He is . . . an anomaly. We have known about him since he was small, when Beatrix discovered him. Only weeks for us, but a lifetime for him.

"For reasons I do not understand, Beatrix did not want Sam exposed to the world, to bond or connect with others. She allowed Sam his mother, but prevented him from leaving home. It was awful. Sam was a prisoner. And, worse perhaps, Sam believed his mother was his prison guard. The one person he was allowed, and he believed she kept him captive."

The trio turned a densely treed corner that opened up into a small meadow. At the edge of the stream, a man with carmine wings and long, auburn hair crouched over a spot on the earth. He did not look up, but greeted them as they approached. "Alma, Selah, and new girl."

Alma greeted him. "Hello, Gideon. What are you examining?"

"I am not certain. The old coyote is dead. It happened here, and in the last hour. Perhaps two. But almost nothing of her remains."

Selah approached his side, inspecting the ground. "How did she die, Gideon?"

"I heard her heart stop when she died. But then, after, I felt her panic. And then, I think, she burned."

Chapter Thirty

The Fountain

Many were on their way to the Fountain.

Ember and Selah and Alma were close.

Miles and his friends were not far behind.

There were also four Philosophers making their way. The group was complete save for Alma. They were grim. Their work was serious and had become urgent.

Gideon would arrive first, accompanied by a number of other Groundskeepers. They were all worried. Some of them were frightened to their cores.

Sam had lost his way.

Save Sam, they would all reach the Fountain, the *whens* would all align, well before nightfall.

However, none of them arrived in time to witness the hungry thing that crawled out of the water and disappeared into the forest beyond. It was a thing that belonged in the depths of the Fountain, a thing that should have been bound there.

A thing that had no business being free.

PART THREE

What Happened There

Chapter Thirty-One

Sam

Sam walked for a short while with his head down. He watched the grass, the stream, his feet. He could not face the sun. He could not face the stream stretching on endlessly before him. He could not face what he had done, what he kept doing.

Sam wondered if the dogs watched him, if the pack followed him from the safety of the trees. He wondered if he would have to kill any more of them. Sam wondered if he could stop his own heart. He wondered if the time would come when he would have to. He wondered if he would like it.

His stomach twisted, turned, and pulled.

He knew he would. He would like it. He wanted it, didn't he?

He had nothing to do but think and follow the stream, and he had no idea how far he had come, or how far he had to go.

It was, all of it, too much. The anger that had spiked in him over and over again had not dissipated. It was a red and steady hum that colored every thought. It was better than feeling lonely and afraid, so he clung to it.

Because there was nothing else to do, Sam ran. He ran hard and fast as he could, he ran until his temples throbbed and his chest burned. His stamina was limited from too many days spent indoors and too few breathing free and wild in the sun. When Sam could no longer run, he staggered just inside the edge of the woods. He was deep enough to be sheltered from the worst of the heat, and, he hoped, sheltered from view of anyone who passed by.

Sam pushed his bag up against the base of a large tree, rested his head upon it, and fell asleep. He did not dream of anything at all.

When Sam woke, he felt better, clearer. He filled his thermos and headed back along the banks of the narrow channel. This time, he would not stop until he found the Fountain. He had water to drink and, if pressed, could protect himself.

Sam walked and allowed his mind to wander. He took in the forest noises around him. The wind in the trees, the creatures that lived in them. Sam listened to the water and its changing quality, how it shifted from a steady babble to a soft gurgle. The sound was peaceful until Sam considered the implications of it. He studied the brook. It was narrower and shallower than it had been before. He looked ahead and walked faster. He told himself not to run again, not to let fright overtake him. But Sam was certain what was coming, and he could not delay what was inevitable.

So he ran again.

He ran until the runnel disappeared in mud and rocks. He had no doubt the stream, had it not dried up, would have led him somewhere. The Fountain, maybe. He now also understood that it took an underground route from the source before resurfacing and becoming the stream he had been following.

It was gone. His best hope to find the Fountain was gone.

There was nothing left for him to do, so he did what he had hoped to avoid.

Sam walked back into the forest.

With no direction, and no goal, the walking was somehow easier. He would go until he reached anything that wasn't a tree or a rock. And there, he would do whatever came next.

When the trees began to thin around him, and more and more sunlight cut through their branches, Sam looked up. In front of him, something broke the monotony of the forest canopy. It was the very topmost triangle of a roof.

Sam moved quickly then.

As he reached the building, he was struck by its size. The structure was enormous. Sam approached the great door and knocked hard. When silence greeted him, he tried again. When there was still no response, he tried the handle. To his surprise, it was unlocked.

The door swung open without sound into the cool, dark building.

Sam stepped inside and closed the door behind him. It was by no means as dark as the hole had been, but his eyes struggled to adjust.

The room was endless and full of the most random assortment of stuff he had ever encountered. Random, yes, but not dusty or unkempt. This room was pristine, as if it were well tended.

He walked deeper into the building and saw it was not truly one large room. There were rooms to the sides, and each of these seemed better organized, more specific, than the great room. Behind the first door he found a huge room full of nothing but dolls. They lined the walls, floor to ceiling, on narrow shelves. Some were decades old and appeared to be made of twine and corn husks. Others were plush and well loved. Still others were brand-new, propped up in heat-sealed plastic boxes. Sam had the absurd but clear sense the dolls were patient and were watching him with interest. It would be ridiculous to even consider it in the regular world but, here, the dolls' eyes were more focused than they should have been. More watchful. Maybe he was imagining it all, but he wasn't imagining the crawling sensation moving up his spine.

He shivered a bit as he hurried out of the room.

The next room had woodwind instruments.

The next, maps.

And the next, eyeglasses.

On and on, rooms dedicated to a single thing.

When Sam opened what might have been the twentieth door, he stopped. The room itself was full of doors. They leaned up against the walls in neat stacks. Bedroom doors, front doors, pantry doors, and even small doors for accessing crawl spaces. He was ready to turn around when one caught his attention. It was made of the same material as the wooden building itself and sat flush against the wall. Two doors leaned against it. Quiet as he could, Sam slid those across the floor and added them to a nearby stack.

Perhaps it should have occurred to Sam that going through the door was a risk, but it did not. Sam tugged at the iron handle and the door swung open on silent hinges. Here he found no room. Only a set of steep stone stairs leading down. A dim flickering beyond told Sam he would not be in absolute darkness when he reached wherever the stairs led to. The air smelled wet, and the temperature dropped as soon as he walked across the threshold.

Sam stepped onto the first of many stairs, closed the door behind himself, and began his descent.

Chapter Thirty-Two

Ember

Ember and her friends crossed through a copse of enormous, gnarly trees and to the clearing just beyond. The Fountain was quiet aside from a group of about a dozen winged men talking in hushed, hurried tones on the far side. Gideon was among them.

Ember had little interest in their conversation. All her attention was on the Fountain before her.

The Fountain was the size of a small pond and almost perfectly round save the side that butted up against a sheer rock face that seemed to reach into the clouds. Water tumbled down the mottled burgundy wall, flowing into the Fountain. Threads of silver ran through the rock, the same as the stone in her pocket. The falls were not loud, but provided a constant sort of white noise that muffled all other sounds. At first glance, the Fountain appeared natural, but as Ember noticed the neat, almost intentional way the rocks and stones were positioned around its edge, she wondered if that were really so.

And there was something else. It took Ember some time to put her finger on it, but when she did, she could not unsee it. The entire island was green and lush, but here, around the Fountain, it was brighter and more verdant and alive, as if enjoying a benefit from proximity to the strange pool. And everything alive and growing that surrounded the Fountain—trees, grass, clumps of wildflowers scattered at the edge of the clearing—bent just a bit toward the Fountain. Every green blade and branch reached out to be closer to the shining pool of silvered water. Without sharp eyes it would be easy to miss.

As she watched, a breeze picked up and pulled the most fragile leaves from the surrounding trees. As they fell, they fell toward the Fountain, regardless of where they had started. None of them landed in the perfect stillness of the water, deferential to the end, but they did make their way as close to its edge as they could as they found a place to rest and fade and eventually be taken back into the earth to add to the rich soil of the island.

Ember felt it, too, the pull.

She did not want to swim in the waters, but she wanted to be near them. To touch a finger to the surface as if to leave her mark, her own story, in the memory of the Fountain. If she touched the water, there could never be any doubt she was truly here, and the Fountain would know her.

As she mused, Ember drew closer to the rocks surrounding the beckoning water. When she reached the edge, she peered in and saw herself looking back up with wide, green eyes. The water was deep. As deep as any lake Ember had ever encountered. She could not see the depth as much as feel it, and the pull was strong now. The peaceful, cool, centered light in her chest grew and spread through her blood and her bones and her breath.

Without wondering if it was the right thing, or even allowed, Ember reached one finger out and tapped the surface. In the moment it seemed the water reached up just above the surface, pressed itself against her fingertip, touching her back. Ember would think later perhaps it had not been the water at all, but a long, pale, sharp-nailed finger. It was a quick and gentle motion, but it created concentric rings that flowed, one after another, until they disappeared into the surface beyond. Her reflection rippled with them. That feeling that had first started at the edge of the lake intensified. Ember was sure she glowed with it.

And then, in a moment so brief a blink would have meant missing it, there was something beneath Ember's wavering reflection. Turquoise eyes looked up and met her own. A hint of a too-wide smile was just visible. In that split second, Ember's suspicion was confirmed: her mermaid and Selah's home were connected. Glancing at the deep red rocks of the Fountain, she also knew where the stone she'd been gifted had come from.

Ember was not sure if she had made a friend in the mermaid, or a grave mistake.

But she thought better than to ask anyone.

Ember's unease was enough to break her out of her trance and bring her attention back to the group surrounding the Fountain. If anyone had seen her touch the water, they did not acknowledge it. And Ember would not mention it. The moment was hers, and she would hold it tight and close. But the powerful feeling remained. It had taken root in her marrow.

Selah motioned for Ember to join her.

When Ember reached Selah, she could feel the tension flowing off her friend in waves.

"What is it?" Ember asked, quiet so as not to be heard by anyone but Selah.

"Something is very wrong."

As the girls watched, Gideon soon approached Alma, the rest of his group walking just behind. Ember now saw there were two women among them. Ember was sure Gideon was in charge, though there was nothing tangible to separate him from the rest. It was in the respectful way the others listened when he spoke, how they nodded at times almost in unison. Yes, Gideon was in charge, but of what, Ember was not certain.

As Ember watched, half the group stayed near the Fountain, the rest greeted Alma then walked toward the trees and disappeared into the woods beyond.

Selah, still at Ember's side, spoke with a low and confidential tone in her ear. "Gideon is the closest thing they have to a captain."

"Who are they?"

"The Groundskeepers. They care for the menagerie. But they also care for the island. They are more attuned to it than the rest of us. It is why Gideon knew about the old coyote, how he heard her die. Twice."

Ember swallowed. *Twice?*

"They seem so . . . fierce?" Ember was not sure she had chosen the right word.

"When they have to be. Sometimes their work is dangerous, and it is often demanding." Selah took Ember by the hand and pulled her forward, toward the group. "Come. I want to hear what is being said. The falls make it difficult."

Despite feeling as though she was forgetting her place, Ember allowed Selah to drag her toward the conversation. She fought the urge to be timid, even though she was fourteen and, as her mother had often reminded her, nearly a woman.

"We do not know why it has happened. There is no precedent for it." Gideon stood stone-still while he spoke, but his voice was agitated.

"Have they hurt anyone else?" Alma's face was unreadable.

"Not yet, but we need to warn the island to stay out of the lake, not to attempt to cross it. I would prefer no one risked the shore unless necessary. Especially alone. Especially at night."

"And we have to warn the seekers," Alma said.

Gideon shook his head. "It would take many to be effective, to go everywhere the seekers might be. And without the Fountain guiding them, we would only be guessing as to where the seekers were coming *from*. Besides, there are few who are strong enough to fly that fast and that far, and we need them here. Protecting the island. I will not leave this place unguarded."

Selah's eyebrows knit together. "What has happened at the lake? Who was injured?"

"Aaron, a Groundskeeper." Gideon's response was clipped. He directed his next question to Alma. "Why would the Jury allow this? Certainly she did not command the creature to attack?"

"No, I am sure Beatrix did not. When the Philosophers arrive, perhaps we will have some answers. Where is Aaron now?"

"At the Infirmary with an Apothecary and a Surgeon. Both of them are capable. Both have seen wild injuries before. They may be able to save the wing, but his arm . . . there is little left."

Selah's hand flew to her mouth in shock.

Alma raised a hand to stop him. "We need to warn the island. And until we can speak with the Jury, I do not know how we reach everyone."

"There is something else."

Alma closed her eyes. "Of course there is." She opened them, but her face was tight with wary expectation. "What else?"

Gideon hesitated. "Something left the Fountain. Today. It is likely in the woods. A half dozen good Groundskeepers have gone to hunt it."

There was muted horror on Alma's face. When Ember turned to Selah, wanting her friend to help her understand, Selah's expression was identical to Alma's.

Alma took Gideon's arm. She locked her hand around it as if her insistence would change what he had said. "No, Gideon, it is impossible. Nothing of the Fountain could leave it, much less survive outside it."

"But something has," he insisted. "And now it is in the forest."

"But the Jury would never. Could never. And the creatures, they lack the . . ." Alma struggled for her words. "They lack the free will to decide to leave the Fountain on their own."

"I can only tell you what I know, Alma. I cannot explain what I do not understand. Something left the Fountain. We know the creatures are deadly in the waters, so we must assume the same is true on land."

Ember listened, wondering what it was that had looked back at her from the Fountain.

Chapter Thirty-Three

The Fountain

What had climbed from the Fountain was not the first to escape. Others like it had already squirmed from the depths and crept into the surrounding forest.

The thing was very old. It had been lithe and powerful in the water. Now, in the sun and air, it was all hard gristle and stiff movement. Its skin tightened and stretched, already beginning to split and seep. It struggled to cross through the trees and over the rocky ground. It hid from the Groundskeepers in the low bushes and brambles, its almost colorless hide serving as camouflage in the dappled shadows.

After the creature gutted and devoured a sun-warmed snake resting on a flat rock, the animals of the island, already wary, hid themselves deeper in the forest. The wild dog pack tracked the thing, but kept their distance. They had already lost one of their own. The dogs were wise enough not to approach it. Even in its current state, it was capable of causing great harm.

It finally arrived at a clear stream. It could smell the Fountain in the water. Home.

With its sharp snout and ten calcified fingers, it burrowed under the rocks and into the wet mud like an exotic toad. Only one eye remained exposed, and that disappeared among the pebbles and the forest debris.

When the time came, it would maul and devour as many of its jailers as it could before it was stopped. And it would be stopped for certain. But, first, there would be blood.

There, in the Fountain mud, it could watch. And it could wait as long as it had to.

Chapter Thirty-Four

Miles

Miles, Simon, and Gabby were the next to arrive. Miles was not sure what he had expected when he reached the Fountain, but a group of worried winged people and a lone, wingless girl were not it. Miles watched as Gabby approached another of her kind and embraced her. Where Gabby was sun-bright with copper hair and golden skin, the other, with her dark hair and skin so pale it took on the lavender cast of her wings, was all twilight.

Simon embraced the pale girl as well, with some embarrassment and a shy "Welcome back, Selah." Miles thought he understood why the boy was blushing. The pale girl was as beautiful as Gabby.

Gabby returned to Miles, took him by the hand, and brought him forward to a small woman with short, dark hair and huge blue-grey wings. "Alma, this is Miles. Ava's boy."

Alma's smile was sad, but her eyes were kind. "Miles, I am so glad to see you again. I knew Ava well, and cared for her very much. You look so much like her."

Then why didn't you send her back to me? Miles thought but then pushed it away. He was being unfair. He had no way of knowing what this small woman had or hadn't done. So he said, "Nice to meet you, too."

With his white-blond hair and blue-green eyes, he did resemble Ava. Miles knew it, had seen pictures. But he also looked a lot like Ava's sister, the woman who chose to be his mom, and it was that resemblance that mattered to him most.

Alma turned to Gabby. "Please introduce Miles to Selah and her companion, Ember. I would like you to join them and keep them all together. Especially tonight."

Selah was talking with the wingless girl who, while tall, looked young. He assumed she was Ember, and he was curious to know why she was here.

It was agreed that everyone should be behind closed doors well before nightfall. Alma asked Selah and Gabby to bring their group to her own cottage. It was, she said, large enough for everyone to find a place to sleep. There they could rest and wait for the sun to return.

Alma would not be joining them, but promised she was certain they would be safe together. Together, and indoors. "I will wait for the other Philosophers. We will go to the Academy and, together, find a way to stop what had been set into motion. And I will wait for the Jury's boy as long as I can. I expect the *whens* will align soon."

Miles understood about half of Alma's short speech, and he would have plenty of questions later. But he was also exhausted to his bones, and the idea of a roof over his head and a warm place to sleep sounded better by the minute.

As Miles left with the others, he heard a man with bloodred wings and an air of authority give directions—commands—to a small group of four tough-looking winged people. They were placed on watch at the Fountain. They would stay through the night. If something tried to leave the water, they would be there to stop it.

Miles wasn't sure what might try to leave the Fountain, but if the strangers coming out of the lake—and the mutants in it—were any indication, it couldn't be anything good.

He walked away thinking the team left behind looked like they could handle themselves and whatever came at them.

Chapter Thirty-Five

Sam

Sam made his way down the staircase. He was cautious, unsure of his footing in the dim light of the place. He considered his flashlight then dismissed the idea. The flashlight would give away his location. If there was something down there to hide from, he wanted the option. At the thirty-seventh step, Sam reached the bottom.

He found himself in a tunnel. It was tall—maybe ten feet—and half again as wide. The stone and mortar walls blended from one to the other, connected by the round arch of the ceiling. The only sounds his own shallow breathing and bass-drum heartbeat.

No, but that wasn't quite right.

There was another sound.

The steady, smooth song of running water filled the emptiness of the tunnel, echoing along the walls and the floor. The sound, and the faint source of light, came from directly ahead of the place Sam stood. Slowly, hugging a wall, he made his way toward them.

The air around Sam grew brighter by degrees as he reached an intersection where his tunnel crossed another. Here he discovered what provided both the light and the sound. In the floor of the perpendicular tunnel was a narrow channel, perhaps five feet from one side to the other. A rock footbridge spanned it, leading to more darkness beyond. To the left and right, the tunnel was more brightly lit. It was, Sam saw, illuminated by the channel itself. The water had a silvery phosphorescence, and provided enough light to see, if not enough to read by.

Sam had a decision to make. Straight ahead, over the bridge and into the darkness, was easily eliminated. He could go right and follow the water to wherever it was leading. Or he could go left, against the flow, and toward the source.

Left was the only choice.

Far below ground and with no sun or landmark to track his progress, Sam had no sense of time. The floor and walls and air were damp with cool humidity. Breathe in the mineral-filled air, breathe out his body heat. Over and over and over again. Soon, he was shivering.

More than once, the channel split and led to two separate tunnels, two separate choices. At each Y was another footbridge. Each time, he stayed to the left, never crossing a bridge. If he were to become stuck, or run into a dead end, Sam would not have to remember which side he had chosen.

The echoes of Sam's footsteps developed echoes of their own and the spaces around him became full with the sound. The effect was hypnotic, and Sam became lost in his own head. The tunnels a tangible extension of the barren grey landscape in his mind.

So lost was Sam, he did not notice the change in the echoes until it was too late to run.

The reverberating sounds of his steps shifted their cadence and pattern as whoever followed him changed their stride, sped up. Not one set of footsteps then, but two. Sam's and those of someone with a long, purposeful gait.

Sam froze, unsure of whether he should run or hide

He didn't have time to decide.

The light of the channel disappeared as a bag, coarse and heavy, was pulled over Sam's head from behind. The force of it drove him to his knees.

"What the—" His words were cut off as the bag cinched tight around his throat. In seconds it was loosened enough Sam knew he wouldn't be strangled—not yet, anyway. But he understood the warning: *No talking. No questions.*

Sam clutched his duffel bag to his chest. His panicked breathing was shallow, and trapped in the sack it was warm on his face.

Sam, once again, was certain he would die underground.

Then, he remembered, he didn't have to.

He thought about killing his assailant, but even as the idea formed, strong hands twisted and yanked the back of the bag, forcing him to stand.

If he stopped the heart of whoever stood behind him, Sam would still be lost in a dark tunnel far beneath a landscape that did not want him treading upon it.

So Sam did not kill his captor then, but nor did he dismiss the idea outright. Instead, he held on to the possibility like a life raft—*a piece of driftwood*—deciding to see where it was the stranger would take him.

A hand shoved the center of his back and Sam stumbled forward. He and his captor began to make their way through the tunnel. With that hand twisting the sack taut against the back of his head, Sam could only face forward. Blind as he was, he had no choice but to trust the person behind him knew the way. And would not run him into the channel or into a wall or, worse, off a precipice and down, down to a place deeper and darker than even the hole in the ground had been. A place as deep and as dark as the dry well in his mind.

Clink.

He tried, once, to speak. Before he could form a full word, the sack was pulled with a sharp snatch, and Sam lost his balance, falling hard.

His back and shoulders burned as he was yanked back off the tunnel floor and pushed once again to move forward.

They walked like that for a while. It might have been a day, or just half an hour, but time was a lost thing for Sam, and he focused solely on the walking.

More than once Sam was turned without warning and walked over the gentle slope of footbridges over the channel. And more than once Sam, disoriented, tripped and fell to his knees. Each time he was pulled back up without a word from his captor and pressed to continue forward. His head pounded and his body ached and he was so cold he might as well have been naked.

Sam's foot struck a barrier, and he stumbled forward, catching himself with his right hand on the sharp corner of what must have been a stone step. Hot blood bloomed on his cold palm, and Sam fought the urge to reach back and wipe it on the person behind him.

As they ascended, Sam had the distinct impression his captor was not walking up the stairs as much as hovering. The air in the staircase shifted and turned as if displaced by giant wings. Insane, of course, but Sam could not shake the sensation.

He counted the steps as he went. At thirty-five, the person behind him reached over Sam's shoulder and the quiet was broken by the metal-on-metal *clank* of a latch being thrown and the shifting sound of a heavy door.

They walked up two more steps—*thirty-seven*—and the air around Sam changed, warmer and drier than in the tunnel. The door they entered through was slammed behind them, and another metal *clank* of what must have been a lock was snapped into place.

Sam was walked forward and pushed to his knees.

Something wound around his neck two, three, four times. A heavy rope or cord. Sure he was about to be hanged, Sam began to thrash. But while the cord felt tight enough to choke him, it did not cut off his air. Instead, it held the sack firmly in place over his head.

He tried to calm himself, and it worked. For a moment. When his duffel bag was snatched from his hands, Sam howled and reached out blindly for it. A leaden foot came down between his shoulders, forcing Sam's chest and face to the floor. Heavy footsteps crossed the floor, and another door was unlocked, closed, and locked once more.

Sam was alone again.

In the dark.

Clink.

ONCE upon a time, quite recently . . .

YASMIN filled the tub. She added more rose-scented bubble bath than was necessary, but that was the way she liked it. Her parents were out for the night, so there would be no one to tell her to hurry up or that she was using all the hot water. In fact, she knew they wouldn't want her taking a bath at all. A shower, sure. But not a bath.

She took the long-handled wooden shower brush off its hook and placed it on the edge of the tub before remembering she'd left her phone in her bedroom. Barefoot and wearing nothing but a soft white robe, Yasmin padded down the hall to her room to retrieve it.

She was gone less than half a minute.

On her way back she heard a slosh, *and the bathroom door swung almost closed.*

Damn it, *she thought.* I let the tub overflow.

Her parents would be pissed.

Yasmin pushed the door open and froze.

Against the back wall of the bathroom stood a woman. She had long straw-colored hair and a dress that was about four decades out of style. The hair covered most of the woman's face, but Yasmin could see her mouth moving. Her words, if that's what they were, were hard to hear over the running water and seemed entirely gibberish.

The woman was soaking wet, water running out of her hair and clothes and onto the floor.

Yasmin knew at once who—or what—she shared a bathroom with.

She'd heard stories about the strangers.

Not taking her eyes off the woman, Yasmin dropped her phone to the floor, slapped the running water off, pulled the knob in the wall that would allow the tub to drain, and snatched the wooden brush off the edge of the bathtub. It was the closest thing she had to a weapon.

The woman, still mumbling, took a shaky step toward Yasmin. Then another. She moved as though she had forgotten how her feet and legs were supposed to work.

Yasmin swung. The wide arc had power behind it, but not enough power to explain what happened next.

When the head of the brush connected with the woman's temple it . . . caved in. Yasmin fought back a wave of nausea as the skin of the woman's forehead sank in around her crushed, too-soft skull. The grey skin split where she'd been hit and instead of red blood, a thick black stinking sludge oozed out of the gash.

The woman's head rocked hard to her shoulder. Something deep in her neck made a nasty cracking crunch *as she straightened it and resumed her plodding, unsteady approach.*

Yasmin turned and ran along the landing and down the stairs to the first floor of her house, still wearing nothing but her robe. The woman, a little surer on her feet now, followed. She stopped at the top of the stairs as if confused about how to navigate them.

Still clutching her makeshift weapon, Yasmin thought, I have to call someone.

But, of course, her phone was on the bathroom floor where she had dropped it, and the woman stood between her and it.

The woman took a hesitant step down the first wooden stair. She put her weight on the leg and it gave out, or her wet foot slipped, or both. Regardless, the result was that the stranger came tumbling down all thirteen steps and landed in a heap on the floor.

Yasmin stepped back just in time to avoid being crushed.

That has to be it. She has to be dead. More dead.

She was not.

The woman lifted her head to expose her now fully crushed forehead, and for the first time Yasmin could clearly see her eyes. There was nothing in them at all except appetite.

She was still muttering through the black stuff that now oozed out of her mouth.

Like an animal, Yasmin froze.

The stranger attempted to push herself up, but her arm was shattered in at least two places. It had far more angles than any arm should. She had more luck with her other, but her legs were beyond use, just as bent and broken as her arm. With her one good arm, the woman pulled herself toward Yasmin.

Yasmin almost ran.

Instead, she swung again.

The first blow missed and connected with the woman's shoulder with a disgusting crunch.

The next landed where it was supposed to. On the top of the woman's head.

There was a sound like the cracking of a rotten egg and more of the black nastiness leaked through her hair and onto the floor.

Yasmin brought the wooden weapon down again. The stranger was still muttering.

And again.

And again.

And again more times than she could count until the stranger stopped twitching and she was covered in black gore, like splatter paint.

Taking shallow and shaking breaths, Yasmin dropped the black-stained brush to the floor.

She waited.

And she watched.

The stranger was still.

Satisfied, Yasmin pulled her robe tight at her neck and went out the back door to her neighbor's house.

She had to call her parents.

She expected a lecture about the bath.

Inside the house, the woman twitched.

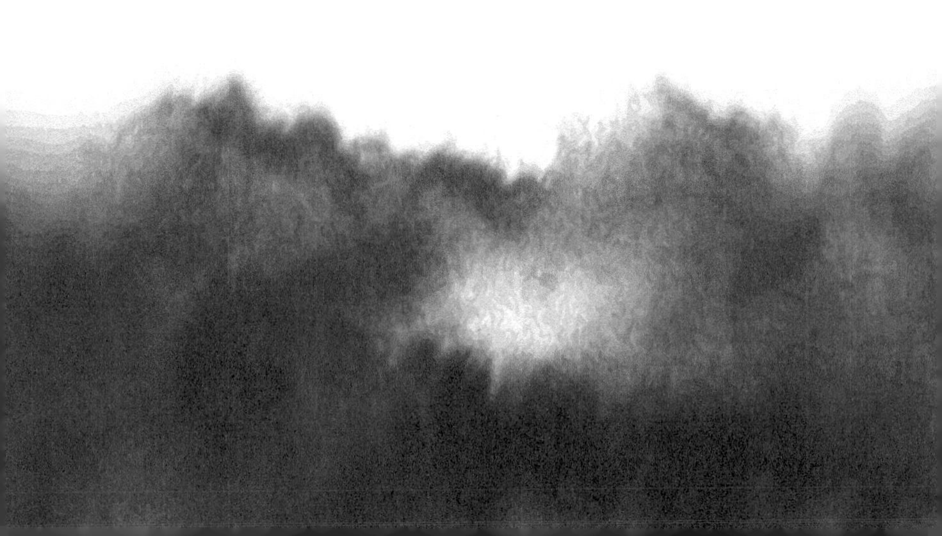

Chapter Thirty-Six

Selah

Everyone went to Alma's cottage as they had been told. But they would not stay for long.

Selah gathered bread and soft cheese, and they sat around the large wooden table in the kitchen. At Gabby's direction, they shared their stories. Miles suspected by the way she hesitated that Ember left some part of hers out. He had. Miles left out the bit about being angry at his birth mother for choosing this place over him and focused instead on the strangers that were invading his *when*, the strangers who seemed to be looking for him.

"It's been happening for weeks, these zombies showing up and just . . . There wasn't any pattern and there wasn't any reason. It's chaos. Curfews in some places, like that means anything. It's not like they only come out at night like vampires." Miles paused, thinking. There was so much else, the floods of poison water and the creatures that lived in it, but it was too much to try and explain. He didn't entirely understand it himself. "So it's good that I'm here. If they're looking for me, maybe they'll stop showing up? Stop hurting people. I hope."

Gabby and Selah exchanged a look. If they meant it to be subtle, they failed as no one at the table missed it.

"What?" Miles asked.

Gabby shook her head, but Selah answered despite the silent direction. "We do not know what it is they want, other than it concerns you. And if it concerns you, it concerns Ava. That much is clear. But you are not the only link between Ava and your *when*. The woman who raised you is as tied to Ava as you are."

Miles paled. "Because they're sisters. Twins."

"We cannot assume the strangers, as you call them, will not come for her if they cannot have you. We do not know what they want, nor who has given them direction. We must find the Jury. She alone can stop this."

Miles's jaw and hands clenched as anger overtook him. For the first time in his life, he was furious with Gabby. "Why didn't you tell me that? I came here to protect people. To protect *them*. Why didn't you tell me that my family—the whole *world*—was still in danger?"

Gabby gave Selah a withering look before answering. "Because I do not believe it. They came after you—at the pool, at the lake, on the bridge. It was you they were after. Not your family. Not your mother."

Gabby's words calmed Miles, but just a little. He didn't like the idea he'd only been told part of the truth, especially by someone he trusted so much.

"How can you be sure?" he asked.

"I . . ." Gabby started.

Ember interrupted in a hesitant voice from across the table. "Can't someone go warn Miles's mother? Protect her? Just in case."

Gabby squared her shoulders, wings opening enough to show the jade green within. "I can."

"No," Simon interrupted. "Remember what Gideon said about the lake. About Aaron. You are fast, but Aaron is faster."

And there might have been an argument there at the table, had Ember not spoken again. "So, we go see for ourselves. We go to the lake. Let's see what's happening there. Maybe it isn't so bad. Maybe Gabby, or someone, can go see your mother, Miles."

Miles gave Ember a tired, grateful half smile. She might be young, but she had good ideas. "Better than sitting here all night. At least we'd be doing something. I've got to do *something*." The last words were a plea.

"But Alma . . ." Simon protested.

"Alma instructed us to stay together. We will stay together. None of us will separate from the others, on the path or at the shore," Gabby said.

Simon raised his hand. "Alma told us to stay together, and to stay inside."

Selah sighed, shaking her head. "We cannot possibly be expected to remember every instruction we are given. We will go to the lake. If it is safe to cross, someone will go to Miles's mother. If it is not, we will find the Jury, and she will stop this."

Miles nodded, grateful. "Either way, it's something."

Chapter Thirty-Seven

Ember

Ember had surprised herself. First, by having the idea. Second, by suggesting it aloud. She was frightened by what might be in the lake, the forest, the dark. But once she had the idea, she knew it would have to be spoken. She did not want anyone else to lose a mother.

And there was something about Miles, in his smile and the way he seemed to really see her, that reminded Ember so much of her brother Hank that it hurt to look at him for too long. But there was something else, too. Someone else he reminded her of. Ember couldn't quite sort it out. The idea darted across her mind like a quicksilver fish, too nimble and slick to grab hold of.

Chapter Thirty-Eight

Miles

It was fully dark when they left Alma's cottage, and his heart raced at the thought of stepping out of the warm home and into the black night.

The little house was the last in a neat semicircle of similar buildings. A neighborhood of sorts, but the windows in the other cottages were black and empty eyes. At Gabby's suggestion they left lamps burning in Alma's home, indicating to anyone who passed that the cottage was occupied, as it was supposed to be.

Gabby went first, followed by Ember and Miles, with Selah and Simon keeping watch from behind.

A path led from the cottages right to the lake, but the group did not take it. Instead, they slipped into the woods where they would be well hidden from anyone who passed. Selah, Gabby, and Simon were silent as they moved through the forest. Miles was as quiet as he could be, but twigs snapped and underbrush rustled as he made his way. Ember, it seemed, had the same problem. She winced with every *crack* and *crunch* beneath her feet.

As they went, they skirted clearings filled with other cottages and small neighborhoods. Some were occupied, warm light pouring out of the windows and breaking up the night that wrapped around them.

The air on the island had changed with the setting sun. It was cooler, and the blanket of humidity lifted enough to make breathing easier for Miles, who was accustomed to the thinner air of a higher elevation. Not that any amount of wet air would have slowed him. Miles pulsed with a sharp urgency. His mom was—both his parents were—in danger, and Miles was not there to protect them. He had no way to even warn them. Every part of him wanted to run until he reached the shore and then swim until he reached the other side. He tried to tamp down the adrenaline that surged through him, knowing what he wanted and what was possible were two very different things.

He couldn't get to his parents but maybe Gabby could, and the only way for her to get to them was to cross the lake. And their only way to the lake was through the dark woods. So Miles went on, one careful, noisy, determined step at a time.

The world around them was not as quiet as Miles had first thought. It was filled with slight, quick sounds of small creatures that lived on the forest floor and scampered about after the larger animals had turned in for the night. The canopy above them housed what must have been birds, with calls that were deeper and lower than any owl Miles had ever heard.

A breeze stirred through the tall grass and the air lightened, filled with the bright, mineral smell of water. Between the trees ahead, the shadows thinned as they approached the shore. Nearing the edge of the forest, Gabby held out a hand behind her. The others drew up alongside her, peering through the trees but not crossing them to the shore beyond.

What Miles saw there made his heart sink and his eyes sting. Gabby would not be reaching his mother this night.

Twenty yards away from them, a dozen or more Groundskeepers lined the water's edge. Each held a staff longer than the wielder was tall. At the ends of the staffs, blades glinted in the starlight. Some were curved, wicked scythes. Others were long with deep serrations.

One, a trident with tips that ended in needle-fine points, was held by a giant of a man. A woman held what looked to be a staff that ended in a ragged corkscrew. One staff lay in the sand, abandoned by its owner. Each Groundskeeper was at the ready. Some stood, feet planted and knees bent slightly. Others were in the air, weapons pointed down and toward the water.

Down toward the mutant that dragged itself out of the lake.

The instinct to flee was so strong Miles had to will his body not to turn and run.

A nightmare crawled onto the shore.

It was skeletal and angular, and at least ten feet long with a narrow, protruding jaw that ended in rows of broken shark's teeth. Its skin was the pale color of a noxious mushroom. The creature's arms were lanky and knobbed, and undeniably human, ending in equally human hands.

Miles recognized those arms and hands, the same as those that had reached for him on the bridge. He shuddered with the knowledge of what was in the waters.

The creature had no discernable eyes, its head made of just that gnarled and pointed snout that was now stretched wide, full of something heavy.

Miles saw the something heavy was a person.

The monster reared up and dropped it at the feet of the nearest Groundskeeper. When the person, a woman, landed in the sand, there was a *thump* heard even by those hiding in the trees. The figure did not move. Her right shoe was missing, as was her right foot. Miles knew by the way she fell, the horrible angle at which she landed, the woman was no longer a person.

She was a body.

"A seeker." Selah's voice was a low moan.

"How?" whispered Simon.

"Maybe she was crossing the lake on her own. Perhaps . . . perhaps she stood on the far shore . . ."

My shore, Miles thought.

As soon as the corpse was dropped, the airborne guards descended with their blades.

They're warriors.

The monster screeched and screamed in a voice that was too familiar to be anything but human. And too alien to be human at all. The sound brought tears of horror to Miles's eyes as a scream tried to rise in his own throat.

The creature swiped at a low flying guard. Caught by a wingtip, the guard was pulled straight down and into the lake. She came up fighting, using her corkscrew blade to her full advantage. She twisted as she stabbed, and the screaming filled the air and became something else. Something worse. Miles had never experienced a sound so visceral and overwhelming. The one clear thought he had—*all blood is black in the moonlight*—ran through his head like the chorus to a song.

Two of the guards on the ground rushed for the body, pulling it up the beach and away from the mutant that thrashed and died in water that languidly lapped the shore. That silvery water so apathetic to the horrors within.

The guards lifted the woman's broken body, flew with her to a place farther down the beach, resting her with somber care on a white cloth. With careful and practiced movements, they wound the woman's corpse in the length of white fabric, protecting her from the elements and providing her the dignity of the quick ritual.

Miles, his brain a half beat behind everything unfolding before his eyes, then saw there were three other shrouded shapes in the sand. Three other white-wrapped bodies.

Back at the lake, the monster half floated in the water. Its form mangled and split wide and now more black than white.

All blood is black in the moonlight.

It was then Miles realized Ember had inched closer to him as the scene on the shore unfolded. As protective as a brother, he reached out with his right arm and pulled the younger, smaller girl against his side. She stiffened at first at being touched, but Miles felt her lean against him, turning her face into his shoulder and shielding her eyes as the next part happened.

Groundskeepers—*soldiers, they're soldiers*—dropped their weapons and dragged the monster onto shore, and away from the neatly laid bodies. When it appeared they had decided the mutant was far enough from the other dead, something was poured over the prone creature. A Groundskeeper with long hair took the lantern he carried and, with an arcing swing of his arm, smashed it against the back of the mushroom-colored hide. It erupted in flame. The smoke that came off the remains was oily and acrid. Miles was certain this time he really would vomit and only hoped he could do so without making too much noise.

The long-haired man stepped backward from the burning creature, moving away from the thick smoke. He turned and strode toward the group hiding in the trees.

Caught. Miles wondered what punishment would come from the man for spying on his terrible work. The urge to flee was back and stronger than ever, but he would not leave the girl who still clung to him for support. He'd always been an only child, but the urge to watch over her like a brother was unexpected but felt natural and right.

Gabby surprised Miles by walking out of the shadows and onto the beach to meet him. In a matter of steps, they were face-to-face, Gabby forced to tilt her head back to make eye contact with the tall man.

"Gabrielle, did you think we did not know you were here?" His voice was angry, but the rage Miles had feared was not there. The man was exhausted, dark circles chiseled under his eyes. And he was filthy, his tunic the color of soot and drying blood—if blood was black as sin—his long hair lank and matted with stuff Miles did not want to think about.

"I had hoped, Gideon." Gabby was not contrite.

"And what were you thinking? Bringing these children into the forest and to the shore at night?" Gideon leaned down, drawing his face closer to Gabby's.

"We needed to know if the lake was safe to cross. Miles's mother may be in danger. Someone needs to go to her."

Miles's stomach sank hearing the words spoken out loud.

Gideon looked over to Miles and the others hidden, not well it turned out, in the shallows of the forest. He motioned to them. "Come down here. All of you."

The group did as they were told. Selah held her head up, a counter to the shame that radiated from Simon's slumped wings. Miles kept his arm around Ember as they walked out together.

"Are you glad you saw this tonight? Are you glad you saw *them*?" Gideon gestured to the row of bodies. "Or *that*?" He thrust a finger in the direction of the burning pile now, fortunately, downwind from them. Miles saw it was not the first carcass to have been burned that night. Two other smoldering piles lay just down shore from the one that still blazed.

"I am." Selah was not cowed by the warrior. "We needed to know the state of things. And now we do. We cannot travel by water."

"You cannot travel *over* the water." Gideon snapped.

"*Why?*" Miles wanted to swallow the word back even as he asked. Gideon clearly had some respect for Gabby. There was no reason to think he felt the same for Miles.

When Gideon turned to him, Miles expected to be reprimanded at the very least. Being hit by the furious man didn't seem out of the question. He tried to brace himself for both.

"Are you Miles?" Gideon asked.

"Yes."

Instead of anger, Miles was surprised to see compassion in the man's eyes. "Then it is your mother we are talking about, and you deserve to know. But I cannot spare our strongest and fastest when the island needs protecting."

Gideon turned to Gabby to say the next part, almost like he could read her mind. "Aaron was injured today in the air, not on the water. There are beasts in this lake that can fly, something we did not know until now. The lake cannot be crossed."

Simon looked up, wide-eyed.

Gabby set her jaw and took a long, deep breath.

"Then we find Beatrix—the Jury." Selah corrected herself and used the honorific, but now Miles knew the Jury had a name.

"Do you not think we are trying? We will find her. And we will end this. But you"—Gideon looked at them in turn, making eye contact with each—"cannot be here."

Gabby nodded. "We will return to Alma's cottage."

"You will not." All Gideon's authority came through in his tone, but there was an undercurrent of dark amusement as well. "You will go to the Academy. Tonight. Now. I will know where you are."

Gabby looked ready to argue, stopped herself. Nodded. "Yes, Gideon."

Selah was not as quick to concede. "Are we to be prisoners, then?"

"You are to be *safe*," Gideon said. Implored, perhaps.

Selah looked toward the small collection of shrouded bodies. "Were they seekers?"

"They have to be," Gideon confirmed. "And the things in the lake were their juries tonight. Do not think they would not happily be yours as well."

Chapter Thirty-Nine

The Fountain

The thing that climbed from the Fountain was hungry, and it grew restless in the mud. It would need to eat something soon. But, since the snake, none of the wild things would come close enough for it to feed.

It needed easy prey.

It listened.

It tested the wind.

It waited.

Chapter Forty

Sam

Even locked in a room with a sack over his head, despite the rasp of his own panicked breathing, Sam heard something cry out as it died. He did not, of course, know what it was. But he recognized the wail, knew it well. It was so much like the sounds, the sounds before the Sounds stopped making their hateful noises and began talking to him. The noise had been the soundtrack to Sam's childhood.

What the hell is this place?

Sam would have his answer soon enough.

A soft rap of knuckles against a wooden door startled him. Sam, who had not moved from his spot on the floor, scooted back and away from the knock.

The rapping came again, three firm knocks against the wooden barrier.

And then a woman's voice, as gentle and firm as the rapping, "I am coming in now. Let us get you out of this place and to somewhere more comfortable."

Then came the now-familiar sounds of a lock turning and a door opening.

Silence. And then, "What is the reason for this?" The woman's voice had developed an edge.

Sam didn't know how to answer, but realized soon he wasn't expected to. The question was not for him.

"I thought it best he did not know the way." A man's deep voice responded, and there was something like sullenness at its fringes.

"You were to fetch him, not terrify him. We need the child's help, not his fear."

"Magdalene said . . ."

The woman sighed. "Please help him up. And let us take him to a room befitting a guest, not a prisoner."

"Magdalene said we are to take him to the others," said the man.

The woman sighed again. "Fine. First to the meeting, then to a proper place for him to rest."

Sam listened to every word, mentally tucking away names and anything else that seemed important. Like this Magdalene. The man seemed to answer to her. The woman, he wasn't so sure.

Strong hands were lifting him from under his arms, no snatch of the bag this time.

He was guided out the door and through what must have been a long corridor. They turned twice as they walked, down equally long stretches.

The two people with him did not speak as they made their way.

At last, another lock and another door. Sam was led, rather than shoved, into a room.

"I am going to take this thing off you now." The woman this time.

Sam felt deft fingers untie the knot at the back of his head, then unwind the cord from around his neck. The bag was lifted, and Sam blinked in the dim light of the room.

The woman in front of him was small, shorter than Sam and maybe his mother's age. She had brown skin and short dark hair and wide silver eyes. And she had wings. Huge blue-grey wings. They looked both soft and substantial, like the wings of some kind of exotic moth.

Sam knew he was in a strange place and had experienced what could only be called otherworldly events his entire life. But being freed by a winged woman was a different kind of weird. He was surprised beyond response and froze instead. The woman had kind eyes, but he had trusted what he thought was kindness from an impossible being before, and that had gotten him exactly here.

She reached out and touched his cheek, frowning at what she saw there. Sam could imagine a bruise was spreading, the result of one of his many falls in the tunnel.

The man was much taller, imposing, with dark hair and a square jaw. Where the woman's silver eyes held a measure of sympathy, his, while a similar color, were cold and hard. He, too, had wings, striated with shades of orange and brown.

It was then Sam looked past the two winged people in front of him and found he was inside a large and barren room. There were windows set high in the walls and Sam was surprised to find it was dark outside. Everything was grey stone, and what lighting there was came from an array of scattered candles and torches on the walls. The center of the room was taken up by a long table where three other people were sitting, watching.

Watching him.

One was a pale, thin woman with grey hair and wings. She wore a pinched expression that looked permanent.

Across from her was another woman, this one golden and beautiful with ivory wings that glimmered even in the low light. For the first time, Sam thought, *fairy*. The woman reminded him of an old, long-dead movie star whose name escaped his whirling brain.

At the head of the table was a man, dark skinned and lean. Even sitting, it was apparent the man was very tall. His wings were a dark yellow.

"Friends," said the blue-winged woman, "this is the Jury's boy." She said nothing else to introduce him, which led Sam to believe they either knew nothing else about him or enough about him that he might need no introduction.

These, he thought, *might be the people behind the Sounds. And what is the jury?* His chest tightened in a combination of excitement and dread.

"And these, child, are the Philosophers."

"Zane," said the man with yellow wings.

"Isabis," said the beautiful woman.

"Magdalene," said the grey woman.

"Zebedee," said the man who'd captured him.

"And I am Alma," said the blue-winged woman.

If any of them recognized him they did not show it. But he had to know.

Sam spoke for the first time since arriving at wherever he was. "Philosophers? Does that make you the Sounds, too?"

There was silence in the room. When Alma answered, Sam heard confusion in her voice, and she seemed to choose her words with care. "No, we are Philosophers. I am not sure what the sounds are."

His stomach sank. It was not the answer he had hoped for. Sam read her eyes as best he could. He thought she was telling the truth.

"Alma," said Magdalene, "we need to discuss this. Now."

"In front of the boy? I will take him to—" Alma started.

"You'll take him nowhere he is not guarded," said Magdalene, her words curt and clipped.

Alma stood to her full height which was not very tall and opened her mouth to respond.

Zane beat her to it. "Alma, Zebedee, stay. There may be things the child knows. We finish this and then, Alma, you may take the boy somewhere he can rest. For now, he stays as well and is, perhaps, helpful."

Sam had assumed Magdalene was in charge, but it appeared it was Zane, instead. *They want to watch me, to know where I am.* Sam wondered how much these people already knew, if they knew about the hole and all the killing he had done since he arrived on their island. Regardless, he was not going to give them anything for free. Not while he was being treated like a trespasser and criminal. In spite of what Zane hoped—or, maybe, just to spite him—whatever they asked, he was not about to be *helpful*.

Zebedee escorted Sam to a chair at the far end of the table, putting as much space between him and the others as was possible.

"Do not run away now," the tall man whispered in a way that suggested he hoped Sam would. "This is an enormous place and quite easy to get lost in. You might never be seen again."

There was a threat in those words, and Sam did not miss it. It made something noxious froth deep inside him. This was a man he would happily burn. Not now but later, maybe.

He watched as Zebedee joined the others at the table already mid-conversation. Sam lowered his eyes to the floor and hoped he looked disinterested. But he listened.

"The girl may well be a gift." Isabis suggested in her musical voice, picking up a conversation that had been dropped when Sam entered the room.

"Or a complication. We should not be surprised Selah has brought us a complication." Magdalene's tone said she was not interested in Isabis's optimism.

"Or a balance. With the Jury's boy—Sam—here, we will need it." That was Zane with his low, calm voice.

"But do not forget Ava's child is here, too. There are too many variables in play for us to wait for something to happen. We have no choice but to act," Magdalene said.

"Do you actually think the Jury brought the boy here thinking he would be—"

"Not now, Zebedee." Zane's voice remained low but it was also outraged and impatient.

They'd been talking about him and Sam would have gladly done terrible things if it meant Zebedee could have finished his sentence. The man seemed to know why Sam was there. Or suspect, at least.

"Sam," said Zane, "do you know why you were brought here?"

"No," said Sam. He did not look up. It was the truth. He could have added he wasn't brought at all, that he had made his own way. But that was more information than he was willing to volunteer.

Zane tried again. "There must have been some explanation, some reason. Certainly the Jury told you *something*."

"No." Sam didn't even know what the jury was.

"Where is the Jury? Hidden? Injured?" A hand struck the table. Magdalene's voice bordered on shrill.

How can an entire jury be missing or hidden? The island can't be that big. And how could they all *be injured?*

Sam said nothing. Instead, he stared at the floor.

"Your silence is not convincing," said Magdalene. "You know more than you would like us to believe. If you will not speak by choice—"

There was a long pause. Sam was sure that if he looked up, he would see a silent conversation happening between the winged people.

It was Alma who next spoke. "We need to talk to them all, not just Sam. And to Selah and Gabrielle as well."

"In time," Zane agreed. "But we have matters to discuss aside from Alma's insubordinate girl and our little collection of outsiders." Zane seemed to take charge of the group without having to raise his voice or address them by name. He spoke almost as if to himself. "This is not a time for frivolous banter. The Jury is missing. That must be our focus."

"Of course you are right, Zane." Zebedee's voice had a too-sugary quality that put Sam's teeth on edge.

"With the Jury absent, the island will look to us for guidance and for action," Magdalene said. "There has been no communication with the Jury for two days. While the silence is not unusual, the silence at the Fountain *is*. There has not been a seeker, or a losting thing, at the

Fountain since she stopped communicating with us. The Jury has not called for anything or anyone, seeking or losting. It is unprecedented."

Sam tried to hear and remember every word. Some of what was being said made sense, but much of it didn't. It made the conversation hard to track.

"With the Jury gone silent, there will be no instructions for the Fountain, for the beasts in the water. It is dangerous," Zane said. "For us and for all the *whens*. It is a wonder Sam made it here at all—"

I almost didn't.

"We do what we are called to do here, but you know as well as I that what matters—what's at stake—is what is on the far side of the lake."

A collective shudder ran through the room.

Curiosity won and Sam glanced up before he could stop himself. It was Isabis whose eyes met his, who answered his unasked question.

"It is Hell." She said the words as though they tasted bitter in her mouth.

Hell? Where am *I?*

Magdalene sneered at the other woman. "Do not be dramatic. It is not *Hell*."

"And what would you call it?" challenged Zane. "A place where those losting things so vile and corrupt as to pollute everything around them go never to be found? The place where the losting people soulless enough to want those things and worse are sent to live for centuries—perhaps longer—in time even slower than ours? If that is not Hell, then I do not know what is.

"Until the Jury is found and this is made right, those things—those wretched, horrible people—stay in their *whens*. And"—Zane's voice grew so low they were hard to make out—"if the beasts that guard the lake are no longer being controlled, no longer have a duty, what is to say all that is imprisoned on the far side of the lake will stay there? They have had more than enough time to plan an escape."

Alma stood so fast her chair nearly toppled over. The woman's hands were on the table, her weight settled on them. "I would like to take the child to a room and away from this discussion. He has had enough for one day, would you not agree, Zebedee?" Her voice was stinging as she addressed the man who had captured Sam.

Zebedee did not respond to Alma's implied accusation.

"In a moment," said Zane. "We are nearly done here."

"If they attempted to leave, they would still be attacked. Eaten," Magdalene said, ignoring Alma as though she'd never spoken. She sounded less sure than she had moments before.

Zane answered Magdalene as he might a child. "They have weapons. Poisons. Access to the worst man has created. Certainly they have used them against one another, so why would they hesitate using them against the beasts in the lake? Against us?"

Magdalene, it seemed, had no reply.

"We *must* find the Jury," Isabis said.

"We've searched all the likely places," said Zebedee.

"It seems it is time to send a discreet group of Groundskeepers to search the forest and shore. Gideon can be trusted to choose wisely from his men and women." Zane stopped as if thinking. "It is only a matter of time until we have righteous panic on the island. A panicked community will not be able to defend itself."

And with that, the bizarre meeting was over.

Zane elected himself to talk to the man he called Gideon.

Isabis, sounding upset, excused herself.

"You two take the boy somewhere safe," Magdalene instructed, but did not sound at all concerned with his well-being.

Safe for who? Sam wondered.

Sam was taken down more hallways and through more doors than he could even begin to keep track of. Alma, holding a torch, led them, and Zebedee walked closely behind, from time to time giving Sam a rough and unnecessary shove to his back.

As they turned a corner and stopped at a door, they were met by a small woman with charcoal wings who was nearly running. She whispered something in Alma's ear. Alma nodded and thanked her, then turned to Miles.

"Zebedee and I have something to attend to," said Alma. "But I will be back soon, and you and I will talk. And I will bring you something to eat. You must be famished. You are our guest here, and I will see to it that you are comfortable."

Sam was, in fact, starving. But he wasn't ready to share even that much with Alma.

Alma opened the door for Sam and ushered him in. She followed behind and lit torches on the walls of the room with the one she carried. The space was larger than Sam had expected, and not a prison cell at all.

When Alma left with more promises to return, she closed the door behind her.

Sam did not miss the sound of the lock engaging.

He was alone again.

Chapter Forty-One

Ember

Having already been discovered, the group had no reason not to take the well-trod path from the lake to the Academy. This time, however, Gabby did not lead. A tall, broad-shouldered Groundskeeper with earthen-brown wings walked ahead of the group. The woman held a short staff that ended in a V of foot-long blades. She glanced back occasionally as if to confirm they were all five still there, that one of them hadn't slipped into the forest in search of another adventure. Yet another Groundskeeper flew ahead, perhaps to notify whoever was waiting at the Academy that they were on their way.

Once, the woman stopped them with an upheld hand. She had heard, or seen, something in the woods beyond. They waited, barely breathing, until the Groundskeeper motioned for them to continue.

Bringing up the rear of the procession—and that's what Ember thought it felt like, a procession—was a short, thick man with wings the same color as the grey mist that crept between their feet. He was armed as well, his staff ending in single metal blades on each end.

"How far?" Ember whispered to Selah, who walked in front of her.

"Sooner than I would like," Selah replied.

Indeed, in only a few minutes time, the Academy loomed above them in the darkness.

Standing alone in what must have been a full-acre clearing, it was an imposing building. From the outside, it was not nearly as large as the Library, or even the Hatchery. Despite being smaller, it was heavier—cold and foreboding where the others were warm and inviting. The difference was in the architecture and the materials. Rather than simple, light wooden construction, the Academy was mud-colored stone and ornamented. It stood three stories with a sharp, mean spire at the top. Lanterns hung at either side of the great double doors, casting writhing shadows all around. The windows were black, blind eyes embedded into the walls of the place. No lights shone through them, but the small hairs on the back of Ember's neck knew without question they were being watched as they approached.

This is a haunted place, Ember thought. *Or a place waiting to be haunted.*

She wondered if it looked different in the light of day, less ominous.

She wondered if she would be allowed to leave to find out.

"I once loved this place, the weirdness and the drama of it." Selah spoke so only Ember was able to hear. "But that veil has lifted. It is a self-important building full of self-important people who want nothing more than to collect power and prestige like pretty rocks, or bullet casings."

"What *is* it?" Ember asked.

"Many things. A school by title, and also in practice. I learned here as a child. It is also home to the Philosophers, with the exception of Alma. She wisely chooses to live alone. And it is our capitol building, I suppose, in as much as we have one. And, from time to time, a prison."

"How can it be all those at once?" It was a large building but, Ember thought, not that large.

Selah wrapped a wing around Ember's shoulder, leaned in close so as not to be overheard. "You will see. There is more to it inside than out. It is . . . disorienting. Do not wander alone. It is very easy to lose your way here."

Lose your way had two meanings, of course, and Ember wondered which her friend intended. *Both. I think she meant both.*

Chapter Forty-Two

Selah

"Wait here." The Groundskeeper at the front left them at the base of the six stone steps leading to the front door. She mounted the stairs alone, lifted the iron knocker and rapped sharply five times with her gloved hand. She waited, lifted her hand to knock again, when the door swung inward. There, Zebedee stood, smiling with too many teeth and smelling of too much perfume. Even at a distance, sage and lavender overwhelmed Selah.

It had to be Zebedee. I had to hand myself over to this vile, groveling weasel.

Zebedee looked past the guard without greeting her, his eyes landing on Selah. "It is wonderful to see you. The others will be delighted." He opened the door fully and smiled a gilded smile at the group standing at the foot of the stairs. "To be quite honest, we thought perhaps we would be forced to hunt you down and drag you here." His smile widened at the idea.

Selah wished she were able to reach up and clean him out as she had Ember's father. She believed she would leave a husk behind. Instead, Selah climbed the stairs, skirted the guard, and pushed past Zebedee, motioning for the others to follow her as she did.

"Manners, girl." There was a forced humor in Zebedee's voice that did not hide his displeasure at the affront. He dismissed the guards, closing the door before they could protest.

The group found themselves in a foyer with high ceilings and dead air. Doorless hallways branched off like fingers from a palm.

The Academy was as unlovely within as it was without. Large grey stones and yellowed marble and time-darkened wood consumed any light that accidentally found its way in. Under the blanket of night, it was lit by tapers and torches and nothing else.

The structure managed to be both claustrophobic and cavernous and was far vaster than it appeared from the outside. Halls and doors spidered into more doors and halls, some leading down endless passages and others looping back where they began. Selah knew many of them at one point in her childhood but had never known them all. Now, time enough had passed since she spent her days roaming this place that she feared she would be lost if left to make her own way.

Zebedee led them with practiced confidence through the labyrinth. When they entered a large, sparse room, four others waited for them there. Alma, Zane, Isabis, and Magdalene were seated around a dense wood table. Thin candlelight struggled to illuminate the thick air giving the room an unclean quality Selah found appropriate. There were benches enough for a much larger group. Zebedee escorted Selah to the seat directly across from Magdalene. Ember, Miles, Gabby, and Simon were left to stand in the shadows behind her.

Zebedee, of course, installed himself at Magdalene's right side, looking as though he hoped to be patted on the head or offered a good-boy treat.

Magdalene ignored him and addressed Selah. "You are very challenging. Difficult, some might say. Others might call you a problem."

"Which do you prefer?" Selah would not be intimidated.

Selah's eyes found Alma's. There was a clear message there: *Do not argue. Do not make this worse.*

Magdalene rested her chin on folded fingers as she looked hard at Selah. Her dove-grey wings beat rhythmically behind her, belying her calm tone. "Me? I think you are a nuisance. Fortunately for you, you are also useful. The other Philosophers see something in you despite your indifference to tradition and your lack of respect. The Jury sees it, too. Or she did. I hope for your sake she still does."

She is pretending to think about this, about what she will do with us. She has already decided. She is taking pleasure in this charade. I will give her as little entertainment as possible.

Selah chose to disregard Alma's warning. "Enough, Magdalene. I am bored. Why are we here?"

"Oh, I assumed Alma told you. But perhaps she did not have time before, well, we do not know, do we? Because you all disappeared into the night like specters when you should have been fast asleep in Alma's little hovel." Magdalene, all feigned distress like a bad mask.

Selah looked around the table. Alma's eyes were tired, but there was also an exasperation there, and Selah knew she would hear about her impropriety another time. Zebedee wore a practiced, simpering smile as he hung on Magdalene's words. Isabis was miserable, her perfect face refined by it. Zane looked somewhere above Selah's head, unwilling to meet her eyes.

"I do not believe Beatrix left us, left the island, to fend for itself. She loves it, and *us*, too much. She *raised* many of us—me, Alma, you, Zebedee. So, which was it, Magdalene? Did you kill her, or did you have her killed?" Selah was going to move this game forward. She was rewarded as Isabis gasped, and Zebedee's awful smile slipped.

Magdalene grew very still and very quiet.

"You are an awful little creature. You do not know your place, nor do you respect mine. I am already tired of you and see no point in softening my words any longer." Magdalene stood, pressed her palms into the table and leaned in toward Selah. "You—all of you—may consider the Academy your home for the foreseeable future. Or consider it a jail. It matters not at all to me. Know only you are not leaving until the Jury is found and you are cleared."

Selah was incredulous. "Cleared of what? Of leaving this place in search of a way to save it? Cleared of bringing back the brightest light I could find?" Selah reached back and pulled Ember by the hand toward her. "Beatrix created something when she toyed with the boy. And if he is now here, on the island, we need a counterbalance to him. Ember is that counterbalance. I am sure of it."

"And how, child, can you possibly know that?" Magdalene had dropped her bad mask, spit her words at Selah.

Selah felt Ember's hand tighten on her own. She squeezed back gently. *I will not give it all away.*

"It is . . . it was a feeling. A feeling that led me to her. A feeling I had upon meeting her." No talk of mermaids and their gifts, nor of the music Ember had no way or right to know so intimately.

"It is remarkable you are prepared to rest the fate of the island on the ragged seams of *feelings* you patched together until you found meaning in them. You are quite enamored with yourself, child, even as you spurn our traditions and our collective wisdom."

"Ah, collective wisdom. And what of the Collective Jury, Magdalene? If we are so much wiser together, where do you stand on that?"

"Beatrix does not approve, and neither do I. We have served the Fountain for generations, so many generations countless are lost to history. And we have always done so with a single Jury to guide us."

"And what of the rest of you?" Selah questioned the Philosophers gathered around the table. Their silence told her nothing other than they were being cowed by Magdalene.

Zane spoke then. "We will not talk theology at this late hour. It is an important topic, but one left for daylight and clear heads."

Chapter Forty-Three

Miles

Miles followed the conversation as best he could. What he took away from it was a deep respect for Selah. She was, in her own way, as formidable as Gabby.

"Take them somewhere deep in the building." Magdalene left the room with her shoulders and wings squared against them all.

Zebedee stood to escort the group.

"I am going to accompany you." Alma spoke to Zebedee much as Magdalene did, as less than an equal.

"I am capable of taking children to a room." Zebedee was indignant.

"They are smart, and, if any of them were to disappear, you would do well to have a witness to your actions. Someone to confirm you did, indeed, deliver all five of them safely." Alma's words were thick with underlying meaning—how Zebedee chose to interpret them was another matter.

"Come, then. Assist and bear witness." Zebedee spoke to Alma, but kept his eyes trained on his wards.

Zebedee again took the lead. Gabby was at his heels, and Miles watched as her hand slid into the deep pocket of her tunic, where he knew her sharp blade was. *How bad is this going to get?*

They turned right.

Miles was tall but struggled to see over or around the larger man's orange and brown wings. As there was not much to be seen, he missed little. The hallways were remarkable only for their ceaseless repetition of torches and doors. The walls were otherwise unadorned, no break in the monotony and no landmarks by which to track their progress. Miles thought it was by design, only those who belonged in the Academy would be able to make their way through it without getting lost.

Simon walked at Miles's side, radiating anxiety. Miles knew while the boy was years older than him, Simon was still a child in many ways that mattered. So Miles ran a brotherly hand through Simon's red hair, and when the boy looked up at him, he gave what he hoped was a reassuring smile.

They turned left down another hallway.

Ember and Selah walked together behind Miles, with Alma trailing them all. In one hand she carried a burlap sack.

Miles turned once and saw Selah and Alma engaged in a silent conversation. They mouthed words to one another, and when Alma gave a sharp nod, it was over. She acknowledged Miles with a lift of her chin, then pointed to her ears—*listen to what I am saying*—and then twirled her finger in tight circles: *turn around so Zebedee does not see that you saw.* Miles did as she instructed, fascinated with what the woman was up to.

As they walked, Alma began speaking to herself. She muttered but was audible in the empty halls. "It would be best to put them together, I think. And near enough we can keep an eye on all of them. Does not much matter if they talk, there is nothing of consequence they can learn from one another. Perhaps in the old dormitory wing . . ."

Gabby glanced back, her face curious. Miles gave a quick shrug.

"Yes," Alma continued, "if they were together, it would be so convenient. Much easier to manage. And Magdalene is so busy. She would be pleased if we did this on our own, took initiative. No reason to ask permission for everything we do."

Miles saw Zebedee cock his head to one side. He was listening.

At another intersection of hallways, Zebedee hesitated. Then another left.

They walked in silence for a few yards when Zebedee spoke. "It seems to me we should put them together in the old dormitory wing. They are no threat, together or separated."

Miles risked a glance back. Selah, Ember, and Alma wore the shadows of smiles just beneath their carefully composed expressions. Alma looked especially pleased with herself, and answered, "Very wise, Zebedee. Magdalene herself might not have thought of it."

"If she asks, do tell her it was my idea."

"I certainly will."

Zebedee stopped at a door and reached to open it.

"The next room, Zebedee. Please." Alma's voice was deferential. And then, apologetic. "The next room has more beds. And a washroom. It will mean they do not need to bother us during the night."

"Are you sure?" Zebedee asked Alma. The question struck Miles as unfinished, as though something unspoken was passing between the two.

"I am," said Alma. "We can lock them in and be done with them until the morning."

Locked in? Miles blanched and looked over his shoulder. Selah gave him a half smirk that disappeared immediately, but it was enough for Miles to believe there was a plan in place.

Zebedee sighed like an unskilled actor. "A point well made, Alma. I am tired. And tired of chaperoning." He opened the next door down the hall and stood aside as they filed through. It was dark when they entered. Alma took a torch from the hallway and brought it into the room, lighting candles and sconces until the room glowed warm.

It was, indeed, a large dorm room. Miles counted six beds, three to a wall. Each was covered in matching ivory fabric, and on the back wall was a heavy wooden cupboard and a narrow window high above.

In the corner opposite the cupboard, another door that must have led to the single bathroom.

Zebedee remained at the door, never entering the room.

Alma embraced each of them in turn, with Simon clinging a bit longer than the others. She surprised Miles by hugging him, as well. Her arms held him tight and squeezed—it was motherly. He was happy for the gesture. If he needed any further convincing she was on their side, the embrace provided it.

"Alma, enough. Let us be done." Zebedee's limited patience had run its course.

On her way out, Alma handed a bag to Selah. "Bread enough to keep you all from going hungry tonight. Water you can get from the washroom. I will see you, *all five of you,* in the morning."

With that, she was gone, the door closed and then bolted behind her.

Miles was the first to speak. "What kind of dorm room locks from the outside?"

"One that has been converted to a jail cell," Gabby responded with venom in her voice.

"Can someone please explain what the hell is going on?" Miles sat heavily on one of the beds nearest the door. It was soft, and he fought the urge to lie down on it. He was shot through with adrenaline, but he was also very, very tired.

"And what is special about this room?" Ember asked.

"And may I please have some bread?" Simon asked quietly.

Selah dropped the burlap bag on a bed and pulled out small parcels of cloth-wrapped bread. She stared in the bottom of the bag for a moment before passing the bread out to the others.

Selah reached once again and brought from it a black metal cylinder. She studied the object for a moment, then held it out so the others could see. "It seems Alma left us something else, although the name escapes me."

Miles crossed the room and took it from her. He pressed a button and light poured out of one end. "It's a flashlight. And a pretty old one, but it's in great shape and seems to work just fine."

Ember's eyes were wide, as though she'd never seen an old flashlight before. Miles handed it to her to inspect. She clicked the button, turning it off and on again, all the while shaking her head a bit in what looked like bewilderment.

"That," Gabby said, "will be useful tonight."

Miles found himself the topic of conversation, a conversation he did not understand.

"I am certain Magdalene is involved," Selah repeated.

Gabby shook her head. "That does little to explain what is happening in Miles's *when.* The things leaving the lake gravitated toward him. Why would Magdalene involve Miles? She had little regard for Ava."

"I do not know," Selah admitted, "but despite what tradition dictates, Magdalene is hungry to be the next Jury. And of course she would want to be in place before the island moves to a Collective Jury."

"That," Miles interjected, pointing a finger at Selah, "What is that? A Collective Jury?"

"As Magdalene said, the Fountain has always been guided by one person, and that person has the title of Jury," Selah responded. "As the world has changed and become more complex, decisions here become more complex as well. The Jury's rulings must be more nuanced, and the shades of grey between right and wrong, deserving and undeserving, are not as clear as they once were. A Collective Jury, a Jury made up of the collective wisdom of a small group, is better suited for a more nuanced world."

Gabby interjected, "Miles, you will best understand this as it is your *when* to which Selah refers."

"Miles, when . . . when is your *when*?" Ember asked the question in a reluctant voice, as if she were afraid of the answer.

Miles told her, then asked, "Why? When's your *when*?"

Ember blinked rapidly, from surprise or to hold back tears, Miles wasn't sure which. "1913" was her simple, but astounding, reply.

Miles shook his head as he processed her words. "Over a hundred years before mine? I don't understand any of this."

Ember stared at the floor, her voice was small. "Am I the past then? Is Miles the future?"

"Neither," answered Selah. "Your *whens* are both present. But Miles lives in the current present, while yours is a present from ago."

"That makes no sense . . ." Miles argued.

Gabby responded with a voice edged in impatience. "I do not know we could explain it in a way that you could easily accept. We certainly cannot tonight. But it does not make it any less true."

Miles rose from the bed he'd been sitting on and began to pace the room. "Fine. So our *whens* are whenever, but they're all right now. And Ava might be the reason your world is falling apart, but she's dead. So it would be her ghost. Or it might be Magdalene. Because she wants to be put in charge before a bunch of other people get put in charge."

Simon nodded, encouraging his friend. "Yes! You do understand!"

Miles's laugh came out a bark, but he did not want to hurt the boy's feelings. "Thanks, Simon. But where does any of that leave us? I mean, what we have to do is find the Jury, right? And then she can make all this stop before . . . before things get worse in my *when* for everyone. Before something happens to my parents. If it hasn't already."

Miles sat back on the bed, bone-tired. It all seemed impossible.

Selah crouched down so she was level with Miles. "Yes, we have to find Beatrix. The first step toward finding her is to find her boy, Sam, the one she brought to the island. And if we are to find him, we are in the right place. The Academy is where every important decision is made."

Miles fell back, his head bouncing on the bed as he landed. "But we're locked in this room. So where does that leave us?"

Gabby smiled. "It is true. The door is locked. But I do not believe anyone said it is the *only* way out."

Chapter Forty-Four

Sam

Sam inspected the room. It was comfortable enough with a small couch and a bed across from each other against the long walls. There was a washroom of sorts behind a door in one corner. He ran cool water from a tap into a basin, scrubbing at his face and hands to get the worst of the grime off.

Leaving the washroom, Sam saw there was a single, slim window on the wall opposite the door. The ceilings of the room were high, and Sam could not reach the lower ledge even when he tried to pull the beds and then the couch underneath it. All were firmly attached to the floor.

Sam collapsed on the couch, his tired body grateful for its softness.

A prisoner, not a guest.

And he waited.

Alma did return with Zebedee at her heels. As promised, she brought food with her. Sam was offered heavy, sweet bread that smelled of almonds as well as sharp cheese and fruit all on a large plate. He ate thankfully, greedily. He ate until he knew he had to stop or would get sick from it.

"Zebedee, please leave us." The woman was curt.

"But what about Magdalene . . ." The man's voice came out a petulant whine.

"I will speak with Magdalene. Leave us now. You have . . . you have done your part. Close the door when you leave."

With a frown, the man turned and slunk out the door, shutting it as he left.

The woman stayed where she was, not moving toward Sam. She then sat on the floor where she stood, her feet tucked under her body and her wings pulled behind.

"Sam, yes?"

He nodded. *How do you know that?*

"Sam, I am Alma. And I am sorry for the reception you received today."

Sam hesitated, then nodded once more.

"Can you tell me why you are here? Why did you come to the Fountain and the island?"

There was a quality to this woman, to her kind eyes and voice, and Sam found he very much wanted to tell her. He was tired of not telling anyone. He was tired of not understanding. And Alma seemed important, the way the man deferred to her confirmed it. If anyone would know why he was here, Sam thought this woman—*Alma*—would.

So he told it all to her. He did not know how much she already knew, so he told it all. Up until the lake. He was not ready to talk about the last two days. "I've never belonged," Sam finished. "Not anywhere. And when my mother tried to help—I guess to protect me and everyone else—she died for it." He couldn't quite bring himself to say the words *I killed her for it*, though he believed that was the truth.

Alma sat without speaking, giving him time and space to continue.

"So along come the Sounds. And they were scary at first, but they became someone I could talk to. Someone who told me I was special. And they weren't afraid of me. All my life they've been telling me there was a better place for me. A place where I would belong and even matter. With Mother gone, there was no one left who wanted me. No one who cared. And this time, when the Sounds asked me to come to this place, they called it home. So I came.

"Except it was a lie." Sam hadn't planned on talking about this part, but the words were flowing now that someone was listening. "This isn't my home, either. No, don't shake your head. It's true. The island itself tried to stop me. Animals attacked me. And then I was captured and thrown in a cell and now I'm here. Even if it doesn't look like a cell, it is."

Sam stopped. He wanted to talk about how angry he was, now that this place had rejected him. How furious he was with the Sounds for lying to him, and how much he wanted to punish everyone who rejected him. But he thought better of saying those words to the woman sitting on the floor. She seemed to pity him if not actually like him, and he didn't want to risk that thin lifeline.

Alma's eyes grew sad as she listened, but she did not speak until he finished his story. "Where to start, Sam? Your mother, she was trying to save you. She loved you, but she did not know how to help you. Did not understand. Do not be angry with her."

"Not with her."

"And do not be angry with yourself. You were a very small child with a very large burden. As you grew, there was no one to help you carry it. Now you are here. Let us help you."

Sam did not respond.

"But you must tell me all of it. Including what has transpired here on the island. I need to know if I am to help you, and perhaps help the Jury."

"What is the Jury?"

The question made Alma pause. Confusion and realization traded places on her face. "What do you know about this place? About the Fountain?"

Sam shook his head. "Not a lot." He told her what little he understood. Sam knew what he had gathered from stories the Sounds had told to him.

It seemed he only knew the darker parts, stories of power and punishment.

So Alma described the rest, telling of the beauty of the island, the generosity of the Fountain, and about the losting and the seeking.

Alma gestured at the seat next to him on the well-worn couch. "May I?"

Sam made room for her, shifting as far to one side as he could.

Alma sat, hands between her knees. Sam thought she was anxious. "What you call the Sounds, we call the Jury. And before that, Beatrix, a Hatchery keeper. She is important—vital—to the Fountain and to the island—"

"Wait. The Sounds are just one person? They—she—always made it seem like it was a bunch of people, a group, talking to me in one voice."

Alma looked puzzled at this. "Perhaps she was trying to keep some distance between you. Perhaps she didn't want to divulge who she was. I do not know. She has been the Jury for many, many years. Do you understand what that means, what she does?"

"Not really. I mean . . . No."

"It means she is the mind and the heart of the Fountain. She has final say on reuniting what is losting with who is seeking. When there is doubt, she decides who can cross the lake. She can make the way easy or difficult. And she alone can control the things that live in the lake and in the Fountain. She is the one who determines reward and punishment."

"So she's like God."

"No, because unlike God, she sometimes requires counsel. Which is where I and the other Philosophers come in. We can help guide her in her decisions when she is conflicted or unsure. Because she is not God, this happens from time to time. But we cannot control what she can; we cannot make final decisions and judgments. We are in frequent contact with her or have been until two days ago."

Sam nodded, and then interrupted Alma with his piece of the story. "I was still talking to the Sounds . . . the Jury . . . Beatrix . . . until yesterday, I think. But they, she, wasn't always there when I expected her, or when I needed her. And she was making things confusing when she could've just helped me. You said she could help people get to the island, but she didn't help me. And there was a hole in the ground . . . I think she could've told me what to do, but she just made it a riddle . . . a game or something."

Alma responded with careful words. "She has changed. Maybe it happened over time and we did not notice it. Or did not want to. I do not know why. Perhaps she is sick and her mind is deteriorating." Alma looked thoughtful, sad and paused before continuing. "Or perhaps I am making excuses for her. She was an exceptional Jury for a very long time. She was kind and just. It has only been recently that she has been . . . different. There has been less kindness from her and more harsh judgment."

Sam stopped Alma as he stood and began to pace the room. A hot rage crept through him. He spoke without looking at her. "But she has been coming to me for years, since I was a little kid. And she messed with my life. All that time. All my life. She made it so I couldn't go anywhere or do anything. I didn't have friends. I mean, at all. No one. My *mom* was scared of me. And I don't know if they—she—made me whatever I am. But she made it worse. She made it worse when she could've made it better?" Now, Sam turned to Alma. His eyes flashed in a reddened face. "I don't see how that's just. And I promise it wasn't kind."

Alma spoke in a low, gentle tone. "Remember, time here is different than it was for you. What was years in your life may have been just weeks for Beatrix. That does not make it any better for you, I know."

"So my whole life was screwed up because some sort-of-god got old and went crazy? That does not make it better at all. It's worse! It's worse because it doesn't *mean* anything. It doesn't. Mean. Anything!" Sam was yelling now.

There was a sharp knock at the door, and it swung open. The man, Zebedee, stood in the doorway. It was clear he had been listening for some sign of trouble, and Sam's yelling had been his cue.

Alma surprised Sam by turning the man away. "We are fine. You may *go*, Zebedee. The boy is upset, and rightly so."

Zebedee stared hard at Sam, deciding perhaps. He nodded, a hint of a snarl on his lips. "As you wish."

The door once again closed behind him.

Alma sighed, continued, "I know nothing I say can make it any better at all. But keep this in mind. Beatrix came to you because there is something in you that drew her. She did not create it; it was already there. You burn so brightly. The Jury is the most powerful among us, but as a child you were able to communicate with her and win her favor. You were strong enough, and brave enough, to push her away. That is astounding. *You* are astounding."

Sam held his face in his hands, mumbled through them. "I'm not. I had to. I was going crazy. I needed to make space in my head or . . . or I don't know."

"Sam, you and I will talk about this again. As much or as little as you like. But now I need to ask you something. Something important."

Sam looked up at her, waiting for what was to come next.

"You were able to push her away, even hold her at bay. You were able to keep the Jury out of your head until you let her back in. Is that right?"

"Yes."

"Do you think it can work the other way? Do you think you can call out to her? Can you make her come to you?"

Sam's frustration reignited. "I can call her all I want. I did at the lake. I did in the hole. I did when the stream ran out. It didn't matter. She didn't care. She didn't come. So, no, I guess I can't. I can't do what you want. Sorry."

The conversation had come to the end of its useful life.

Alma stood. "I cannot promise I will not ask you again. In fact, I assure you I will. But for now, for tonight, I will let you rest. It has, I think, been a very difficult time for you, and I know you are tired."

As Alma went to leave the room, and Sam alone in it, he stopped her.

"I want my bag. The one Zebedee took from me."

Alma did not turn around to face him. "I will see what I can do about that."

She left then, again locking the door behind her.

One might think Sam had become accustomed to being a prisoner. He had, after all, spent his life in an invisible cell. But over the previous days, Sam had experienced freedom, a wild and terrifying sort, but freedom nonetheless. It began with the death of his mother, freeing him from any human bonds. Then there had been the freedom of crossing the lake and surviving the island and the fierce, intoxicating freedom of taking life and extinguishing it. Sam had only just experienced it all, and he was not ready to relinquish it. And then there was his life, so unfair. Chosen and reared into madness. So in the hours that passed, he paced his room like a caged animal, and the anger in him simmered. And so many fragments fell down the deep, dry well in the grey place, each was lost in the echo of the last.

Clink.

Clinkclinkclinkclink.

This, he understood, was not so unlike the hole in the ground. It was a place he could kill his way out of. He made up his mind to stop the heart of the next person to walk through the door. And the next, and anyone else who stood in his way as he made his escape.

But then what?

Even as the question persisted, pulling at his sleeve, an answer arose. It was clear, and he was certain. He had not been entirely honest with Alma and thought, perhaps, he *could* find the person who had destroyed his life. *I find Beatrix. And I get some answers. And we'll see what happens then.*

Escape first, then a plan.

It was still night outside the high, narrow window when the metal-on-metal *clank* of the lock's mechanism froze Sam in place. He turned to face the door, preparing.

When it was Alma who crossed the threshold, Sam deflated. She was the one person he was not prepared to kill. She had shown him kindness of a sort, and compassion. And, besides, she knew where his duffel bag was.

Alma brought with her more food. She did not have his bag.

She sat down on the couch, looked up at him. "Join me?" she asked, patting the couch beside her.

He shook his head and sat on the bed opposite her.

"All right," she answered. "Have you considered my request?"

"No." It was a lie, of course he had. But he was not yet willing to help this woman, to help any of them. And he was not prepared to face failure if he were unsuccessful at his attempt to reach out to the Jury.

Alma's blue wings were wrapped around her shoulders like a great shawl. She held Sam's dark eyes with her own as she spoke. "Without the Jury, there is no one to control what lives in the lake. Sometimes, sometimes people who seek losting things find the island and the Fountain on their own. Sometimes, they try to cross the lake. Now, even if they deserve whatever it is they are seeking, there is nothing to stop the creatures from attacking them. Because they are nothing but appetite and are always hungry. Sam, people are being killed. Slaughtered. If we cannot locate the Jury and bring her home, the deaths will continue to multiply."

"I don't know what to tell you. I can't *do* anything."

"I believe you can."

"I don't see how it's my problem."

Alma rocked back a little. "I am choosing to believe you do not mean that."

Sam narrowed his eyes. "What if I don't want to?"

Alma straightened in her seat, her posture formal and stiff. "Well, that is a different thing entirely, is it not?" She leaned forward and spoke, her voice heavy with meaning. "Sam, I may well be the only friend you have on this island. The only one who does not believe you are a monster. Please do not convince me otherwise."

"Maybe I am a monster. Maybe you're wrong."

"Perhaps," Alma admitted. "But I think not. I think you are frightened and exhausted and so very alone."

"I want my bag."

"I need your help."

"I want to leave."

"Your mother would be sad, ashamed, to see the person you have proven to be."

Sam froze then. He took Alma's words in, turned them over in his mind. He thought about the way she had known his name when he'd never told it to her. His next words were frigid with anger. "You read my letter."

Alma nodded. "I did. Did you? Because it seems you have ignored your mother's last wishes for you."

"Get out. Get *out*. I want my bag, and my letter." He turned away from her.

They were done.

He was done.

Clink.

Clink.

Clink.

ONCE upon a time, a few days ago . . .

ANTHONY almost never skipped school to go fishing, but this was one of those rare exceptions. It was a perfect late-spring morning, and he'd meant to just stay out for an hour or so and then head to first period, but the fish were biting and there was nothing in his biology class he couldn't learn by gutting his own catch. He'd hear about it later from his folks, but they wouldn't do too much about it other than bitch at him.

When Anthony's boat rocked, it was strange but not so strange that he thought much about it. You couldn't always predict what the water would do, even in just a largish pond.

When his boat lifted what felt like a good two feet, well, that caught his attention.

Anthony surveyed the pond looking for another boat that might have joined him (even though that wouldn't have explained it). What he saw instead were fish. A lot of them. Popping up to the surface and floating there. Anthony's well-trained eyes knew a dead fish when they saw one.

There was a thump *on the underside of his boat. And then another. Soon, two fish floated just feet away from him, one with his hook in its dead mouth.*

Anthony lowered his oars meaning to get back to shore and away from whatever toxin had invaded the pond. Fish would sink after they died and not surface until their innards began to decompose. Either that process had happened very quickly, or these fish had been dead for a while. Either way, something in the pond was poisoning them.

The water surged again and, this time, it was strong. Strong enough to push Anthony's small boat closer to shore. He tried to help it by paddling, but when another surge came, stronger yet, it shoved his boat all the way to shore and grounded it there.

The new shore, anyway.

On a normal day, there was half a football field between the dense trees that made this place a perfect spot to hide from the busy road and the water. Now, there was half that. The pond had, somehow, become larger. Like it was being filled up by an invisible source.

He looked back and saw what must be all the fish in the pond, more than he had imagined there could be, at the surface. Some of them clumped together and formed masses that glistened in the perfect sunlight.

Anthony looked down at the fish still on his line. A black blight that looked a lot like the bad kind of mold was beginning to spot its scales. He thought better than to try to rescue his hook. He wanted nothing to do with whatever the black stuff was. He pulled out more line from the reel until he had enough to safely cut it without touching any of the thin strand that had touched the water, then snapped it with his pocket knife.

He carefully stepped onto dry land and inspected his boat as best he could. Some of the black mold was climbing the sides starting where the boat had been submerged in the lake. It grew faster than Anthony thought it should probably be able to. As he watched, something interesting happened. When the mold reached dry wood, it slowed and then stopped growing completely. Then it shriveled and turned an ashen grey, dying before his eyes. Anthony wasn't sure if it was the sun or the lack of moisture that killed it, but he didn't have time to ponder the question.

Another surge came, the strongest yet. Anthony backpedaled toward his truck, not wanting to take his eyes off the water's edge. When it stopped and receded a bit, there was just about five yards of dry shore remaining, the edge of it littered with dead and blackening fish.

A squelching, slopping sound that could only be described as the shifting of an enormous amount of pudding came from Anthony's right. The sound was followed by an almost human scream. When he spun to see who it was, Anthony found he was no longer alone on the shore.

Not thirty feet away, a creature that looked very much like an enormous jellyfish had been beached by the last surge. It writhed on the rocky ground, and with each movement came that nasty, gelatinous sucking sound. It continued its awful screaming, but the noises were already weaker and sounded more pain-filled than threatening. Anthony took his phone out of the front pocket of his flannel shirt. Without pictures, no one would believe what he was seeing. The strangers were one thing but this? This was something else.

The jellyfish continued to shift and twitch, but it was clear by the way its tentacles spasmed uselessly that it wasn't going anywhere. It did not look like it was in any condition to attack him.

Anthony approached with measured steps, wanting the best shots he could get. Closer, he could see it was not a jellyfish. Not exactly. Its body, longer than he was tall, was both thin and bloated with skin so pale its organs were visible.

Anthony drew closer, taking pictures with every step.

Like a jellyfish it did have tentacles, but there was something else—hard, angular limbs where some of the tentacles should be.

Anthony drew closer and one of those limbs lashed out at him. He cursed and almost fell backward. The end of the limb appeared to have a human hand that ended in sharp, nearly translucent claws.

"What are *you?" Anthony whispered.*

At the sound of his voice, the not-a-jellyfish turned its head to face him and let loose with another scream. This one sounded furious. And hungry.

Anthony would go no closer, so he looked at it through his phone's camera and zoomed in. The face was that of an angler fish, a creature he had seen only in textbooks and on screens. It was half taken up with a gaping mouth filled with transparent, needle teeth.

But its eyes.

Its eyes were human.

Even as Anthony watched, the creature's skin began to break out in yellow, oozing sores that went black at their edges in a matter of seconds. Without warning, its body deflated and something clear but thicker than water poured out of it and onto the ground. That stuff began yellowing and blackening as well. The smell was worse than the insides of anything Anthony had ever gutted.

Once again, he found himself backpedaling to his truck, taking pictures as he went.

By the time Anthony reached the truck and was safely inside, the not-a-jellyfish was nothing more than a twitching pile of yellow-black slime. He was almost certain he spotted pieces of a human skeleton in the mass.

Another surge was forming in the center of the pond, its surface now gone pitch black with sludge. Anthony started his truck, threw it in reverse, and made his way as fast as he dared to the road that would lead him away from the water and toward, he hoped, someone who would believe him.

He was not about to wait and see what else might be birthed by the pond.

Chapter Forty-Five

Ember

"What do you mean? There are other ways out?" Ember asked. A tiny spark of hope ignited in her. She grasped the stone in her pocket. The calm and powerful feeling still ran through her, but it was more subdued since they arrived at the Academy. As if the building itself were a damper.

"Selah and I lived here, in this room, while we were in school. We became friends here. We caused our share of mischief as well. On long nights we grew restless, as children do, and we looked for ways to amuse ourselves. We took this room apart, knew every stone and board." Gabby rose from her bed, snatched the flashlight from next to Miles, and went to the cupboard in the back corner.

Could it be so easy? Ember wondered.

When Gabby opened the cupboard door, disappointment washed over Ember. It was, after all, just an empty cupboard.

Gabby stepped into it and closed the door behind her. There was silence. When a confused Ember glanced at Selah, her friend wore a wry smile.

A shifting, dry sound of wood scraping wood came from inside the cupboard. A silent minute passed, then two.

Miles tried once to speak, but Selah shushed him. She was listening for something.

And then the shifting came again.

The cupboard door opened, and Gabby stepped out. Her smile was triumphant. "It's all still there. Even the marks we made. I do not think anyone has been there since."

"*What* is still there?" Ember asked.

"Come," Selah said. "It is easier to show you."

Gabby returned to the open cupboard, leaned into it. The others gathered around behind her, watching. She took her thin blade and ran it along a seam Ember could not see. With a deft twist, the back of the cupboard seemed to split along a straight line. Gabby pushed, and a door swung away from them. It was perhaps four feet tall and three feet wide, and when Gabby ducked through it, she disappeared into the dark. "Bring a torch," Gabby called in a hushed voice.

Selah took a torch from the wall and crawled in after Gabby. Miles followed, then Simon and Ember.

Ember experienced something akin to dizziness as she moved through the cupboard. The room she entered was massive. *This should not*, Ember thought, *be possible.* The cupboard stood against a wall with a window—an exterior wall. There was no place for the room to be. But this was far from the first unlikely thing to happen to her since coming to the island, and she had herself experienced the strange physics of the buildings here. There was, as Selah had told her, far more to this building inside than out.

The room was an enormous circle, the same stone and mortar as the rest of the Academy and was lined with dozens of wooden doors. Each door was as small as the cupboard door, but on this side there were iron rings that served as handles.

As Selah moved around lighting a few of the room's many wall torches, markings could be seen on most of the doors. They were, in fact, words. Each door was labeled, presumably with the name of the room behind it. In addition to a word or two, some rooms had a giant black *X* from one corner to the other.

Simon turned to Gabby, his young face furrowed with hurt. "You never told me about this!"

"I would have. In time. Perhaps."

"We found this place when we were just a bit older than Simon," Selah told them. "Not all these doors are useful. Some open up into rooms where chances are we would be caught. There is a door to the meeting room we were all in earlier, and that would be a bad place to go crawling into as it is generally occupied. There is a door to the kitchen, and that is often busy as well. But there are doors for classrooms, sleeping quarters, studies."

"Does one of these go outside?" Miles asked.

"No," answered Gabby, "all the doors open in. But not every room will be locked. There are ways out of the Academy if we need them."

"What are we looking for?" Ember stood at the door nearest their own.

Gabby shrugged. "Answers."

Ember moved to the next door, put her hand on it then snatched it away. She looked at her fingertips in the shifting light. They were pink. The door had burned her. "Why is this door so hot? Is there a furnace here?"

Selah frowned. "No. This is another sleeping quarter." She placed her hand on the wood, left it there. "It is not warm, Ember."

Ember reached down, touched the door, this time pressing her full hand against it. Her palm burned, but there was no pain. Even as the heat pulsed in her fingers, and, strangely, through the scars on her back, the now familiar cool and calm surged from deep in her body. It came in great waves, washing through her. It pushed back against the heat, was a response to it. *I should be scared—of all this—but I have never been less afraid.* She put her still-warm fingers on Selah's arm. "It *is* hot. We shouldn't go in that room. You can't feel it, but I can."

Selah stared at Ember for a long moment, seemed to find something in her eyes that surprised her, then nodded. "We stay out of this room," she told the others, "at least for now."

They split up then. Ember and Selah a pair, the others a trio. The pair carried the flashlight while the others carried a torch.

Ember and Selah first tried a room marked *classroom*. Then two marked *storage*. Each door opened easily and almost without sound. And each room proved a disappointment.

Selah went to the door nearest their own—the door between theirs and Ember's hot door—and pulled on the iron ring. Ember played the flashlight through the opening and found the inside of another cupboard. When that door opened, they were in a room identical to their own. It was empty and dark. Selah turned to leave when Ember's flashlight caught something on the bed nearest the door to the hallway.

"Wait," Ember whispered. She moved with caution toward the lump on the bed. As she approached it, Ember found it was a long bag. The fabric was slick and smooth, unlike any she had felt before. It was open at the top, and when Ember shone the flashlight inside, she saw a folded sheet of paper resting on top of a small collection of items.

Curious, Ember handed the flashlight to Selah who directed it over Ember's shoulder. She took the paper, unfolded it, and found it was not one sheet but two.

It was a letter.

My Sammy—

I hate that I am writing you a letter, but I can't talk to you anymore. You won't even let me close enough to touch you. The voices you are putting in my head are awful, and I am so, so sorry you have heard them for so long. And for everything else. I am SO SORRY. And sad. And tired. This is not what I wanted for you, or for us. I LOVE YOU. No matter what you believe. No matter what you are.

Sammy, I am crying while I write this, I don't want to tell you, I never did. I want to fix it so you never have to know. More than anything, I want to protect you and keep you safe. But I don't have time. I can feel you in my head more and more. Sometimes it is hard to breathe, and I think that is you, too. I know you don't mean it, but you can't control it when you sleep. Some morning soon, I think you are going to wake up and I'm not. I am so scared to go to sleep, but I am so tired. I could leave, but where would I go? And I don't want to be anywhere without you, no matter how frightened I am.

It was always you, Sammy. You had all the power always. You just didn't have any control. I know you didn't mean to. I hate that you have to know.

I believe you could take all you can do and do something wonderful with it. I also think you could do very, very bad things. What terrifies me, maybe what scares me the most, is I don't know if you are a good person or not. I don't know what kind of man you will be.

I don't know what you are, but I do know you are my son, and I love you. I have always loved you. I always will.

There are some things you HAVE TO DO.

Be good, and kind. You don't have to hurt anyone.

Don't be afraid of what you are. But find out, it is important you know. I'm sorry I couldn't help you.

When I die, they will take you away. You'll go somewhere else. Run if you have to, but don't hurt the people trying to take care of you. Even if you are scared. Even if you hate them.

Sammy, I don't know what else to say. I am so tired. It has been days since I slept. I'm going to close my eyes soon.

I never blamed you. I hope you can forgive me.

I love you,
Mommy

Ember folded the letter with shaking hands, returned it to the top of the bag. She felt dirty for having read it. The words it contained had not been meant for her. And she was heartsick for the mother and the son. "Sammy . . ." she said, almost inaudible.

"Sam," Selah answered. "The Jury's boy. He is here, then. Somewhere in the Academy."

Ember turned to face her friend. "I know why the door is so hot."

Out of the silence beyond the hallway door came footsteps.

Selah grabbed Ember by the hand and pulled her across the room and into the cupboard, shutting off the flashlight as they climbed in. She closed the door behind them. Instead of slipping through the door to the great chamber, the girls sat in the dark of the cupboard, barely breathing. Listening.

A bolt was thrown, and Ember could hear the door to the hall open into the room.

Footsteps, muttering.

There was a rustling sound as the footsteps retreated and the door was again closed.

When long seconds passed in silence, Selah slowly opened the cupboard door. She risked the flashlight.

The room was empty.

The bag was gone.

Chapter Forty-Six

Miles

Miles watched as the two girls slipped through a small door and into the room beyond. "Which one?" he asked, considering the chamber full of doors from which to choose.

Gabby's steps echoed as she made her way to a door with the word *Study* scrawled across the center. It was between two doors, each marked with a large *X*. "This one," she answered.

"Whose study is it?" Miles was apprehensive; they would be placing themselves between two rooms that were unsafe.

"Magdalene's."

"This is a terrible idea," Simon muttered from behind Miles as they caught up with Gabby.

She ignored him and pulled the door open until a seam of silver light filled the space between it and the frame. After a half minute, she seemed satisfied the room was empty and threw the door wide.

They stepped not into a cupboard, but right into the room.

From the study, the door was masked by stone and mortar. No, not masked, it *was* stone and mortar. Miles shook his head, left the mystery for another time.

An enormous wooden desk took up half of one wall and was covered in books and stacks of paper. The walls themselves were hung with charts and maps, many overlapped, and some Miles recognized. Others were entirely foreign.

There was no discernible order to them. A map of the New York City subway system was adjacent to what appeared to be a centuries-old ink drawing of a large body of water with the words *Here There Be Monstyrs* written in elegant and faded script across the top.

The study glowed with a silver light, the source of which was an open cistern in the center of the floor. It was maybe seven feet across and three feet high. The water it held came almost to the top of its stone sides.

"Why?" Miles asked as he peered into the water. The surface was still, although the glow that came from the water made it impossible to see very far into. There were four stone benches built into the inner sides of the cistern, maybe two feet below the surface. Seats for bathing or relaxing, Miles wasn't sure. As bizarre as the place was, Magdalene might have slept there like some kind of a weird vampire for all Miles knew.

Gabby looked as perplexed as Miles had ever seen her. "I do not know. I would expect this, a direct connection to the Fountain, in the Jury's study. Not a Philosopher's. Not Magdalene's."

"You're sure it's hers?" Miles asked.

Gabby answered his doubt with that withering look.

"Maybe she really is the next Jury?" Miles suggested.

"Then our problems have just begun," Gabby retorted.

"What is the Jury's boy's name?" Simon asked from the desk.

"Sam. Why?" Gabby crossed the room to join her brother.

"Because Magdalene has been tracking him."

Miles made his way to his friends, looked over their shoulders. Simon turned the pages of a ledger. In precise handwriting was a log of sorts. It contained dates, times, and notes, some brief and some more extensive.

September, 1978
Evening

Sam is quite remarkable. The mother is aware, but she does not know what is to be done about it. She appears ordinary, entirely unremarkable. His gifts are likely not inherited.
An anomaly of some sort, perhaps.
A mutation.

April, 1984
Morning
Sam was able to push me back today. It was painful, and I hope not to repeat the experience. Though I think I likely will. If I am to keep him in line, to groom him, I may need to be more persuasive.

I find it most effective when I relax in the cistern while communicating with him. It is the Fountain's influence, I am sure.

March, 1989
Evening

I believe Sam will be ready soon.
He continues to push the mother away.
He has begun punishing her.
She is frightened of him. As she should be.
There are nights he stands over her bed while she sleeps.
He is conflicted.

There were hundreds of entries. There was no time to read them all, but even a quick scan was damning. Together the entries told the story, with clinical detachment, of an entire life. Magdalene saw

Sam as a science project, not a child. She seemed content to watch the boy's childhood collapse and decay while she sat by taking copious notes.

Miles shuddered. "Why do you call him the Jury's boy? Seems to me like he's Magdalene's."

Gabby shook her head. "I do not know what this means. Beatrix would never allow it if she knew."

Miles left the desk and returned to look at the chaos of maps on the wall. His eyes ran over them, barely taking them in. He'd just about given up on them when one caught his eye. It was a map of the United States, the sort with the states sketched in rather than the geography. Across the map were tens of tiny circles, and next to each a date written in the same hand as the ledger. All the dates were current, from the last two months of Miles's *when*. As Miles studied the map, it occurred to him what the places and dates were.

What they had to be.

His heart pounded in his temples but seemed to stop cold when he saw the map to the right. It was a map of a town. His town. And there were circles there, all but two dated weeks after the day he had left for the island.

Which was, by his count, maybe two days prior.

At least, two days here on the island.

Time is different here . . .

The seven circles on his hometown map were random, except a small cluster that centered on the south side of town. His side of town. Next to the date marking each circle was a single scrawled word: *No.*

Many things raced through Miles's mind at once.

Magdalene was tracking the attacks.

Or causing them?

The attacks were still happening in his town.

The attacks were now happening in his neighborhood.

The zombies from the lake—the strangers—had not found his mother. Yet.

If he believed the dates on this map, he had been away from home for weeks.

His dad.

His mom.

His mom.

Maybe his parents had left town, fled the violence that was circling them. But Miles disregarded the thought. It was absurd to think his parents would leave now. He was missing, had been for weeks, and they wouldn't abandon the house until he came home. They would be there, heartbroken and afraid, waiting for him. And where was he? He was chasing after the ghost of the woman who had left him. Like understanding her would finish something in him that had no business being incomplete. His parents had done and been everything he needed, and yet he was still here and they were in danger.

Miles was consumed by a guilt that started in his stomach and snaked its way through his chest. He felt hot tears run down his face and did nothing to hide them as he called with a broken voice for Gabby and Simon. "Guys, we have to fix this. Figure it out. My family is out of time."

Chapter Forty-Seven

Ember

Ember and Selah stepped through the door in the rear of the cupboard and back into the chamber. Selah shut it behind them. The two girls looked at one another, and then they both looked toward the door that burned Ember.

Ember went to it.

"No!" Selah ordered.

"I'm checking. Making sure he's still there." This time, Ember placed both hands on the wooden surface. It radiated heat. Sam was, then, still in the room. Again, her body responded by filling, cooling. If anything, it was stronger than before. Ember closed her eyes and allowed herself to be swept up in it. When Selah spoke her name, Ember had to find her focus before she could turn to respond.

Selah studied Ember. "What color are your eyes?"

Ember furrowed her brows, confused. "Green," she answered with a bemused smile. She was sure there was enough light here for her friend to see the color of her eyes.

"And silver?" Selah prompted.

"No. Not silver. Not like yours, not like everyone's here. Just green."

"Then it appears there has been a change. You have silver streaks in your eyes. They cut through the green like lightning. They are," Selah conceded, "beautiful. Whatever is happening to you here is real."

Ember could not recall ever having been called beautiful. A foreign feeling, incandescent and glittering, rose within her, but she blushed all the same. Uncomfortable with both the attention and the compliment and confused by the change she herself felt, Ember looked back to the door of Sam's room. "What now? Do we go to him?"

"We go to Alma. She will already know, but she needs to know about your . . . reaction . . . to him as well. As strong as it is with a door between you . . . and if he killed his mother . . ." Selah appeared to gather herself. "We should go find the others."

The finding was simple enough. Only one other door stood open.

Entering the room, Ember took in her friends gathered around something on one well-papered wall. Gabby leaned close to Miles, rubbing his shoulder with a gentle hand. And then there was the cistern, glowing in the center of the room and completely out of place.

Ember approached the water. Shades of liquid silver and white and palest blue spun lazy circles. The effect was hypnotic. Ember reached out a single finger to touch the water. The water, as it had at the Fountain, reached out and touched her in return. Music coursed through her veins. A symphony rose in her soul. Water poured from the cistern and onto the floor of the study. Lightheaded, Ember had just begun to pull away when a sharp-nailed hand grasped her own.

Another hand reached up over the wall of the cistern and then someone familiar was pulling herself up and out of the water. She smiled her sharp-toothed smile at Ember.

The room had grown silent.

"Ember," Selah said with forced calm, "is this your mermaid?"

"Yes," Ember replied. "Isn't she lovely?"

Chapter Forty-Eight

Miles

Miles was still wiping his eyes when he heard water sloshing onto the floor of the room.

He turned to see something ghoulish latched onto Ember's hand. It had long, pale hair and even lighter skin. He could only see it from the back, but it was enough for him to know a monster had hold of the girl.

"Ember!" He pulled himself together and shoved down the emotion he'd allow to climb to the surface.

At the sound of his voice, the thing released Ember and whipped around. Its features were like an unfinished statue—the impression of a face, but none of the requisite detail that would make it human. It—*she, the monster is a* she—moved across the cistern toward Miles. He could see the eyes, at least, were human. And that made it all the worse.

Blade drawn, Gabby circled the monster from behind trying to reach it without being seen. *Here There Be Monstyrs.* The thought stuck in his head like glue as Gabby circled. But the circumference of the cistern was too broad, making it impossible for her to reach it undetected.

Gabby, being Gabby, tried anyway. The girl rose into the air, her copper hair trailing behind her like the flame of an avenging angel. As she dove toward the thing, it spun and swiped, knocking her to the floor.

After that, everything happened in a matter of seconds.

Simon ran to Gabby's side.

Selah rushed to pull Ember away from the cistern.

And the mutant moved toward Miles.

It was, they all saw, no mermaid.

The creature pulled a long leg out of the water, stepped over the stone boundary, and onto the floor. Her feet were huge and webbed, with toes that tapered into wicked claws. The creature's torso was elongated and narrow, with the same unfinished quality as its face. Her joints and clavicle and hip bones protruded from smooth skin, skeletal and sharp.

At its full height, the monster was over seven feet tall. As she approached, she trembled on rickety knees and unsure feet, as though she were not accustomed to leaving the water and walking on solid ground.

With his back against the map-covered wall, Miles was unable to use the creature's instability to his advantage. And then, in a lifetime, in a half second, the thing towered over him. She leaned low, almost a bow, and took his hand in one of her own. She inspected his hand, ran a careful claw over his palm.

Miles's own skin grew cold at her touch. She was ice.

When she looked up, her eyes level with his and his heart racing with certainty, Miles managed a single word. "Ava?"

Even as he asked, he knew it was true. It was her turquoise eyes. They were the same as her sister's, the sister who had raised Miles and become his mother. They were the same as his. And tears ran from those familiar—familial—eyes as she lifted a pale hand to stroke his face.

Ava smiled at Miles. It was a hideous red smile, far too wide with far too many white teeth.

But Miles was not afraid.

He was many, many things, but he was not afraid.

Miles smiled back.

Something broken in his heart clicked back together like a long-lost puzzle piece.

He reached up and held her porcelain face in his hand. She leaned into his touch and closed her streaming eyes.

Miles cried then, for the second time in less than an hour. He cried so hard he became lightheaded with it.

With a finger under his chin, Ava lifted Miles's head, tilting his face up toward her. She leaned down and kissed his forehead as best she could. She cupped his face in both her hands and wiped away tears with a taloned thumb. *Don't be sad, baby.*

"Mo— Ava?" Miles's voice quaked as he began. "Can you talk?"

Ava shook her head, opened her mouth wide to show him why. In all that bloodred, she had no tongue. Whether it had been taken from her or was never there after she . . . changed . . . Miles could not be sure.

He had to close his eyes, steady himself. When he opened them again, her mouth was closed. Miles blew out a short breath, relieved. "Did you send the strangers from the lake to get me?"

Ava's eyes were confused. She shook her head again. *No.*

"People—monsters—are coming from the lake, to my world. To my *when.* They're hurting people. Killing them. I think they want me. And now I think they want my mo— Hannah."

This time Ava nodded before shaking her head again. *Yes, I know. No, it is not me.*

"Do you know who's making it happen?"

Ava looked around the room, indicating the chamber with one long, outstretched hand. *She is. Not me, her.*

Somewhere in the hallway a door slammed. Someone was coming.

Ava gave Miles a terrified look. *Go now!* She squeezed his hand and was back at the cistern, slipping without a splash into the water. Gone, with no trace she had ever been there save the water pooled on the stone floor.

The five friends ran to the open door in the wall, fell through, and closed it behind them in seconds.

Miles collapsed hard on the stone floor, everything in him now exhausted, hands on the back of his head, forehead pressed against bent knees. He was no longer crying, but his breathing was rapid and shallow. The room was silent, and he could feel four sets of eyes on him, but Miles was not ready to meet any of their gazes.

He could sit there like that forever. Still and silent. If he didn't move, didn't look at anyone, nothing else could happen.

Someone sat next to him, close enough their sides touched. A hand touched his then pulled away.

"Miles . . . I . . ." Ember's voice was tender, distraught. "I . . . I don't know what to do for you."

Miles took a deep, ragged breath. He looked up into the younger girl's eyes and noticed for the first time how weird they were. Beautiful, but weird. "Nothing. I mean. What do I even say? I just met my dead mom. Except she's—not a ghost—she's a monster. But she's in there, too. I could see her in there. And. And why can't she just be *dead*?" His voice cracked on the last word. "Is this Hell? Is she in Hell? Why is she that *thing*? What'd she do to deserve that? Because she left me? But I'm okay! If this is for me, someone has to take it the hell back. I'm okay. But she . . . she shouldn't . . ." And this time he cried with his entire body. Cried until he gagged. He hyperventilated and gagged and swore. And though she'd known Miles less than a day, Ember held him through it all.

Gabby knelt down beside them, wrapped a hand around Miles's calf. "Miles, this is what happens when one dies in the Fountain. A part of you stays behind, the essence. Perhaps, as you said, the soul. And it becomes . . . something else."

"But why that? She was . . . awful."

"No." She rubbed a hand on his shoulder. "You said she is in there. You saw her. I *know* you did. The body, well, that makes sense."

"What are you talking about? You *saw* her!"

Miles sobbed, confused.

"The things in the Fountain are cruel and hungry and will kill for sport. Of course her body has to be fierce. How else could she mean to survive? If she were soft and small, she would be unable to defend herself. She would be killed. Eaten."

"Enough, Gabby," Simon snapped. His tone made them all turn his way. Even Miles looked up. "It is *enough*. Not everything has to be a lesson. Leave him alone. Let him mourn." Simon reached down and took Miles's hands, pulled him to his feet. When Miles was steady enough, Simon wrapped his small arms around the bigger boy's waist, wrapped his wings up around the taller boy's shoulders. "I am sorry," he said.

Then Simon took one of Miles's hands in his own and led him to the door that would return them to their dormitory. Without looking back, he said, "The rest of you can keep looking for whatever it is you think you will find. Miles needs rest."

Just before ducking to go through the cupboard door, Miles turned to Simon, his eyes red and dry and haunted. "What if both my moms are dead?"

Chapter Forty-Nine

Ember

Ember watched Miles walk away.

Her mermaid was not a mermaid at all. She was *Ava*? Why had Ava sought her out, more than a year ago, a girl on a failing farm in the middle of nowhere? Why seek her out rather than Miles?

"Why me?" she said, turning to the girls. "Why did she come to me and not her son?" Coming to the island made Ember realize how little she knew about everything, but the one thing she *did* know was that mothers were supposed to love their sons. Hadn't her own mother given her whole heart to Hank? *With none left for me,* she thought. All of it dead and buried with her brother. Anger and sadness fought for space in Ember's chest.

Why on earth and why in all the *whens* would Ava choose her over Miles?

"Why?" she repeated.

She was met with heavy silence.

Gabby sighed, her head bending low, like the question hurt her. She would not answer.

As the quiet grew uncomfortable, Selah spoke. "I think . . ." She sounded uncertain. "I think she would not have wanted Miles here, on the island. Not after everything that occurred for her here. She would have wanted to keep him from ever stepping foot on the shore, from even knowing it exists."

"But then Simon found him." Gabby's words sounded confessional. "He found him, and we both became his friends. So when the chaos began in his *when*, when it began to center around him, we knew he was somehow a part of it all. When he was attacked, we knew we could no longer protect him and made the decision on our own to bring him here, to see if he could help us find the Jury." Gabby sighed, looked toward the floor. "I grew certain Ava had something to do with the Jury's disappearance. I see now I was wrong."

"So was Ava," Ember said. "She was wrong to seek me out. I don't have anything to offer here. I'm a problem. I'm nothing."

"No, you are a solution." Selah was forceful. "I see it. Ava saw it as well. We were both drawn to you. Perhaps I do not yet know why, but I know it to be true."

When the girls returned to their dormitory, they entered with more knowledge but even more questions. Ava did not have Beatrix. Magdalene reeked of guilt. She had a decade of notes on Sam and a map of the attacks happening in Miles's *when*.

Once in the room, Ember was startled to find not two, but three people talking in hushed voices. Miles and Simon were there, as was Alma.

Ember sat on the bed next to Alma, Selah sat on Alma's other side. When the woman turned to Ember, she looked at her for a long moment. Ember could see Alma was contemplating something, deciding something.

There was a riot of noise in the hall—the sounds of a fight, of something being thrown. Or falling. Short, violent chaos. A male voice screamed something unintelligible. Another, deeper, voice yelled, "Sit back down!"

Then, silence.

Alma stared at the door but spoke to the group gathered in the room. "Stay here. Do not open this door. Not for me, not for anyone. Block the door however you can. If someone tries to get in, go out that cupboard door and do not come back. Find a safe place and stay there. Better to be lost in the tunnels than to hand yourselves over to what is outside this door."

"Alma . . ." Selah grabbed onto her hand. "Do not go out there."

Alma kissed her on the forehead. "I must. I will find you when this is over."

Alma then leaned over and said something into Ember's ear that only Ember could hear. Ember paled but nodded. When Alma pulled away from her, she said, "I am so very sorry. We never knew. Not until Selah found you."

The words Ember spoke next would cause all the heads to turn. "How could you? But Ava knew. And the Hatchery knew. It has called to me, all my life. I just didn't know how to answer it. I didn't know I was supposed to."

Alma stepped through the door and into the hallway, locking it behind her as she went.

ONCE upon a time, yesterday . . .

NOEMI pulled a glass out of the cabinet. She let the water run from the faucet until it was as cold as it could get. She filled the glass, turned off the water, and glanced up at the clock as she brought it to her lips.

Three things happened almost at once:

Something sharp scratched the inside of Noemi's cheek.

She spat out the water. It was warm and filthy—like the stagnant water Miles had tossed at her last summer at Kayla's lake house, after they won State.

And, when she saw what was in the glass, she dropped it to the floor.

What Noemi saw was murky, disgusting water. Bits of dark debris floated in it.

And then there were the fingers. Three of them, far too long and tipped with sharp black claws. The fingers reached for her even as the glass fell.

Noemi tasted blood where the fingers had gouged the inside of her mouth.

When the glass hit the tile floor it exploded and left a pool of water on the hard surface.

As the water spread, the tile below seemed to morph and melt and sink until it disappeared, and Noemi found herself looking into a small, dark pool.

She took one step back, but then her muscles froze.

The fingers belonged to an arm, and the arm belonged to something that wasn't quite a person. Noemi saw enough of its pallid face to know that it was all long snout and needle-sharp teeth.

With one wicked hand, the monster pulled itself up and with the other it grabbed Noemi's ankle.

The creature was strong, and when it yanked, Noemi went down to the floor. It pulled her toward the pool, which was not wide, but just wide enough *to allow her narrow teenage frame.*

Noemi grasped for something to hold on to, and when that failed, she grasped for something to defend herself with. A large shard of broken glass was the best she could manage. Her heart in her throat, adrenaline racing through her blood, fear coursing silent and frigid and overwhelming inside her.

She flailed at the thing's arm, but it didn't react as she plunged the glass into its too-soft flesh. The glass came away smeared black but still the monster pulled.

She screamed.

Half in the pool, half out, the bottom portion of her body the same temperature as the water around it. Noemi tried to grip the tile at the edge of the water. Desperation took her voice. Still screaming but warbled and wrong. She succeeded only in cutting her own hands.

With one more tug, no time even for a deep breath, she was submerged.

It was terrible but it was over with a merciful quickness.

Noemi didn't even have time to drown.

Chapter Fifty

Sam

Sam reclined in his cell. The bed, he decided, really was comfortable. It was a shame he wouldn't spend another night sleeping on it.

The door, now opened wide, was blocked by the prone figure of a large winged man.

Sam wanted to touch the man's taupe wings, to see what they felt like between his fingers. He wondered if they would turn to powder when crushed, like the wings of the idiot moths that circled the porch light back home. They would dance around the bare bulb until they ran into it, by accident or on purpose Sam didn't know. Even when they watched their friends die, they kept dancing and diving and cremating themselves. Maybe they thought the bulb was a god, and they were a happy sacrifice. Or maybe they were just idiot moths.

He wished he could go back in time and burn them himself.

He smiled.

Clink.

But Sam did not touch the dead man's wings. He didn't want to get carried away and burn him. He needed others to see what he could do. What he *would* do.

A door closed down the hall, not far from his own room. Soft feet hurried on the stone floor. When it was Alma who appeared in the doorway, Sam was glad.

Alma stood, frozen. She placed a hand over her mouth, looked from Sam to the man and back again. Never taking her eyes off Sam, Alma crouched and touched the man's throat. She would not find what she was hoping for.

Standing again, Alma whispered, "What did you do?"

Sam smiled at her. "I guess I made a point."

"You did not have to . . . I could have helped . . ."

"You read my letter."

"I would not have allowed them to keep you here."

"*You* locked me in."

Alma began to speak, stopped herself, nodded. "I did."

"I want to leave."

"Sam . . ."

"Help me leave, or I'll kill the next person I see . . ."

"Sam . . ."

". . . and the next and the next and the next until you help me leave."

"Where will you go?"

"I'm going to find the Sounds—Beatrix—and she's going to tell me why I'm here."

"Can you find her?" There was a hope in her voice that made him want to laugh.

"If not, I'll kill you all, and it won't matter. Get in here so I can move him. I don't want anyone to see him too soon."

Alma stepped over the man, entered the room. Sam directed her to sit on the bed. Standing in front of him, he breathed deep. *Do not burn him. Do not burn him. Do not burn him, even if you want to.* He took the man by one arm and pulled. Something popped, high and deep in the man's shoulder, so Sam moved to his leg and pulled that instead. It was heavy work, but Sam managed to move the body far enough into the room that he could close the door.

He only singed him a little.

Alma's eyes were closed, her lips moved without sound. If Sam didn't know better, he would have thought she was praying. *Maybe she is. But she's not praying for me.*

When Alma opened her eyes, she scanned the room. Sam saw the moment she recognized what was on the couch. He was amused it had taken her so long.

"You have your bag."

"Yeah, he brought it." Sam gave the body a nudge with his foot.

"Then why?"

"My flashlight is missing."

Alma blanched but said nothing.

"Okay. Let's go. I want out. Maybe to that tunnel I came through? It seemed pretty empty."

"If someone sees us . . ."

"Either you lie and they believe you, or I kill them."

Alma nodded.

"Can the tunnel get me to the Fountain?"

Alma paused, then, "Yes." The word fell heavy from her throat.

"Let's go, then."

They skirted the man, his wings limp and meaningless, and walked out of the room. Alma closed the door as they left.

"Lock it," instructed Sam. "Wouldn't want anyone to think I escaped."

Sam and Alma traveled down the corridor, past the room in which Ember and Miles and the others waited.

At an intersection they crossed paths with an armed Groundskeeper. He didn't acknowledge Sam but addressed the woman with a nod. "All right, Alma?"

"Fine," Alma replied. "The Philosophers have requested another audience with the boy, and I am bringing him to them."

"I could accompany you . . ."

"No," Alma replied, her voice cutting, "I am more than capable."

The man's eyes widened as he recoiled a bit at her tone, but he remained courteous, "Of course, Alma. No disrespect intended." He continued on his way, Alma and Sam theirs.

Alma stopped at a plain door lacking ornamentation. Sam noted it also had no lock. She twisted the handle and there was a metallic *clank* deep in the frame. The door swung into a glorified closet.

"Do you think this is funny?" Sam asked in a low voice.

"No, not at all funny," Alma responded.

Sam took in the room around him. Racks of tools—*no, weapons*—lined one wall. Otherwise, the room was bare save a second door on the back wall. It was toward the second door Alma led him.

"Is this the door I came in?"

"The same."

Sam considered taking a weapon off the wall, thought of the damage and the pain he could inflict with such a sharp blade. He smiled at the images surfacing in his mind. He disregarded the idea and thought, not without pleasure. *I* am *a weapon.* "Let's go, then."

He pulled the door open and held it for Alma. It was not a chivalrous act. He wanted to make sure she did not shut him in and bar the door or shove him down the thirty-seven steps he knew were waiting on the other side.

Once down the stairs, he followed Alma as she made her way through the tunnel. Sam had been right to take a guide; he would have been lost on his own. When he was little, his mother bought him the game Chutes and Ladders. This was much the same, a twisting maze of ups and downs with a destination—a prize. There were occasional staircases leading up and, Sam presumed, out to somewhere on the island. Mostly there was just more tunnel, every corridor unremarkable save for its similarity to the last.

Without warning, Alma stopped at a staircase and turned to Sam. "Here."

"Are you sure?"

"I am certain."

Sam began to make his way up the stairs. He hesitated, looked down on Alma. "You shouldn't have read my letter."

"Sammy, I only wanted . . ."

Sentimental, manipulative words.

"I don't need you anymore. Don't you call me Sammy. Don't try to mother me. Besides, I kill all my mothers."

Alma's eyes grew wide, and Sam had the satisfaction of knowing she knew in that last moment what he was about to do.

Alma fell to the floor of the tunnel, collapsed in an ungraceful heap. She was dead before the tips of her wings fell soundlessly to the stone. Her face was a mask, eyes wide and blank and glassy.

"And you shouldn't have locked me in."

Sam hurried up the stairs. The Fountain was waiting. And if Beatrix was not there, perhaps some other sort of answer would be.

He threw the door wide but froze before walking through it.

Sam stepped over the threshold and onto sand. The door opened through a boulder, the very boulder on which he had rested his first night on the island.

Water lapped the shore.

The *shore.*

The door closed behind him. There was no handle, not even a seam.

Sam was back where he started.

He screamed and screamed and screamed.

Clink.

Chapter Fifty-One

Miles

The night dragged on.

In the locked dormitory room, Miles and the others waited for Alma to return. Despite what she had said, they did not bar the door. The sky outside the room was just beginning to lighten when it opened. For a short moment, Miles was relieved. Alma had come back, and maybe whatever was happening outside the room had come to an end. When he saw the hulking silhouette in the doorway, he knew it was not so.

It was not Alma, but Zebedee. And he was grim. "Selah, you are to come with me."

"No, I do not think I will." Selah stood to her full height, which brought her to Zebedee's shoulder. Sitting on the bed, Ember took hold of her friend's hand. Her message was clear: *Don't go.* Miles felt like he was watching the same scene play out over and over again. First Alma, now Selah.

"I am taking you to Magdalene. I would prefer if you did not make this difficult. Either way, you will accompany me."

"What does she want with me?"

Zebedee did not respond. Instead, he stood aside, holding the door open for her.

Miles watched as Selah removed Ember's hand from her arm, fingers squeezing tight before they released each other. Tears ran down the girl's cheeks, and Miles went to sit next to her. "It'll be okay," he told her as he put his arm around her shoulders and pulled her against him. "Selah's tough. She'll be okay." His words felt hollow. He had no way to know if Selah would be okay or not, but Ember needed comforting. She had done the same for him not an hour before.

Thoughts of his mother—his mothers—began to creep along the edges of his mind. Miles pushed them away as best he could, he didn't have room for them and everything else.

Selah went to the door, then turned to look at the four remaining in the room. She opened her mouth to speak, seemed to think better of it, then walked without a word into the hallway, shaking Zebedee off as he reached for her.

When the door closed behind them, Ember let out a short sob. "What are they going to do to her?"

"I do not know, but we are not going to wait here doing nothing and be removed one by one." Gabby was standing now, making her way to the cupboard.

Chapter Fifty-Two

Selah

Selah was not surprised when Zebedee retrieved a heavy set of chains and bound her hands and wings, wrapping them tight enough she could not move without hurting some tender part. She was, however, surprised when Zebedee walked her past the room with the great table, down long halls, and, finally, out the front door of the Academy.

They had no audience, no one to bear witness to their exit. It was that tired time between night and morning, and all those who could be asleep were.

The walk to the Fountain was short. The Academy had been built nearby by generations prior, as the Philosophers could never know when they would be called upon. When Selah and Zebedee reached the clearing, the falls still ran. *Beatrix is still alive then, somewhere.* While the falls and the Fountain were as they should be, the clearing had become a makeshift slaughterhouse.

Her wings may have been bound, but her mouth was not, and it dropped open at the sight.

A monster, or what remained of it, was in a bloody pile near a stone bench. Selah could not see through the gore well enough to describe the beast, but it had been taller and broader than a tall, broad man, and was armed with wicked talons on both its hands and its feet.

Those feet, Selah saw, very much resembled Ava's. This beast was not Ava, though. It was—had been—much wider and heavier than she.

In the grass, between the dead beast and the Fountain, were the bodies of four Groundskeepers. Selah did not recognize them, but in fairness there was little left to recognize. They had been slaughtered—torn apart and, to Selah's horror, apparently chewed. The parts missing surely eaten. She turned away from the carnage to find Zebedee taking it all in with an inconvenienced half frown.

"I had hoped they would help me, but it appears they will be unable to assist." He pushed Selah down in the grass. "Stay here or I will kill you." He then went to the edge of the Fountain, dug around in the tall grass and low bushes that thrived in the soil there. Soon, Zebedee's face lit up as he found what he was looking for. It was a chain, longer and heavier than the one that bound Selah.

Zebedee rose into the air, struggling to pull something heavy out of the water. When he succeeded, sweating and breathing hard, Selah began to understand what was about to happen.

Balanced now on the rock ledge at the midpoint of the Fountain was a cage. It was inches taller than Selah and half again as long and wide. The chain was attached to its top.

Selah began to panic, her thoughts spiraled and beat against one another. She would be able to move in the cage, but not open her wings completely. *No matter. You will not be doing any flying at the bottom of the Fountain.*

Zebedee pulled her up by the chains binding her, marched her to the open door of the cage. "In. Now." He pushed Selah up and into the open metal box. He made a show of closing and latching it behind her.

The space seemed to shrink in on itself. That the floor was made of mesh rather than bars was one small relief. She would at least be able to sit.

"Beatrix, are you watching?" Zebedee spoke aloud, but there was no one there to respond to him. *Where does he think Beatrix is?* He approached the cage and peered in, his face close to Selah's. He could have been a nasty child inspecting a bug in a glass jar.

Zebedee continued speaking to the air, "Selah is going in soon. She will start dying right away, but it might take hours and hours. It is going to be *just* appalling."

What had happened to Zebedee to poison him so? He had never been kind, and had always been a narcissist, but this was a new level of cruelty for even him.

They had been raised together and despite herself, Selah had always seen Zebedee as an older brother of sorts. She had been wrong, and the loss surprised her with its sharpness.

He stroked the bars of the cage. Zebedee spoke as if to someone, but he was not talking to her. "We will know soon if Beatrix is still aware enough to save the girl. If she has gone mad, Selah will die. If she did not love her very much, Selah will die. Me? I think Selah will die down there with the creatures and the seekers greedy enough to require punishment. In time we will pull her up, and it will be very sad. Then we will get Ava's boy and try with him. And if that does not work, we will bide our time until the Jury dies in whatever hole she is hiding in and can be replaced."

Selah's laugh was almost authentic. "I thought perhaps you and Magdalene had her, the Jury. But you do not know where she is, do you? You have been outmatched by a crazy, dying old woman. You are pathetic."

Zebedee stared at Selah for a moment. His eyes burned with purest hate. "Let me tell you a story, a true one." His eyes shone like fire. "In a long ago *when*, the humans did something I have always found ingenious in its stupidity. When people in a village believed a fellow villager to be a witch, and the person in question was almost always a woman, they would strip her, bind her hands and feet, tie her to a heavy stone, and throw her in a lake. If she floated, she was determined a witch, and they would find some other way to kill her. Mind you, this never happened. If she sank and drowned, she was innocent. Either way, the people had their answer and were rid of their problem. Soon enough, we shall see if you are a witch or an innocent, insolent little girl."

"You are not pathetic," Selah whispered. "You are mad."

Saying nothing, Zebedee pushed the cage into the Fountain and, with it, Selah.

For the briefest of surreal moments, Selah thought the metal contraption was going to float. Then, of course, it sank, fast and straight down.

Chapter Fifty-Three

Zebedee

The chain *clank, clank, clanked* over the side of the Fountain as it was pulled over by the weight of the falling cage. There was still plenty left on the ground near the Fountain; it had been a long chain. Zebedee secured the end with heavy stones winding it between the rocks bordering the Fountain, then fed the remainder into the water. It was almost invisible.

There were bubbles, many at first, then fewer. The Fountain became still, the water reflecting the new morning sun. With the chain well hidden, there was nothing to tell anyone a girl was dying directly below them.

He stood in silence, arms crossed, wings restless, and considered what he had just done.

It was not right.

Zebedee walked to the chain almost hidden in the rocks and unwound it. It was heavy in his hands. He tugged at the metal links. He would not be able to pull Selah out on his own, but a strong team could. How long would it take for the chain to be found? Would they free her before Beatrix came to her rescue? Before she drowned? Zebedee thought they might.

He took the length of chain and fed what remained into the Fountain. It sank without a sound.

Zebedee sat on the stone bench nearest the Fountain and waited for Magdalene. He had left her a note, albeit a cryptic one, and expected she would arrive soon. She would be impressed by his initiative.

And he waited for Beatrix. He felt sure she, too, would respond to the message he'd left for her.

Beatrix would return, Magdalene would be the next Jury, and he would be the reason for it all.

Zebedee looked forward to being a hero.

Flies, warmed by the rising sun, began to gather around the corpses littering the clearing. They were drawn in black, buzzing clumps to the wet bits now on the outside that belonged on the inside. From time to time, one would land on Zebedee. He didn't notice.

Chapter Fifty-Four

Ember

"We should wait for Alma. And for Selah," Simon said. He remained seated on an ivory-covered bed while Ember, Miles, and Gabby stood by the cupboard arguing in hushed tones.

Staying in the Academy was out of the question. It was something her mother would say, but the words were right. Staying was foolish. With Selah taken at Magdalene's request, and Alma gone, the walls of the building were closing in around them. On that, at least, three of the four agreed.

"She would have returned by now," Gabby said from across the room, "if she were able."

Simon grew smaller by degrees, wrapping his wings about himself. Ember went to him, sat next to him on the bed. She leaned into him, nudging his wing-draped shoulder. He ignored her until she did it again, a second then a third time. *Hank used to do this. I hated it—loved it, too.*

When Simon looked up at her, the beginning of a smile tugged at the corner of his mouth. "We cannot leave them," he said, serious again.

"No, we can't," agreed Ember. "We've got to *find* them. They might need us."

Simon sighed, nodded, and joined the others at the cupboard.

In the chamber of doors, Ember went without hesitation to the door that had burned her earlier in the night. It was warm to her touch, but no longer scalded her hand. "He's gone," Ember told the others, "and Alma is with him. She has to be."

"Can you track him?" Gabby asked.

"How do you *know*?" Miles asked at the same time.

"Maybe, and I don't know. Selah said something was coming to the island, and I was the . . . the counterbalance, she called me. Alma said Sam burns hot. It just . . . it just makes sense."

Miles agreed. "It makes as much sense as anything else."

"Can you track him?" Gabby repeated.

"I can try."

Gabby was first through the door. She stood aside as the others entered the room. Ember held the flashlight, but the weak light through the single, narrow window was enough for them to see the Groundskeeper on the floor.

Gabby touched the man's throat, verified he was dead. "We must find Alma."

As Gabby stepped over the man toward the door, Simon pulled her wing. "We have to move him. We cannot leave him like this."

Gabby opened her mouth to argue but Ember spoke first. If she was going to help keep Simon safe—even keep him with them at all—Ember knew she would have to allow him such kindnesses. "Yes, of course we can do that for him."

"Quickly," conceded Gabby.

The four of them worked together to lift the man from the floor and rest him on the room's single bed.

Satisfied, Simon said, "We can go now."

Miles turned to Ember. "Can you feel him here? Is this going to work?"

Ember stood still and quiet. Eyes closed, she felt the room, opened herself up to it. "Yes, but he's fading. If there's a . . . a trail to follow, it won't last forever."

There was an agonizing moment when the door to the hallway proved to be locked, something they had not anticipated in their haste. Gabby moved like quicksilver through the cupboard and the chamber of rooms, through the adjacent dorm room, and unlocked the door from the outside. She motioned for the others to join her.

When Ember exited, she asked Gabby, "Was a bag in there? On the bed by the door?"

Gabby shook her head. "Nothing. It was empty."

"He's gone, then. And not planning on coming back."

Gabby leaned in and breathed into her ear, "You lead. I will be with you. Do not rush. Listen at corners."

Ember understood.

She touched the wall just left of the door; it was cool. The stone and mortar to the right radiated a subtle, infected heat. The feeling was revolting, but Ember did not pull away. Fingers grazing the wall, she followed it. They made their way like this, Ember leading, the four of them silent as shadows through the halls of the Academy.

No one crossed their path as Ember tracked Sam through the labyrinthine building. *We won't stay so lucky much longer.*

The light coming through the few windows they encountered had changed from violet and rose to a weak morning gold tinged with blue. The Academy would wake up soon, and Ember did not want to be found wandering the halls when she should have been behind a locked door. She was not afraid of being caught nearly as much as she was terrified at the prospect of being split up from the rest of her friends. Without Selah, Ember was untethered. Without any of them, she would be truly lost. Her fear intensified her focus, and, with that, her ability to feel and follow Sam.

Left to her own devices, she would have been unable to find her way back to their room. The Academy, large as it was, closed in around Ember as she led her friends deeper into its bowels. When she stopped at a door, Ember turned to Gabby. "Through here."

"I expected," Gabby replied, "but did not want to suggest it, did not want to interfere or misdirect you in case I was wrong."

Gabby opened the door and ushered the others through before closing it behind them. They were in a small room.

On one wall hung weapons like those Ember had seen carried—*wielded*—by the Groundskeepers at the shore.

"Take one," Gabby instructed them, gesturing at the shelves of weaponry. "Not so big you cannot manage it."

Miles selected a short staff with a serrated blade on one end. He spun it back and forth in his hand, then slipped it into a belt loop.

Ember chose a blade similar to the one Gabby carried, shorter than most on the wall but honed to the sharpest edge. Like Gabby, Ember slipped it into the pocket of her tunic opposite the one holding the flashlight and the stone. She said a brief, silent prayer asking that she would never need to use it.

Simon refused to take a blade from the wall.

Gabby leaned down, spoke in his ear. "You may need to protect someone, perhaps Miles or Ember."

Simon seemed to consider his sister's words, then took down a small hatchet and slipped it into the belt he wore slung across his hips.

Gabby made her way to a door at the back of the room. "It will be cold down there, but I hope we will not be in the tunnels long."

"Tunnels?" Miles asked.

"A system, to be accurate. It was built with the Academy, I am sure. Much of the island can be accessed from it. It is primarily used by the Philosophers, the Jury, and the Groundskeepers. It is not forbidden to others, but it is not practice, either."

Ember felt the door, placed both hands on its timeworn wood. It was as hot as the door to Sam's room had been. Like an answer to a question, her body responded. The calm power coursed through her bones and her nerves and the beds of her nails. With her eyes closed, she felt both lighter and more dense, taller and more lithe. The cool white filled her limbs and chest and bones, leaving the palms of her hands and the scars on her back to burn.

"He was here. And . . . something. I don't know. But . . . something . . ." Ember clenched her jaw, frustrated at the almost knowing.

"Then we go." Gabby pulled the door wide.

From deep in the tunnels and up thirty-seven steps, a wave of heat that only Ember could feel came pouring out. She grimaced, turned her face away. "We have to find Alma. Now."

By the time the four reached the bottom of the stone staircase, three of them were chilled, arms speckled with gooseflesh. Ember alone was running with sweat. The channels of water coursing down the center of the stone walkways provided light to the enclosed space, but they also provided an endless supply of moisture. The tunnels, humid and close, grew suffocating for Ember as she led her shivering friends toward something she wanted nothing more than to run from.

Ember fell into a lull, a trance, as she followed Sam through the tunnels. She led the way over bridges as the path branched and then branched again. Her thoughts became intertwined, diseased plants, sending off wicked little shoots and multiplying. *Mama is alone now. Alone in the house, on the farm. Did she get help? No, she had no one to ask. She moved Uncle Joe alone, somehow. Buried him alone, too. And Daddy. Is she nursing him? On the front-room couch because he's too heavy to get up the stairs to their bedroom? Maybe he won't eat. Won't drink. How much time has passed? Two days here, three? Weeks—months at home. Daddy is dead now. And Mama is alone. And Selah—where are you? Alma, I'm coming. And Ava, I'm glad you found me. But I'm sorry you didn't die. Is it better to be dead or a monster? Daddy was a monster and now he's dead. Which would you choose? Ava's a monster, and she loves Miles more than Mama ever loved me. Because maybe I'm already a monster. A broken monster—*

A pitiful keening filled the air, snatching Ember out of her fog. Somewhere ahead of them, someone was hurt, dying.

Chapter Fifty-Five

Miles

Miles had left his house in a black T-shirt and jeans and his best broken-in shoes. They had served him well on the warm island and had been fine in the cooler Academy. In the tunnels, however, he might as well have been wearing nothing at all. The cold, damp air pulled the heat from his exposed skin, and his body responded by shivering violently. Ahead of him, Ember was flushed and sweating. The hair that escaped her bun was stuck to her forehead and neck. She looked miserable, but he found he was jealous all the same. He toyed with the idea of walking next to her, putting his arm around her, and using her as a sort of human hot-water bottle. He didn't, but he thought about it.

When Miles wasn't thinking about how damned cold he was, he was thinking about his moms. He'd never thought of them that way before. There had always been Mom—the woman who raised him—and Ava. Up until a few hours ago, Ava had been an idea, the suggestion of a person. She'd been in his mom's stories and in old photographs. She'd been a memory that sometimes made tears come to her sister's eyes.

For Miles, she hadn't even been that.

She had been a ghost. *And she's still a ghost. And a monster.* Miles was ashamed even before the thought was finished. The way Ava looked at him, the way her head fell heavy in his hands when he held her face. That was no monster. That was a mother. *But she* is *a ghost, just not the kind anyone has dreamed up before.* So now Miles had two moms. One was dead. The other might be, too.

A small, black marble of dread had been lodged heavy in his chest for hours, since seeing the map in Magdalene's study. Now, the black marble swelled and metastasized and Miles knew if he didn't get it under control—

A sound cut through his churning thoughts. It wasn't loud enough to be a scream. It was a wail. *Alma.*

They had come to a crossing of tunnels. Miles could hear Alma off to the left. He turned to follow the sounds, to help her.

"No," Ember whispered. "That's the wrong way. I can still feel him, Sam, but we have to go right."

Gabby made a quick decision. "Ember, Simon, go. Follow Sam. We will catch up with you. Miles, we will go see . . ."

But Miles was already gone, and Miles was fast. He broke away from the group, running toward the sounds.

"Go," Gabby repeated. And then she was off after Miles, leaving Ember and Simon alone.

Chapter Fifty-Six

The Fountain

The thing that had crawled from the Fountain was tired of waiting.

It was ravenous.

It crawled from the mud and began to follow the scent carried on the wind. It would eat well and soon.

The thing dragged one hand, attached to an arm much longer than the other, on the dirt and rocks as it went.

The dragging hand was soon ruined. Knuckles bloodied and open wounds collected filth and grit as the thing noiselessly skulked through the woods, following the smell of a promised meal. Its claws, however, were still sharp. And the thing did not mind a little discomfort, a small measure of pain.

It was accustomed to both.

PART FOUR

The Fountain

Chapter Fifty-Seven

Selah

The cage fell, and with it, Selah.

Faster than she could have imagined, water replaced air.

Selah stretched as tall as the cage would allow, struggling for one last good breath. But she was too slow, or the water too fast, and she was submerged in the churning deluge.

The metal prison landed hard but did not stop moving, gradually but steadily tipping forward.

Selah found herself on an underwater ledge, and the cage extended beyond its brink. Beyond the ledge, down, there was nothing but an eternity of dark water. She was on the precipice of nothing at all. Desperate to stop the tipping, Selah crawled on her knees to the back of the cage, righting it with her added weight.

Hopeless and absurd as it was, she searched for some hidden pocket of air.

Of course, there was none.

Then her body refused to wait any longer.

She breathed in.

Selah's first breath underwater was the worst hurt and horror she had ever experienced. All the lightness she took for granted in the center of her chest became heavy and dense. The water filled her nose and lungs and throat and all the spaces in between.

She burned and ached.

Her body thrashed.

She coughed and choked and gagged.

She had no control, and there was nothing she could do but panic.

Somehow, her body forced another liquid breath in and then out. A third.

She was not breathing exactly.

She also was not dying right away.

As Zebedee had predicted, the process of drowning would be drawn out for her kind.

The water tasted of rock and blood and rotting things.

Some of Selah's winged friends did well in water. They were made for it, able to maneuver almost as if they were in flight. Aaron, the mauled Groundskeeper, was one of those. He could pull his wings in so close they almost disappeared against his body and dive, midflight, through the water like a dart.

Selah was not like Aaron. She was made for land and air, not the water. And even though she could not use them, she needed her wings free. She needed her *hands* free.

Selah managed to get her left thumb through a link in the chain that bound her. She worked it down incrementally as she twisted and pulled her other hand up. Delicate skin on her wrists stretched and tore in strips, the seams in the links catching and biting as they moved. Thin eddies of blood spun into pink clouds in the water.

With tedious progress, Selah was able to pull her right hand up while her left did the work of keeping the chain down. When her hand slipped free, the rest of the chain was easily discarded. Selah was still drowning in increments, but she would not die with her hands and wings bound.

Submerged, her wings were useless. They billowed, heavy in the water. She tried to keep them tight to her body, but the water worked in and around them, pulling them at odd angles. She thought if she made it back to dry land, she would be unable to stand under their weight.

Selah looked around her cell. The cage was big enough for a sharp turn but not much else. Through the bars above, she could see daylight hazy and filtered through the Fountain.

How far up? Forty feet? Fifty? The shifting currents made the perspective unreliable.

More than a third of the cage floor reached past the ledge and into nothingness. Beyond the cage was endless water.

How far down the Fountain went, Selah could not be sure. There was a part of her, the ever-growing part threatening to go insane, that was convinced the water never ended. She hoped she never found out.

Just beyond the limits of her vision, things were moving in that water. Some appeared to be as massive as the leviathan in the lake. Others, much faster, did not look any larger than her. They were graceful dancers and beautiful in their own way. But it was a facade. The beasts in the water had no purpose aside from guarding and slaughtering and consuming.

And there was something on the ledge with her. She was sure of it. In the shadows, it blended against the rock, but Selah was certain it was there. Watching her.

Selah tried pushing on the bars of the cage. They were solid, did not give at all. She was methodical, pressing against each one at a time. She tried the bars above. No reward there, either. Standing as close to the center of the cage as she could so as not to tip it over, Selah grasped the door with both hands. It shifted, but only a little, on its hinges. The hinges might be a point of weakness, but she had no tools, not even a rock. She inspected them anyway.

Then the gap around the door.

Then the latch.

Then the . . .

The lock.

The lock hung open.

Selah stared at the latch. It was a metal slide that lifted up and over. She could reach through, move it up and to the left, and then she would be free.

She almost threw the door open and began swimming up, up toward the sun and land and air. But something gave her pause. She considered the door again and backed away from it.

Here, in the cage, she was trapped but she was relatively safe aside from the problem of drowning. Beyond the cage was whatever swam in the distance. And there were her useless, useless wings. When she stepped off the ledge, would they sink her like a stone? Selah thought they might. She had a clear vision of herself falling through the water beyond the ledge. Falling so far there was no filtered sunlight left. Falling and never stopping. Or falling until she did stop and met whatever lived on the unexplored floor of the Fountain. And even if she *did* manage to avoid sinking, and even if she *did* manage slow, slow progress up and toward the sun, there was the matter of whatever it was that shared the ledge with her. That was what convinced her to stay. Selah knew, with no doubt at all, whatever was on the ledge was waiting patiently for her to leave her cage.

She was trapped, a prisoner in an unlocked box.

April, 1989
Morning

He has killed the mother.
It is time to bring him here. To show the others.

Tradition is the thing that will keep us safe.
All else is a threat.
Progress for its own sake is a cancer.

The notion of a Collective Jury has gained ground. The work takes one brave and decisive mind, not a committee and endless compromise.

Sam is a threat, but I have him contained.
I raised him alongside the mother. I raised him when the mother could not.
I nurtured the seed in him. Bid it grow and bloom.
The others will meet him, will fear him and they will understand why I selected him. We cannot allow ourselves to grow soft. Cannot allow our ways to change. They have worked always. They will continue.

Sam is a threat, but he shows great promise and could, in time, be a detached and decisive Jury. At worst, he will be a useful tool. An object lesson.

Ava's boy is a threat of a different sort. The children are enchanted with him, and the island will become beguiled in time as they were with Ava. His kindness and compassion and morality will draw them to him, and they will celebrate what is only weakness. He can be allowed to become Jury no more than Ava was. He can be contained. Dealt with.

I have much to do.

Chapter Fifty-Eight

Sam

Sam sat against the boulder. He was soaked through from the wet sand and the mist that poured off the lake. He had screamed until his throat was raw as butchered meat, screamed until the birds in the trees became silent and watchful. Now the only sounds were those of the waves grasping and pulling at the sandy shore.

Farther down the beach, blackened heaps of flesh marred the landscape. The smell of them surrounded him when the breeze from the lake was just right, a smell of both rotten flesh and of flesh purified by fire.

Fire made everything cleaner. Fire fixed things, made problems go away. Fire, quick and controlled, was a tool. Sam toyed with the idea of going to the burned creatures to see if he could finish the job, to see if he could burn the heaps until they were nothing but ash and smudged grease in the sand. *But what's the point of killing something that's already dead?*

Sam closed his eyes and went to the barren grey. It was as it always was, bleak and without temperature or atmosphere. He sat in the sand, while in the empty landscape he stood and turned a slow circle. Sam looked in every direction, not that the place had directions in any way he understood, for some sign he was not alone.

And . . .

This time . . .

There was something on the horizon.

Or, maybe, someone.

A noise brought Sam out of his trance, out of the bleak landscape and back to the shore.

A horror was crawling out of the lake. It was deformed and hideous, a fat body and arms and legs so long and thin they belonged to something else entirely. It tried once to stand upright, but the skeletal legs refused to support it, and it fell hard and ungracefully into the rocks and the sand. The creature's face was little more than a long snout and teeth that hung over its bottom jaw.

Sam sat very still.

The thing got up, tried again, then managed to take trembling steps on all fours to the nearest burned pile and circled it. It bent its head low, sniffing and then rooting in the remains like some kind of nightmare feral hog.

Sam's stomach turned as the creature opened its mouth—its maw—so wide the rest of its face was obscured. It began to eat the dead heap in the sand.

Was that one of you, one of your buddies? I could burn you up, too.

As the thing ate, two more monsters rose up from the lake and onto the beach. They were smaller than the first monster, but not by much. They approached the pile to join in the meal, but the first creature, still eating, made a guttural warning sound. The others held back.

Greedy bastard.

Sam stared hard at the gorging atrocity. He stared and he hated and he thought about stopping the creature's heart, squeezing it in his fist until it exploded.

The monster continued eating.

Sam tried again to kill the thing on the beach. And when that failed, he tried to kill one of the smaller, weaker creatures.

They refused to die. They didn't even look his way.

This was a new complication, but better to learn it now than later. Sam now knew to avoid the lake creatures, to keep his distance.

Done cannibalizing the burned corpse, the thing began to move away from the lake and toward the forest. The two smaller creatures followed a few lengths behind. As they disappeared into the trees, Sam stood and picked up his bag.

The lake monsters were going somewhere. Sam didn't see any reason not to follow them. The change in the barren grey of his mind temporarily forgotten.

Chapter Fifty-Nine

Miles

Miles ran.

Miles ran as hard and as fast as he could. His arms and legs, stiff with cold, protested, but he ignored them and pushed harder. Once he almost went down when his tennis shoes slipped on the moist tunnel floor. And only once did he look behind to see Gabby, flying silently down the center of the tunnel, at his heels.

He came to another intersection, and as the sounds grew louder, Miles was convinced Alma was not hurt. She was dying. Nothing else could explain the noise she was making, both high pitched and rasping.

Miles turned the corner and saw Alma on the stone floor, twenty yards away.

He "turned it up" like his coach would say, running harder, and as the gap between them closed, Miles realized he had been wrong.

Someone—*something*—was dying, but it wasn't Alma.

Miles slowed.

The monstrosity on the floor writhed. It seemed to be attacking itself, hands slashing at its own bulbous body.

Miles saw many things at once.

The creature had far too many hands, too many arms. There were six, at least, and all but two of them were motionless and hung at the mutant's sides. Its skin was grey and slick in the weak light of the channel water. And it had not one head, but four, three of which were as lifeless as its surplus arms. The extra heads hung down, jerked and rolled as the thing moved. The eyes on the dead heads were both wide and open, the irises gone milk white. Miles thought of Cerberus, that three-headed guard dog of Greek mythology. Except Cerberus's three heads had all been alive and dangerous.

Miles stopped.

The monster reached with its elongated face and began to chew at one of the lifeless limbs as its two good arms continued to grab and tear. It saw Miles then, and a low growl came from somewhere deep, bloody teeth a rictus around the arm it held. The creature's living eyes were hidden in shadows, but Miles could feel them on him all the same.

Gabby landed next to Miles.

Miles swore loudly before asking, "What is it?"

"One of the Fountain's creatures. The strangers from your *when*. What they are before they return to your side of the lake."

"But why . . ."

Before Miles could ask his question, a question about the arms—*the heads*—the creature began to drag itself toward them. It was fast. Faster than Miles would have believed such a bloated, broken thing could be.

It twitched and gibbered as it came.

Miles recognized the gibbering. If he'd dared close his eyes, he might have mistaken it for the man at the pool or the woman on the bridge. If he needed evidence that his *when*'s strangers and this mutant were one and the same, he now had it.

The gap closing between them, Miles reached for his bladed staff. Gabby already had her knife in hand.

Miles had never killed anything larger than a mouse, and that had been an accident when he'd tried to catch and release the animal before his mom could get to it first. This, however, would have to die.

His entire body knotted, ready to lunge when the monster was close enough to strike.

As Miles reared back, something else crept soundlessly from the channel. It was tall and pale and thin, and it moved with perfect stealth toward the gibbering monster.

Ava.

She attacked it before the creature could turn its unwieldy body.

It lashed out at her with its working hands, human hands that ended in thick talons. Ava dodged, but the abomination still managed to open up her side. Blood ran in a curtain. Then Ava was on it.

Miles could no longer see the mother for the monster. She was all claws and teeth and bloodstained skin. The mutant's wail became a screech and then a new scream, this one Ava's. The creature had her by the hair and was pulling her face to its mouth.

Miles didn't think.

He brought down his blade and pulled the razor edge through hide and gristle and snagged on something that might have been a tendon or a fine bone. Miles tore out the creature's throat, and then there was silence.

It had all taken only moments.

Miles stumbled back, still holding his now-bloody spear in bloodier hands at the ready. It was not until Gabby touched his shoulder that he relaxed his arm and returned the weapon to his belt loop.

He shook with something he'd never experienced before and hoped he never would again—the power and the madness of taking a life. It was nauseating and terrifying and it filled him so completely there was room for nothing else.

A blood-soaked Ava stood over the corpse, holding her side and breathing hard. She turned toward him, and he saw horror and pity in her eyes.

Perhaps Miles should have been afraid of the mother-monster. Perhaps he should have been cautious. But Miles was neither of those things. It was he who had taken a life, not her.

He walked on unsteady feet toward Ava, and toward what he had just slaughtered.

The creature was not like Cerberus at all. It was like a rat king.

Somehow, the thing had become entangled with three others. Their long arms intertwined, their many-jointed legs a hopeless knot of limbs. Three of them had been dead long enough to begin to putrefy, and the smell of decay was overpowering.

The creature had not been attacking itself after all. It had been trying to relieve the burden of its dead mates, chewing and gnashing at the parts it could reach.

Miles vomited into the channel. Then, in a different kind of frenzy, he fell to his knees and tried to wash the blood off his hands and arms.

He felt a hand on his back. Ava stood over him now, a mother once more. When he was again drawn toward the pile on the tunnel floor, she turned his face away with a bloody, maternal hand. *Do not look at this. Do not look at what you had to do.*

She reached under his arm and pulled him to his shaking feet.

Ava took Miles, still dazed and thrumming, by the hand and began to lead him deeper into the tunnel.

"Let him go, Ava." Gabby stepped in front of them, blade extended.

Something dangerous flashed in Ava's eyes. Then they softened. Ava dropped Miles's hand and took a step away from him, then two. Instead of lashing out at Gabby, or grasping for Miles, Ava beckoned them both with long fingers. *Follow me.*

Gabby held her ground. "No. Ava, I'm sorry."

Miles saw tears standing in Gabby's eyes. Lost in his own turmoil, he had forgotten his friend once loved Ava, knew her better than he ever had.

"We cannot . . . I cannot let Miles go with you. I want to trust you but . . ." She paused and floundered for her next words. "We have to find the others, Simon and Ember. And we have to find Alma. And Selah. You remember?"

Ava nodded. She beckoned for them both, insistent now, to come with her.

"I'm going with her." Miles's breathing became more regular, and his shaking was reduced to a tremor. He moved toward the mother-monster, shook Gabby off when she reached for him.

"No, Miles, you are not." Gabby reached for Miles again with her free hand, the other still held her blade toward Ava.

Miles might have blinked, or Ava might have been that fast. Either way, one second Gabby was standing, armed. The next instant she was on the ground, pinned by Ava. Gabby dropped her blade in the fall, metal clattering on the stone floor.

Ava, never taking her eyes from Gabby's, reached out and wrapped her fingers around the handle of the weapon.

Miles was certain Gabby was dead already, that he had been wrong about who he believed Ava still was.

Ava leaned in closer to Gabby, their faces nearly touching. She took the blade, reached across Gabby, and placed it in the pocket of Gabby's tunic. Ava stood then, and when she did Gabby lay staring up at her, as frozen as Miles.

Ava reached down and offered Gabby her hand, and Miles was shocked when the winged girl took it. Ava helped Gabby to her feet. She beckoned again. *I did not kill you. Follow me. Now.* And then Ava began to move on quick feet down the corridor.

"Well, damn," Miles said. It was all he could manage.

Gabby nodded. "Let us see what she has to show us," she said, as if nothing had transpired between them. As if he had not just committed murder.

No, not murder. People get murdered. That was . . . something else.

Miles knew he had just witnessed some silent conversation between Ava and Gabby that he did not understand. He didn't in that moment have the capacity to even try. He hesitated long enough for Gabby to look back over her shoulder at him, and then he followed them both.

They did not walk far.

After a short while, Ava stopped at a set of stone stairs. She looked up toward the door at the top, and then down at Miles and Gabby.

Gabby shook her head. "We cannot go through that door."

"Why?"

"Because it will be barred. Or locked. Or both."

Ava pointed one long finger up the staircase. With that gesture, she was an impatient, weary mother. Gabby sighed but led the way up. At the top, Miles looked over her shoulder.

It was clear the door *had* been barred. Lengths of wood, pulled from the nails that once held them to the frame, littered the small landing. Heavy chain had been torn from iron rings embedded in the door and in the stone wall.

"Did you do this?" Gabby looked back down at Ava who stood halfway up the staircase.

Ava shook her head. *No.*

"Thank you, Ava, for showing us."

"Are we going through there?" Miles asked.

"I think we must," Gabby replied. And she pushed the door open.

The silence of the tunnel crumbled as the air was filled with a deafening, thunderous sound. The world outside the door was a torrent, nothing but the mad rush of water.

Without a word, Gabby stepped into it and disappeared.

Miles glanced back at Ava, who nodded. *Go with her.*

He took a deep breath, held it for a beat, then followed Gabby into the deluge.

He stayed under the rushing water until he could no longer hold his breath, hoping it would cleanse his body and soul.

Chapter Sixty

Ember

"We should wait for them." Simon spoke in a small voice, face turned to the tunnel floor rather than toward Ember.

"We can't." Ember reconsidered her words. "*I* can't. If I don't follow Sam, I'm going to lose him. And if I lose him, we lose Alma, too."

Simon did not look up. "We are safer with Gabby."

"I know, but she's not here. Maybe you and I are safer together than alone?" Ember paused, wanting to say something that would move the small boy. She worried what would happen to him if he were left alone. "Maybe I am safer with you."

Simon looked up to her then. "It is true you do not know your way."

"I don't."

Simon nodded, convinced. "We should go, then. Before you lose the trail."

"Thank you, Simon, for coming with me."

Ember reached down and took his hand. Together they moved quick as they could through the tunnel.

It was still hot. If anything, hotter than before. Ember was as hot as she had ever been, hotter than her worst days working the fields with Daddy. *Daddy's dead now, and the fields were no good this year, anyway.*

Simon wrapped himself tight in his green wings, doing his best to stay warm.

Ember followed the heat until it concentrated, pooled. They were at the base of a staircase. "I think this is it. Where does the door go?"

Simon thought for a moment. "The lake. This takes you to the shore where you arrived with Selah."

The beach, with the promise of a cool, clean breeze off the water, called to Ember. She needed to be away from this fevered place. She started up a stair, then took another before she looked down and to the side. There, almost lost in the shadows, was a body.

Ember's heart stopped. She tried very hard not to believe what she knew to be true, what she was seeing.

"Alma." Ember spoke the word like a dirge.

"Alma?" Simon's voice was terribly, horribly light. Ember could hear the boy's relief. It broke her heart.

Before she could tell him, Simon saw for himself. "Oh. Alma. *Alma.*" He rushed to the dead woman's side, threw himself to the floor with enough force the sound of his knees hitting the stone echoed.

Simon touched Alma's face. Her wing. And then her hand. He held her hand while he repeated her name over and over again. When his voice broke and he could say it no longer, Simon sobbed into Alma's beautiful, blue-grey wing.

Ember ached for the kind woman lying dead on the floor of the tunnels. She hurt more for the little boy who mourned her. Ember didn't know if Alma had been Simon's keeper in the Hatchery, but she surely had a hand in raising him. *Another mother lost.*

Ember gave Simon a short minute to grieve. Then she sat next to him, put her hands on his shoulders. "We have to go."

"I will not leave her."

"There's nothing you can do. She's gone."

"I will not *leave* her."

Ember took Simon by the chin, lifted his face so he had to see her. Her voice was stern. "We have to go. We have to find Sam. He's the one who did this. He took her. We have to find him before he hurts someone else."

"I'm scared."

"So am I. But we'll be together. And I might not be Gabby, but I promise you. I *promise* you, Sam will not hurt you. I won't let him."

"You can stop him?"

Ember nodded. *I don't know. I hope so.*

At Simon's insistence, they took the time to wrap Alma's wings as best they could around her small frame. With as much reverence as the situation afforded, Ember wrapped one wing low, covering most of Alma's body. Simon wrapped the opposite wing high. Before he covered her face, Simon leaned down and kissed Alma's cheek. "I love you," he whispered.

Now Ember cried along with Simon as they finished the job. It was not right, Simon told her, but it would do for now.

"We'll send someone down as soon as we can," Ember promised. "Someone to take care of her properly."

Once again hand in hand, Ember and Simon made their way up the stone staircase.

The door opened through what turned out to be an enormous rock on the beach.

Ember stepped through first, cautious. She expected to finally meet Sam there on the shore, and she did not expect it to go well.

The door closed behind them and vanished.

Ember was met with the cool breeze she'd hoped for, but it carried with it the stench of the burning pyres she had witnessed the previous night. *Was it just last night?* Ember's bones ached as though she'd been awake and frantic for a week.

Aside from Ember and Simon and the burned things, the beach was empty.

There was no sign of the elusive Sam.

Except . . .

"Simon, has there been some sort of blight on the island? Something killing the plants?" Ember ran her fingers along blades of grass growing close to the camouflaged door in the boulder. The grass was grey, nearly black, and brittle to the touch. Blight had infected Daddy's wheat fields one spring, turning what should have been supple green plants weak and white. The whole field had been a loss. This was the wrong color, but the grass had been infected with something.

"No, nothing. The island is healthy."

Ember lifted her fingers to smell them. She was met with the unmistakable scent of ash. *Not infected. Burned.*

While she had lost Sam's telltale heat in the winds of the shore, Ember had an idea. She looked toward the edge of the forest and the tall grasses and low plants that grew there below the branches of the trees.

"We need to look for something like this." Ember showed Simon the desiccated grass. "We might still have a way to follow him."

They scoured the place where the greenery began to overtake the shore. With so much growing, and so many shadows drifting and playing among the plants, finding a patch of grey felt like a lost cause.

A number of frustrating minutes passed before Ember remembered the flashlight. She pushed the rubber button on the side of the cylinder and a beam shone from the end. It was so much better than the lanterns they carried on the farm, the light bright and direct. Ember began to make her way around the edge of the forest, shining light on the foliage that illuminated brighter green in the glow.

"Simon! Come here!"

Simon flew from the other side of the trees to join Ember. She said nothing as she trained the light on a clump of bushes. For the most part, it was covered in dark green leaves and berries the color of small, round rubies. Ember thought they might be currants, but she was not about to taste one to find out. A portion of the plant had gone a sickly grey, the berries black and shriveled. When Ember took one between her fingers, the berry turned to powder. Charcoal.

"Let's start here," Ember said. "We know what to look for."

Simon looked grim but nodded.

They pushed through the plants and into the dense woods. The forest closed in behind them, and much of the daylight disappeared.

Ember was glad for the flashlight.

She was glad for Simon at her side.

She hoped she could truly track Sam.

She hoped she could keep her promise to Simon.

She hoped she would know what to do next.

April, 1989
Evening

The boy pushed me away, out. After the mother died.
I have always had access to the empty place in his mind.
For two of his days, there was no door. No way in.
This is a development, and a worrying one.

Tonight I was allowed back in. But that is not the point.
The point is I am losing control.

He is coming. I told him the way.

I will not help him cross the lake.
I cannot kill him, but I will not help him to live.
If he learns he is enough on his own . . .

Chapter Sixty-One

Selah

Selah had hours at best.

She began drifting off into a half sleep as her body gradually shut down.

She would wake, forgetting for just a moment she was in a cage in the Fountain, dying. Then the horror of the situation would accost her, and she would gasp for air, taking in lungsful of brackish water. Her heart, having slowed, would race. Her eyes and hands would pulse along with it. Then she would calm herself, force herself back to center.

And there were the hallucinations.

Sometimes, Selah thought she could see the creatures that shared the water with her lined up in a row, vague silhouettes just too far out for her to perceive with any clarity. Other times, she thought there was someone there with her. Alma, maybe. A feeling, something warm and almost like love, would overtake her. And, before long, she would fall asleep, and it would all begin again.

Selah knew there was little time left. She was growing slow in her thoughts. When she woke, there was less terror now, and her heart no longer had the power to race.

Her vision was narrowing, the periphery disappearing, and Selah might have been looking into the water through a poorly focused telescope.

She was too tired to be horrified.

When a thing with Beatrix's eyes came to the door of her cage, Selah smiled. *Beatrix, what are you doing in that beast's body? Did you die after all? Is this what is left? Is this what I will be?*

The idea should have terrified Selah, the notion of dying in the Fountain, only her soul left behind. Trapped in the body of a monster until she died again. But Selah's thoughts disappeared as soon as she had them. She could not focus long enough to be afraid.

The Beatrix thing was sleek and piebald, white mottled against taupe flesh. She still looked more Beatrix than creature. *She's not been a creature for long. Perhaps it takes time . . .*

The Beatrix thing smiled. Selah knew the smile well, but the teeth within it were new. And sharp.

Selah smiled back. She reached a hand through the bars of her cage.

The Beatrix thing looked at her hand with interest but did not take it.

I wonder if she would prefer to hold it or bite it off. The idea made Selah giggle, mad and mirthless.

When the Beatrix thing reached for the lock hanging from the door of the cage, Selah was certain she was saved by the only one who could keep the creatures in the Fountain at bay.

When the Beatrix thing looked right in her eyes as she engaged the lock, tugged on it to be sure it was fast, Selah knew she was going to die.

Selah watched the Beatrix thing swim silently away.

She cried, then, hot tears disappearing into the cool forever of the Fountain.

Strange. Why am I crying?

Selah drifted off again.

Chapter Sixty-Two

Miles

The view from the door had been an illusion.

Miles stepped out the door and behind a curtain of water rather than into one. It was a waterfall, the mist around him so thick it was a dense fog. The sun, now well into the sky, illuminated the falling water. It was liquid crystal. Gabby was there, waiting for him. She glowed white in the filtered sunlight.

Gabby did not bother trying to speak over the roar of the cascade. Instead, she motioned for Miles to follow her across the slick burgundy rock.

Around the edge of the waterfall was a perfect day. Never had a morning been as green and blue and gold as this. The chill of the tunnel let loose its hold on his bones, and Miles took in the scene around him.

He was on a platform of red stone, made smooth and flat from untold time under the rush of the falls. The platform was at one end of the Fountain. It tapered and stretched well beyond the reach of the water, creating a narrow but serviceable path to the clearing beyond.

The Fountain, and the glade between it and the woods, were silent save for a constant buzzing. Silent, but far from abandoned.

A bloody clump, what remained of one of the monsters from the lake, was a pile on the ground. Miles thought of what he had just done, and the feeling of the blade catching on something tough and gristly. His gorge rose, but he swallowed it back.

Four bodies were strewn across the grass. They had been Grounds-keepers judging by the weaponry that lay abandoned near them. Drying blood and a horde of blue-black flies masked their identities.

Zebedee sat on one of the many stone benches arranged in a neat semicircle.

There was no sign of Selah.

"With caution," Gabby warned Miles as they crossed the stone ledge to the edge of the Fountain.

Miles did not need to be told.

Zebedee carried no weapon Miles could see, but the look he wore was dangerous. Despite the carnage surrounding him, Zebedee appeared serene. No sane man could be serene in the presence of all that butchery.

"Gabrielle. And . . . boy. You are supposed to be in the Academy, all tucked away safe and sound like good children." Zebedee did not bother to stand as he addressed them.

"Where is Selah?" Gabby demanded.

"She is on a mission. A rather urgent one."

"Where is she?" Gabby repeated.

Zebedee sighed with theatrical exasperation. "I do not answer to you, girl. Speaking of missing friends, where is your little brother? I rarely see the two of you apart, him always hanging off your wing. And the other girl. You did not send them off together, did you? Alone and vulnerable? I thought you a more conscientious caretaker, Gabrielle."

Miles and Gabby were near enough to Zebedee to smell his perfume, but it did nothing to mask the stench coming off the corpses in the grass.

When a figure emerged from the woods, Miles was relieved they were no longer alone with the unhinged man. When he saw who it was, his heart sank.

"Magdalene," Gabby said. The word was a curse and an accusation. "Where is Selah?"

Magdalene looked around the clearing, taking in the scene. Miles thought he saw her composure slip, whether it due to the bloody mess or the reek of sun-warmed death, he wasn't sure. But she recovered quickly and strode with purpose toward Zebedee, her thundercloud wings spread wide.

"She is in the Academy, I suppose. As *you* should be."

"You lie," spat Gabby. "Zebedee came for her before the sun was up. He would not have done so without your order."

Magdalene looked at Zebedee with an impressed sort of disapproval on her narrow face. "Did you, then? Is that what your enigmatic note was referring to?"

Zebedee nodded. "We have wasted too much time talking about finding the Jury. It was time action be taken. If you are to be her successor, she must name you. I am getting the Jury back for you, Magdalene."

Gabby made a scoffing noise. "Magdalene will never be Jury. Surely you know that?"

She was ignored so completely Miles wasn't even sure the other two had heard her.

Miles saw two truths. Zebedee was insane, and Magdalene was an excellent actress. Her dumbfounded expression could have passed for real. Had Miles not been in her study, not seen the copious notes on Sam and the map of his own town, he might have believed her.

"How, Zebedee, are you accomplishing this? By sitting on a bench in the sun, waiting for her to come out of the Fountain to wish you a good morning?" Magdalene's face was twisted in a snarl of contempt.

Zebedee shrugged. "Essentially, yes."

Miles was growing more and more worried. A madman sat, unfazed by corpses surrounding him, and he had been the last person seen with Selah. "Where is she?" asked Miles.

Zebedee leaned back, stretched his wings behind him. He spoke with precision, as if explaining himself to a person he thought slow. "Early this morning I brought your friend here. And then I put her in a cage. The cage was heavy, especially with Selah in it. It was quite difficult to manage."

"Where is Selah?" Gabby took a meaningful step forward, stood with her blade drawn.

But Miles knew and the knowing made him shake with rage and fear. "She's in there, isn't she?" Miles pointed to the Fountain. "You put her in a cage and dropped her in."

With a nod, Zebedee said, "I did. And she sank like a stone. But she was very brave. She did not scream at all."

Even Magdalene had the decency to look horrified. "You put the child in the Fountain? Zebedee, why?"

"To draw out the Jury, of course. Beatrix would not let her darling drown. Not after Ava drowned in this very place. She could not bear it. Losing Ava almost broke her. Losing Selah the same way would finish the job."

"When?" Gabby's voice was quiet.

"Oh, an hour. Perhaps two. She still has time. But how much, who can say?"

An hour? *Two?*

"She's dead already!" Miles screamed. He started toward Zebedee unsure what he would do when he reached the smiling man.

Gabby grabbed his arm to stop him.

"No," she said as Miles turned to shake her off. "Not dead. Not yet. She still has time. Some. Not much."

Miles stated what he thought was obvious. "We'll get Gideon. The Groundskeepers will bring her up."

Magdalene began to speak but was stopped by Zebedee. "How will they reach her? There was a chain. Sadly, now there is not. I . . . accidentally . . . dropped it all in."

Magdalene's eyes widened at the news. "Zebedee, what have you done? This is not the way of things. There is no tradition in sacrificing a child."

Gabby recovered enough to be enraged. "Enough. Magdalene, we know you had a hand in this. Zebedee would not think to do this alone. We know you have been watching Sam. We know you have been tracking the strangers in Miles's *when,* waiting for them to find him. Or his mother."

Magdalene's scorn had returned. "What are you rambling about, Gabrielle?"

"Your study," said Miles. "We went to your study last night. Found your books and your maps. We know you're the one who brought Sam here. Studied him like a bug. And we know you've been sending the strangers into my *when,* looking for me. Trying to kill me."

"My study," Magdalene said with growing anger, "has no maps and certainly has no books about the Jury's pet. Where . . ." A thin, humorless smile played across her lips. "Was there a cistern in the study? Walls papered in charts and books in piles in the corners?"

"You know there was," Miles spat.

"Idiot children. *That* was not my study. *That* room belongs to the Jury. If anyone has been trying to kill you off, it was her."

"You lie." Gabby nearly yelled it.

"Do I? And what, pray tell, led you to believe the study was mine?"

"I . . . I remembered. From my time at the Academy."

"All these baseless accusations come from a flawed childhood memory? You remembered wrong, Gabrielle." Magdalene was joyful. Miles wanted to slap the expression off her face.

The growing look of doubt on Gabby's face told Miles it was true. A simple, understandable mistake. She had the wrong room. The evidence did not point to Magdalene after all, but to Beatrix. If Beatrix had been set on killing children, Miles did not believe she would rush to save Selah. "We have to get her out."

"She has hours at best, maybe much less," Gabby said. "Selah is not made for the water, she will not last."

Magdalene, recovered now from Zebedee's announcement, shrugged. "Then we must hope the Jury loves her dearly. Because I do not believe any of you are going in after her."

"It is suicide, as you are well aware. The beasts in the Fountain would tear us apart." Gabby's voice was still and level, low with anger.

Miles made a decision and began acting before he could talk himself out of it.

"I am," Miles said, removing the bladed staff from his belt loop.

"You are what?" asked Gabby.

"I'm going in after her." He sat and began taking his tennis shoes off.

Zebedee chuckled. The sound was grotesque. "Selah is deep. Deep in the Fountain. And there are many things in all that water between you and her."

"I can swim. I'm fast. And I can hold my breath a long time." *I didn't win State for nothing,* he thought. "I can get in and at least see where she is. If she's alive." Miles stripped down to his underwear as he spoke. "We can't do nothing."

"Maybe she is down there. Or not. Are you going to risk it? Are you going to feed yourself to the beasts in the Fountain based on *Zebedee's* word? He is not very honest, you know." Magdalene turned to Zebedee. She had not forgotten he had acted without approval, without permission. "Or very bright."

Zebedee's Cheshire smile faltered at Magdalene's words, but he did not argue with her.

"Miles, do not do this," Gabby pled with him. "We will get Gideon. Perhaps Alma is with him now. She will know what to do."

"I have to do something," Miles told her. "She might not have time to wait."

Barefoot and almost naked, carrying a weapon he didn't know how to use, he walked to the edge of the Fountain.

This is insane, Miles thought as he dove in.

Chapter Sixty-Three

Ember

Ember and Simon made their way through the forest.

They no longer needed the flashlight to follow Sam. The trail he left was clear. Trees and grass, blackened and scorched, marked the way every few feet.

"Like Hansel and Gretel," Ember murmured.

"Who?" Simon asked.

"Children in an old story, a fairy tale. They went into the woods but left a trail so they could find their way home."

"Did it work?

"Not really. They got lost anyway. Deep in the woods, they found what they thought was a safe place, but it turned out to be a witch's house."

"Did they escape?"

"Sometimes," Ember replied. "Sometimes, they survived. Sometimes, the little boy got eaten. It depends on who's telling the story."

Simon shuddered.

Ember put her arm around him. "Sam isn't a witch. Besides, you know how to get us out of the woods."

"I also know where we are going. This way will lead us to the Library."

And soon, Simon was proven right. The trees around them thinned, and a clearing opened up. Within it, the Library.

There was no sign of Sam. No sign of anyone at all.

Ember went to the massive Library door and placed her hand on it. It was cool to the touch. "He's not here," she said. Urgency and frustration churned in her stomach, "Maybe I was wrong. Maybe . . ."

Simon stood at the edge of the ridge overlooking the Hatchery. "Ember." His whisper was urgent. "We must—"

"I *know*," she interrupted. "I'm trying."

"No. Now!"

Ember left the maddeningly empty Library and joined him at the ridge. What she saw took her breath away. A half dozen monsters were making their way down the steep slope. They moved in a pack like wolves. And they were headed for the Hatchery. Unsteady on their too-thin limbs, the creatures made slow progress down the rocky terrain of the slope. But they made progress nonetheless.

In no time, they would be upon the Hatchery.

And the children within.

Ember wanted nothing more than to continue tracking Sam, to stop him from hurting anyone else. To make him answer for Alma. But she also recalled Selah's words: *If we have to choose, we protect the Hatchery. We protect this place to the very end.*

The choice had been made for her.

"We have to warn them," Ember said.

"I can fly."

"You're not going alone." Ember put her face in her hands. *Think. How do you get past a pack of monsters without being seen? How do you save a building full of babies?* And then, "The tunnels. They connect everything, right?"

"Yes."

"The Library?"

"Yes."

"And the Hatchery?"

"*Yes.*" Simon was flushed with annoyance. Then, in the next moment, he understood. "We just have to . . ."

"Don't tell me. Go. I'll follow."

They threw open the Library door and ran down the great room in the center. Simon stopped at a door and ran through it as well.

Ember was disoriented. It was yet another room full of doors, but these were stacked and piled. Only one was a proper, working door. Through it and down thirty-seven steps, Ember and Simon ran.

The tunnels branched and split, but Simon knew the way. They were moving down, under the valley and to the Hatchery. Up another set of stairs.

Ember and Simon burst into a small storage room. It opened up into the Nursery.

Hatchery keepers looked up in surprise. The room was full of soft music and sleeping babies.

An older woman with red wings and stern eyes passed the child she was holding to another keeper and stood to meet Ember and Simon. "What are you thinking? The tunnels are not—"

"You have to get them out now. All the little ones. There are beasts from the lake on their way here. Now. Get them out now," Simon yelled, his face as red as his hair.

"Coming here? From the lake?" The woman was stunned, but, thankfully, not disbelieving.

"Take them through the tunnels, somewhere. Anywhere safe. You have to do it now." Ember looked around the room. There were too many little ones, not enough adults. Maybe if they each took two . . .

And then she remembered the Hatchery itself. The room was full of dozens of babies, still growing in their cocoons. There was no way to get them all out in time. "Send someone for help," Ember said. "Someone fast."

The woman nodded. She knelt in front of a younger, yellow-winged woman in a rocking chair and said something to her Ember could not hear. As the red-winged woman spoke, Ember saw the younger woman's expression change from disbelief to horror and then to determination. She handed the child she held to the older woman and left the room.

"She is our best flyer. She will reach the Groundskeepers and bring them here."

Then the woman took charge. She sent Hatchery keepers into the tunnels with as many little ones as they could manage. Many of the babies slept as they were carried out. The ones old enough to be afraid began to cry. They sensed something was wrong, and they were frightened, their downy wings fluttering too fast. Soon, the room was full of sobbing children.

Ember picked up the first child she reached. Imre. He looked at her with solemn grey eyes, screwed up his face, and began to whimper.

Ember did the only thing that came to mind. She began to hum along with the music in the Nursery, the music that now filled her head like a gentle friend. When the music in the room began to swell, Ember did not notice. She hummed and the music grew not louder, but *more*. Still she did not notice. It was not until the last child in the room stopped wailing that Ember registered something had changed. She stopped humming and looked up. Every silver eye in the room was watching her.

Simon called softly from a window, "Keep singing. The monsters do not like the music. They have stopped."

Ember didn't question him, she began again. This time there were words to her song, words in a language she could not have known. A language that had died generations before. The cool and calm did not fill her now. It *became* her, and she it.

Ember sang and from her mouth the song was a prayer. A few at a time, the babies were taken through the tunnel door to safety.

Imre was the last. Ember handed him to the red-winged woman. She stopped singing. “What about the others? The little ones in the Hatchery?”

“We will come back for them.”

Ember nodded. “Simon and I will stay until . . .”

But Ember did not finish. As she looked around the room, Simon was nowhere to be found.

Chapter Sixty-Four

Simon

As Ember sang, Simon slipped unseen from the Nursery and into the great room of the Hatchery. It was empty as the keepers were all occupied moving the little ones into the tunnel and away from the approaching beasts.

He looked at all the tiny bundles filled with little ones waiting to be born. There would be no way to get them all out. No chance to save them all before the creatures found a way past the music and into the building. His heart mourned at the thought; he could not bear the idea of it. Could not allow it to happen.

Simon knew others would be coming. But he did not believe they would come in time. Or if they did, they would make the situation more dire.

He thought the Groundskeepers, as fast and as strong as they were, would make too much noise as they approached. The creatures from the lake would hear them as they drew near and would finally attack the building. The babies.

Simon reasoned he was small and young, would pose no threat to the coming army of creatures. If Simon could keep their attention, he might be able to distract them until the Groundskeepers arrived.

Simon stepped out the front door and closed it softly. He wished for a way to lock them all in. But all he had was his small hatchet and his drummed-up courage. He stood still at the top of the steps and looked across the clearing. There were more of the beasts than before, over a dozen now. They watched him with something that vacillated between hatred and curiosity.

It was quiet, as if all the living things in the forest held their collective breath.

There was movement behind him.

Simon had not anticipated something may have already made its way to the great porch of the Hatchery. In his haste, he hadn't bothered to look around the corner where the porch wrapped behind the building.

Simon had time to turn and see the thing approaching him. It was shriveled and cracked, and its mottled skin seeped yellow pus. One of its arms was far too long, and it left a trail of blood where it dragged across the porch. It gibbered as it came, as fast and twitching as a nightmare.

The monster reached a long, clawed hand out and swung hard.

Simon felt something in his abdomen tear and open up.

He felt hot blood pour down on his feet.

Then, he felt nothing at all.

Chapter Sixty-Five

Ember

Ember came flying out the Hatchery door. When she found it unlocked, she knew where Simon had gone.

She staggered over him, bloody and still, and almost collided with the thing leaning in with a wide maw to begin its small meal.

Ember's own words flooded back to her in a black wave: *Sometimes, the little boy gets eaten. It depends on who tells the story.*

Ember was telling this story. It would not end that way.

Everything that happened next happened quickly.

Ember reached into her pocket and wrapped her hand around the mermaid's—*Ava's*—stone. She closed her eyes and thought about the calm, powerful place that grew in her chest, and she filled her bones and her blood and her tiniest nerve endings with it. The scars on her back pulsed.

She said the words to the prayer song. She thought about time, and all the spaces between time, and about the languid way it moved. In her mind, she slid into one of those spaces. And all the while, Ember thought about being invisible while a symphony filled all the spaces the calm and powerful hadn't.

The monster lost interest in Simon, turned its attention toward Ember.

Eyes closed, she couldn't see the creature that breathed, thick and wet, on her arms and shoulders and the vulnerable skin under the slits in her tunic. She couldn't see the creature while it circled her, but she could smell it. And the smell was rotten and fetid, all spoiled vegetables and grey, filmy meat. The creature was teeming with infection.

It *was* infection.

A blight.

The thing circled around and stood before her. Ember felt it, much taller than she was, lower its face until it was inches from her own. The smell intensified, and its cold wet breath left tiny beads of condensation on her cheeks and her eyelashes.

She thought of Selah, and her father and Uncle Joe, and what Selah had done to them. She could not empty this thing; she didn't know how. But she thought, perhaps, she could fill it.

With a speed that came with moving in the spaces between moments, Ember pressed her free hand against the beast's face. The skin was cold and loose on its skull. She pressed gently and, instead of emptying the creature, she filled it. She passed on calm and music and bright, white light. She filled the thing. And in filling it, she filled herself. And through the music that passed between them, she could just hear the beast scream its wretched, human scream. And still she did not open her eyes, did not see the monster that shuddered under her touch, and writhed, and pulled itself away, gravely injured.

She only opened her eyes again when she heard it *thump* to the wooden porch.

Simon was still there, lifeless at her feet.

Ember could not make a sound, could not force the prayer song from her throat. So she held him instead, the scared, brave little boy who was now gone to somewhere else. All that remained was a broken and bloodied shell. Ember held him anyway. She tried to fill him with the calm and the music and the bright, white light.

But instead of filling Simon, the light flowed through him, and out of him like smoke through a sieve.

Ember held Simon, and she cried. She cried for him, and for Gabby who might break in two when she learned her little brother was dead. She cried for Alma and for Selah, who would soon learn her friend was gone, if she didn't already know—if she wasn't gone, too. She cried for Hank who would have known what to do and for Mama who now had no children at all.

Ember cried because she had come to a place that was supposed to help her find herself, but she only kept losing everyone.

And then the forest erupted.

A battalion of Groundskeepers—warriors—crested the ridge and flew down toward the Hatchery.

April, 1989
Morning

I fear I have made a mistake.

I asked the island to swallow him.

I will go to him.

If he has grown too strong, I will leave him there.
If I must, I will kill him myself and end this experiment.
I can drown him like I drowned Ava when she became a problem.
It is ugly work, but a leader's burden sometimes means doing things others would not understand.
I fear I have made a mistake.

Chapter Sixty-Six

Sam

Following the monsters through the forest, Sam had done his best to keep what he thought was a safe distance. He did not anticipate more creatures might still be coming from the lake, coming behind him. When a pack of four approached through the woods, Sam heard them before he saw them. It gave him time enough to hide.

As they passed, he tried again to kill one. He chose what he took to be the frailest and weakest of the creatures. He focused all his hate and rage and directed it at the monster in the woods.

He could not kill it.

He could not injure it.

He did, however, piss it off.

The thing growled. Stock-still, it seemed to listen, and then sniff the air delicately with its absurd, horrible maw.

The creature approached Sam's hiding spot. It stared at him, into him, with deep-set eyes draped in skin and shadows. Sam could not see those eyes, but he felt them. Those eyes saw him.

Sam knew it was wary of him by the way it slunk forward, low to the ground. But forward it came. Close enough Sam could see open yellow sores where overhanging teeth bit into its lower jaw, pink drool seeping and running down either side. It gurgled somewhere deep in its throat, a noise both hungry and alien. The smell of the creature was all rancid lake water and entrails, sick and meaty.

Sam was saved when the leader of the small pack jabbered something, a high-pitched chattering that drilled into his bones, set his teeth on edge.

The thing snarled at Sam, a long, low sound, before it twisted away and lurched into the forest to follow the apparent alpha.

Sam waited until he felt reasonably sure the creature had gone. When he began again to follow them, he did it with more caution. And he was more aware of his surroundings, both ahead and behind.

As the trees thinned and the spaces between the trunks grew, Sam became more cautious still. He allowed the pack to get farther ahead of him, attempting a balance between safe distance and losing them entirely.

The forest ended and the enormous building full of random stuff—losting things, he now knew—loomed. The clearing was empty save the haunches of one of the beasts, visible for a moment as it disappeared over a ridge.

Sam ran for the trees behind the building. He would figure out his next move when he was sure no more of the impossible-to-kill creatures weren't following behind.

In the relative safety of the trees, with the monsters otherwise occupied, he took what he thought would be just a moment to enter the barren grey landscape of his mind.

A woman stood waiting for him there.

She was old and everything about her from her hair to her clothing to her papery skin was white. She had the look of a woman who had been strong in her youth, but age had stolen it from her and left her frail.

Most interesting of all, she was wingless.

"Beatrix."

"Ah, you've learned a thing or two since arriving. Yes, Beatrix." Her voice was strong.

"Why?" The one word was heavy with meaning, but it was all Sam could manage. He had always expected a group—a tribunal—was behind the Sounds. When he found out it was a single powerful woman, he expected her to be godlike. What he had not anticipated was this—an ancient and very human woman with a grandmother's face. *But not those eyes*, Sam thought. *Those are not grandmotherly eyes.*

"The short answer? Because I am finally dying and must choose a successor. As you can see by my lack of extra appendages, I am human. The Jury always is."

Sam began to stutter another question but was cut off.

"The Jury is human because the residents of the island are, for the most part, a kind and moral people. With their long lives and simple existence, they know they can't rightfully judge a human for their wants and desires. In our *whens*, our lives are short and nasty and often pointless. It is beyond the people of this island to understand why we treasure what we do, why we long for what seems to them inconsequential bits and baubles that we've lost. For that reason, a human is always selected as Jury. So that we may judge our own with better understanding and empathy."

Sam did not miss the mocking tone she used as she spoke the last words of her short speech.

"But *why*? Why torture me and destroy my life?" Sam heard his own voice rising, but it was beyond his control.

"Torture? Sam, don't be so dramatic. I wasn't torturing you; I was *grooming* you."

Sam faltered at that word.

"You have gifts that have nothing to do with this place, gifts that make you different and could make you very important or very dangerous depending upon how they are used. And this place is in need of a strong hand. The seekers seem to just want and whine more as the years pass, and the people of the island are soft and growing softer. We must punish seekers who deserve it, otherwise the far side of the lake would be left unguarded. Punishment is what they need. Punishment is what you'll give them."

Sam's mother's words flashed through his head. *I don't know if you are a good person or not. I don't know what kind of man you will be*, and shame washed over him. "There seem to be plenty of those monsters to guard anything the island needs them to. Even the far side. Even if it really is Hell." Sam was shaking. He wanted to punish this woman who had destroyed his life but, in that moment, he wanted answers more.

"You've met Isabis, then. Or Zane. They are the worst of the bunch, always debating what isn't theirs to question. Decisions belonging to those more important than them. Than even me." She shook her head. "We are permitted to serve the losting and the seeking—we are permitted to *exist*—only because we serve a purpose. We create the monsters that guard the lake. And as for the guardians, well, they eat one another, don't they? Without a constant supply we'd soon enough . . . run out." Beatrix lifted her hands with an indifferent *So what else can we do?* gesture. The woman's apathy stoked Sam's anger. "But we are off topic. We were talking about you."

"I want to hear it all. Who are you serving?" Sam said.

Beatrix dismissed him with a wave that made him want to reach out and hit her. "Where was I? Right. You, my friend, surprised me. When I lost control of you, I knew there was no way I could select you as Jury. But I also couldn't leave you as you were, a poorly made bomb waiting to go off. What if you had found this place on your own? What if you had found *me*? With all that righteous fury and splendid skill, I certainly couldn't let that happen. So I brought you to the lake and left you to your own devices."

"You thought I would die." Sam spat the words. The shame was long forgotten, and the familiar rage intensified, metastasized into something bigger. More.

"I did. Had every intention of killing you myself. But I must admit I let myself get distracted when you had your little insect massacre. It was terribly impressive and amusing, but I never believed you'd get far. I thought surely the island, or the lake guardians, or the people who live here would stop you before long. They'd never let you stay, you know. If they didn't kill you, they'd banish you to the far side of the lake. And it may not be Hell, but it's close enough."

"But you knew I could hurt them. Kill them."

Beatrix shrugged. "Yes, but I thought not *too* many before they managed to get rid of you. I see that I was wrong because you're still breathing, and here we are."

"Why didn't *you* kill me?"

"I don't have the power. Not in this place." There was real regret in Beatrix's voice as she gestured around the vast grey landscape. "I'm not gifted the way you are. Besides, when I visit you here—even as whole as I appear now—I make sure to leave a part behind where it will be safe. If I were to die here, it wouldn't be all of me. You do the same. There is part of you on the island right now."

"They've been looking for you, you know." Sam wasn't sure if he was threatening Beatrix or warning her. He hoped she was afraid.

She was not.

"They won't find me. I left myself in the Fountain. After making the . . . necessary adjustments, of course."

Much of what she was saying made little sense, but Sam understood what mattered. Beatrix hadn't made him what he was, but she had shaped him—groomed him. And then, when her *experiment* hadn't worked the way she'd hoped, Beatrix had abandoned him. Left him to die rather than face what she had created. Sam was a corrupted, lonely weapon, and Beatrix was the weaponsmith.

She must have read in Sam's eyes some of what he was thinking, because she said, "Remember, I can't fully die here."

And there, maybe, a hint of the alarm he wanted to see.

"Maybe. But this is the only you I know. The you in this place. This is where you tortured me. And where you left me." He stepped toward her, closing what little distance was between them.

Her eyes grew wary then, but she stood her ground. "You can't kill me. I made you. I won't allow it."

Sam leaned in close. He was gratified to see, at last, there was real fear in Beatrix's eyes. "Careless people get killed by their own guns all the time."

He watched the light in her silver eyes go out as he ended the part of her life he could reach.

Sam crouched now on the ridge overlooking the Hatchery, although he did not know the place had a name.

He was still shaking, adrenaline coursing through him where blood should be. He had found out the truth and had punished Beatrix for it. He would find the rest of the old woman and punish that part, too. And then, he thought, the rest of the island. Beatrix had made him, but this place and these people made her.

He would burn it all to the ground.

Even if that meant unleashing whatever hell was living on the other side of the island.

When Sam braved the ridge, he saw that the creatures had spread across the small valley, positioning themselves around the Hatchery.

Why the monsters were so interested in the wooden building at the base of the valley, Sam had no idea. He didn't particularly care aside from the fact they were now more interested in it than in him.

They were making steady progress until, without warning, they all stopped. There was something happening in the building below. Sam could not see it, nor could he hear it, but he felt it all the same. It was a vibration in the air, a disruption of the most basic specks and stuff he was made of. His very cells recoiled from it. It was now Sam who was suddenly and profoundly afraid.

When the winged child came out the front door, Sam supposed he could have warned him about the monster he shared the porch with. But that would have meant giving up his location to the horde, and to anyone else who might be interested. Sam did not intend to be caught; he had too much to do.

So, instead, Sam watched as the monster attacked the small figure. It was fast. There was a gush of blood and the child fell and was still. The lake monster bent over the form, to eat it, Sam was sure, when a second figure emerged from the door. This time it was a young woman—a girl. And she was wingless.

As Sam watched from his perch on the ridge, the girl flickered. There was no better word for it. Sam could see her, but she became less—less solid and less consistent. Like the end of a reel-to-reel film just before it runs out. Sam could almost hear the *click click clicking* of her. For a moment she disappeared entirely. Then there was a blinding pulse of white. It filled the porch she stood on. It filled the valley around the building. It filled Sam with a noise worse than the Sounds had ever made. The things in the valley recoiled as their comrade on the porch writhed and flailed and fell.

When it was over, the girl knelt on the porch, holding the dead child. The white light came again, but this time it swirled and eddied around the two figures.

Before Sam could recover, a flock of winged people passed overhead in such a rush that he felt the wind created by the rhythm of their wings, strong enough to stir the ground beneath them. They were in formation, and armed. They landed in the valley and began to slaughter the abominations that cowered there.

Some of the creatures fought back with tooth and claw, but they were outmatched. The day was full of the dying wails of monsters. And when they screamed, they sounded like people. Soon, the valley floor was matted with the thick black blood of the creatures from the lake, seeping down into the very fabric of the island itself.

The girl remained on the porch. She held the boy, and the white light still swirled, until one of the soldiers approached her. He crouched down, pulled her away. She struggled for a moment, then collapsed against him.

Sam raised himself up from the precipice of the ridge, ready to put distance between himself and the massacre in the valley. Whatever this was. Whatever *she* was, he needed to finish this. He needed to find the rest of Beatrix.

As he stood, the girl looked up.

Despite the distance between them, Sam could feel her eyes on him.

And, now seen, Sam knew he was marked.

Chapter Sixty-Seven

Ember

Ember felt hot eyes upon her.

She turned her face from Gideon's chest, looked past the bloodbath in the valley and up to the ridge above.

A dark-haired figure stood at the edge.

Fury, wild and dangerous, bloomed in her chest. The white calm was replaced by red, malignant rage.

Sam.

But something first.

Ember pulled away from Gideon, leaned over Simon. She kissed him tenderly on the temple.

As they had done for Alma, Ember would do for Simon. She pulled one of his wings as low as she could, covering the blood and the gaping hole in his stomach. The other wing she pulled up over his face, protecting his still-open eyes from the relentless sun and the growing heat of the day. In the small ritual she found her calm and power again. Heard the music of the white light.

"We will care for him," Gideon promised her.

"Where will you take him?"

"To the Fountain. He will be bathed there, blessed. The others will pay their respects."

"But the monsters . . ."

"Nothing else will harm him. You have my word."

Ember nodded. She had no choice but to believe the man with the now sad eyes. "I will meet you there."

Gideon knelt down to tend to Simon, then looking up thought of another question. "Where are you . . ." But the question would go unfinished. Because the girl who could have answered it was gone.

Ember moved in the spaces between moments. They were not so small after all, those spaces. They were vast. They were infinite.

Ember did not have wings of her own any longer, but she found she could, in her own way, fly.

Chapter Sixty-Eight

Miles

Miles dove in.

The Fountain was warm, and the boundaries between his skin and the water seemed to disappear.

He was at home in the water. He was fast, even while holding the staff in his hand. Miles swam straight down.

Light streamed through the clear water, enough to illuminate the way as he went deeper into the Fountain.

Like so many things on the island, the Fountain didn't make sense. From the outside it was contained in a neat circle in a small clearing. From within, it was endless. Miles hugged close to the side he had entered, could still see a wall of jagged rock there.

The world around Miles was silent, but he was far from alone. In the distance, vague silhouettes shifted with the gentle currents. Some were almost human. Others looked like the mutants from the lake. One could have been the double of the rat king in the tunnel, with too many arms and legs. They did not approach, nor did they swim away. They bobbed there, rising and dipping but staying where they were. *For now.*

Below and to the left, a shape emerged in the water. It was straight and square, not a jutting of rocks from the Fountain's wall. It was a cage. And there was something swimming in front of it. A white hand reached out of the cage, toward the thing.

Selah.

As humanoid as Ava, with a tilted head the creature peered at the hand and beyond it, into the cage. It reached out to touch the door.

As Miles approached, the creature took notice of him. It looked up and Miles was close enough to see it had a woman's eyes. The thing seemed to take him in, to consider him. Then it smiled a shark's smile before swimming away into the void of the Fountain.

Miles's lungs burned with the want of breath. He didn't have much time, would soon need to surface and get air.

First, he had to be sure.

The cage hung dangerously over the lip of a shallow ledge. He did not touch it for fear of tipping it over into the hungry gullet of the abyss below.

Inside, Selah sat near the back of the cage, leaned against its bars. She was, somehow, breathing. Not dead, not yet anyway. Miles could not tell if Selah saw him or not.

When she closed her eyes, a smile played on her lips. Her eyes rolled beneath their lids.

She's shutting down.

Miles reached for the door, prepared to open it just enough to get in the cage and get Selah out. The door, however, was locked.

Zebedee. That bastard.

When Miles broke the surface of the Fountain, all he could do was breathe.

Air filled his lungs and the spots that had formed before his eyes exploded into frenzied black swarms before fading and falling like dead stars.

Gabby leaned over to pull him out. Miles took her hand, then dragged himself over the rocks surrounding the Fountain and collapsed on the ground. He dropped his staff as he landed. The rocks had been biting and mean. Thin red lines now bled into one another on his stomach and chest.

"Locked." He gasped the accusation at Zebedee.

Zebedee, still at ease on the stone bench, raised an arched eyebrow. "The cage? Of course it is not. I left it unlocked. If Beatrix was to get to the girl, she could not very well do it through a locked door."

"Liar." Even as he said the word, doubt clouded Miles's mind. Maybe Zebedee was telling the truth. *The thing at the cage.*

It didn't matter. Right then all Miles cared about was getting Selah out of the cage and out of the Fountain. He could figure out the rest later.

"Give me the keys," Miles barked.

Zebedee scoffed. "I do not take orders from you, boy—"

"Give him the keys, Zebedee." Magdalene's voice, low and flat, was terrifying. Miles could not imagine saying no to that voice.

Neither, it seemed, could Zebedee. He reached into his tunic and pulled out a single key. "This is the only one." Zebedee dangled it before Miles. "Do be careful with it."

Gabby snatched the key from the man's fingers. She spun to Miles. "Do not do this. I will go find Gideon. You cannot . . ."

Miles, in turn, took the key from her. "No time. I saw her. Selah. She's dying. It's got to be now."

Gabby began to speak again, but Miles ignored her.

He breathed in deeply, out slowly. Another long breath and he was back in the water, going down.

The swimming was easier this time. He had, in his haste, left the staff in the grass now far above him. In his hand was just the small iron key.

The monsters in the water were still there, and they did not attack. But they were closer than before. Miles was sure of it.

At the cage again.

Selah had fallen over, was bent in half at the waist. Her dark hair rippled and hung over her face like the promise of a black shroud.

Out of time.

Miles moved the key to the lock as carefully as he could. An action complicated by his feet, which kicked in practiced rhythm, working to keep him from sinking into the blackness below.

The key and the lock made contact, but the key slipped over and away from the hole.

Miles tried again and missed completely.

Again, and this time the key began to slide in. As it did, Miles felt something glide against his right calf. He spasmed, jerked away from the thing that had caressed him.

And he dropped the key.

It sank straight down into the liquid night.

Miles turned to the face of a monster inches from his own. He screamed, as best as one can scream underwater, and pulled away. He did not get far. The monster with the woman's eyes grabbed his wrist and snatched him toward her.

As he freed himself from her grasp many things happened at once.

From below Miles, out of the midnight water, came a familiar white shape. Her pale hair streamed behind her. In an outstretched hand, Ava held the dropped key.

Miles took it from her. In their brief contact, Ava squeezed his hand.

He went back to the cage, but the monster grabbed him by the ankle and jerked him away.

Ava turned on the creature.

With claws extended, his mother-monster slashed at the arm holding Miles. Thick, dark blood defied gravity as it flowed up from the wound.

The creature released him and set after Ava.

Miles had no desire to watch the horror that must be happening between Ava and the other.

Selah was out of time. And so was he.

Miles knew whether he wanted to or not, he would have to surface soon. His body would demand it, would take over.

Miles grabbed the lock and inserted the key. Turned it. It stuck and he turned it again.

Stuck.

He turned it the other way, and the motion of the mechanism was smooth.

Idiot.

Miles went to Selah. He was careful not to step on the free hanging floor of the cage. He did not, however, consider what would happen when Selah's weight was removed from the other end. Miles drug her both back and up. He might later consider how he'd done it, where the stamina had come from, but there was no room for such thoughts in those long moments.

As Miles moved Selah, the cage began to list forward. It tipped to a forty-five-degree angle. Then farther still. With one last, impossible effort, Miles grabbed Selah under both her arms and swam through the moving target of the cage door. And because it continued to tip, Miles was forced to swim down and toward the black before he could move out of the shadow of the cage and then, finally, up toward the light. As Miles passed the cage, it stopped listing and, instead, fell straight down.

As he fought to make his way to the surface, Selah growing ever heavier, he passed Ava and the other. Ava seemed to have the upper hand, but the creatures in the distance were fast approaching.

Just before reaching the surface, Miles glanced into the deep one last time. Selah's eyes met his. And then she looked down.

Chapter Sixty-Nine

Selah

When Selah looked down, everything around her became focused and sharp. She was being brought to the surface. She saw the ledge she had rested on was long and shallow. She saw how deep—infinite, maybe—the water just past the ledge was.

And the cage. It was gone.

Two creatures tore at one another. Selah thought one of them might be Ava, the other the Beatrix thing. But before she could be sure, her face broke the water and sunlight flooded all around, blessing and blinding her.

Chapter Seventy

Sam

When the girl disappeared from the porch like a magician's trick, Sam knew he should run.

He turned toward the building looming behind him. It was a place to get lost in. A place to hide.

But between Sam and the building stood the girl. And she *was* just a girl, maybe fourteen. Tall and dark-haired, she had no wings on her broad shoulders, but she had the same silver-grey eyes of everyone he had encountered on the island. He thought her clothes might have been green, but they had gone almost black with the blood that still dried on them. The winged boy's blood.

"I've been looking for you." Her voice was low and rich with something both calm and enraged. And in that voice was the echo of the ghastly sound, the music, he had heard when she destroyed the monster on the porch. Her expression was impassive, aloof, and it, above all, scared him.

Sam was very afraid.

He wasted no time in trying to kill her.

All his hatred and anger and, now, fear, were directed at the center of the young woman's chest. He looked forward to burning her when he was done. But maybe he'd bring her back first. Make her dance and twitch a little like that rabbit.

"What are you trying to do, Sam?"

How did she know his name?

Sam reached in, pulled up all the hate for his father, the sick and broken love for his mother, all his loneliness, all the terrible nights lying awake wondering why the hell he was what he was. He pulled it all up, packed it into a bullet casing, and aimed it toward the center of the girl's chest.

He fired and, at last, a reaction.

A look of fatigued annoyance crossed her face.

It was maddening.

"I don't think you can kill me. Not like you killed the coyote. Not like you killed Alma. Not with your mind. If you want to kill me, you're going to have to use your hands."

She would have to burn, then.

Sam charged.

She stood her ground, waiting for him.

Sam did not stop to consider what that might mean, her willingness to be caught. He focused on nothing but grabbing hold of her and igniting her.

He seized her right, blood-streaked forearm. Her skin was weirdly cold in the growing heat of the day. Repulsive.

She did not burn.

Instead, she took hold of his forearm. They stood there, locked in a strange sort of handshake.

Then she smiled. It was a smile that held a secret, a surprise.

Still latched onto his arm, she pushed forward, shoving him and forcing him to backpedal, with speed and strength Sam was not prepared for.

Sam felt the ridge behind him disappear from under his feet. And then they were falling down the steep slope of the valley.

Chapter Seventy-One

Ember

Ember held tight to Sam.

His touch seared her arm. She expected it would leave a mark when he finally released her.

She knew Gideon was heading to the Fountain and would be taking Simon with him. She thought, hoped, others would be there as well. So in the languid swaths of time between falling from the ridge and landing on the steep slope of the valley, Ember guided Sam to the Fountain.

She put only gentle pressure on Sam's back, but it was enough to keep him walking alongside her.

The shocked expression he wore never changed. Eyes wide and lips parted, Sam was preparing for a scream that refused to break free. Ember wondered if in his mind they were still falling. She wondered what that was like for him. A part of herself she was not proud of hoped it was terrible. The mottled bruise spreading across the side of his face, the scratches and contusions on his arms, and the filthy clothes he wore told her his time on the island had already *been* terrible.

As Ember led Sam to the Fountain, she could not help but take in the beauty that surrounded them. In these wide, timeless spaces the world took on a watercolor quality. Trees bled into grasses into sky into shadows and flashes of pale gold sun. There were no hard lines here, and everything was connected, a part of everything else.

I could live in this place forever.

And, perhaps, she really could.

Time must have moved in the spaces between moments, but how quickly, or even in what direction, was a mystery to unravel. Ember thought she might be like a leaf on a stream, twisting in the eddies of time, bouncing occasionally off the random moment of a stone that broke the surface. She might live forever here, but it would be a long and lonely life.

No. It was not a life she wanted, but it made for a lovely morning walk.

When they reached the Fountain, Ember took in the scene around her. Dead monsters and Groundskeepers. Zebedee on a bench. Magdalene standing with wide eyes and a hand over her mouth. Gabby reaching for Miles. No, Gabby was reaching for Selah as Miles struggled to lift her out of the Fountain. Selah was alive and the look on her face told Ember she was seeing the end of something terrible.

Taking a deep breath, Ember prepared to step back into time.

When she did, chaos spun around her.

And Sam released the scream he'd been holding in for so, so long.

Chapter Seventy-Two

Selah

When Selah broke the surface of the Fountain, she tried to breathe and found she could not. Her body was entirely full of water. So she coughed and gagged instead. Water poured out of her. There was more water than seemed possible, it came out of her lungs and her stomach and her sinuses. When the air finally replaced water, it seared her saturated throat. She coughed and coughed with almost no time for breath in between, and it was the breath she so craved.

As she fought her own body for air, bright lights exploded behind her closed eyes. Her oxygen-starved brain began to fire rapidly and epileptically. She saw flashes of the hallucinations that plagued her in the Fountain. Of the water monsters, great and small, lined up like soldiers in the deep. Of the thing that shared her ledge, skulking in the farthest corners.

Of the glimpses of a smile and a hand.

Of the thing with Beatrix's eyes.

And then she knew. Or she knew part of it, anyway.

She forced her body to take a deep, steady breath. Then another. She opened her eyes and saw the Fountain was surrounded. Among the crowd was Zebedee, and Magdalene leaning over him shouting about something Selah did not understand.

Miles was climbing out of the Fountain dressed in his undergarments.

Ember held a strange boy by the arm, and he held on to hers.

There was a calm strength in Ember's eyes Selah had never seen before.

The boy screamed like a caught animal.

And Gabby. Gabby locked eyes with Selah and broke into an exhausted smile.

And where was Simon?

But Selah could think of nothing but Beatrix in the Fountain. She was not gone, not yet. Without the benefit of what the others knew, she still believed her leader and former keeper to be in danger.

Beatrix was at the cage. Trying to unlock it. Is that right? That must be right.

Selah did not have time to debate with herself.

Beatrix, whatever remained of her, needed saving.

Then, without allowing herself the opportunity to reconsider, Selah dove from the rock ledge and back into the Fountain. In the brief moment, she registered a scream, but was unsure if it belonged to Gabby or to Miles. It was impossible to tell over her own.

Chapter Seventy-Three

Ember

Ember had made a mistake.

Bringing Sam to the crowded Fountain had put them all in danger. He could not kill her, but he had proven she was the exception.

So Ember tightened her grip on his arm. She stepped back into the in-between spaces, moved Sam away from the Fountain before he turned it into an abattoir.

As she pulled, Sam surprised Ember by pulling back. He did not pull away from her, instead, he pulled her toward him.

He wore the smile of one who had just remembered a nasty joke and couldn't wait to share it with someone else. That someone was Ember. He reached up with his free hand, pulled her head toward him roughly so he could speak in her ear. "My turn."

The watercolor forest disappeared. Ember found herself in a grey place. Sky and land the same color, the color of nothing at all. The landscape, unblemished, went on forever in every direction.

Except.

Except there was one thing that stood out against the bleak and blank.

A woman, crumpled and clearly dead, was in a heap almost at their feet. She lay in a puddle the same color as the ground around her, water running in lazy rivulets down her narrow body.

It was Ember's turn to be afraid.

Chapter Seventy-Four

Sam

Sam was not sure it would work, bringing Ember to his barren landscape.

When it did, he was rewarded with the abject fear that replaced her smug smile.

Sam knew if he could kill her at all, it could only be in this place. Whatever the girl was, she was different. Different like him, and not like him at all.

Sam smiled, a real smile that for a moment made his gaunt face handsome. "I'm a little sorry to kill you. You're interesting." He released her then. She took two steps back and tripped over the body on the ground.

The girl landed hard, but the ground had an unpleasant, spongy quality that broke her fall. "Who was she? Your mother?"

Sam laughed. "Sort of. She raised me in a way. Brought me here."

Her eyes grew wide, as if his words made sense to her. "*Beatrix?*" she asked.

The girl knew far more about him than he did her. "Part of her, anyway. I'll be looking for the rest when I'm done with you." Sam pulled his foot back and kicked the dead woman like he was punting a ball.

The girl winced.

"Don't be sad for Beatrix. She was evil. I might be evil, but she . . . She. Made. Me." Sam kicked the body with every word.

"Stop it!" the girl cried.

Beatrix had warned him the people here were soft. Sam shrugged. "Okay." And then he did the one thing he knew he could do in this place; he killed the girl.

Only, she still wouldn't die.

He rushed at her then, tackled her. He put both hands on her shoulders and turned all the fierce and flaming thoughts into her.

In her own way, she burned.

Chapter Seventy-Five

Selah

Selah had been wrong. Her wings did not sink her like a stone, but they were heavy and unwieldy in the water. She headed straight down, knowing the ledge she had rested on must be below her.

To the right, Ava was punishing what was left of the creatures that had been lined up like soldiers in the distance. Even as Selah watched, a number of them drifted down, into the deep black forever of the Fountain. Strings and bubbles of dark blood poured from their mangled carcasses. Two remained, and Ava seemed to be making quick work of them.

Selah saw the ledge approaching, and the figure resting on it. The Beatrix thing was not yet dead, but she was very close. Her body was gashed and broken. It bled little now, which Selah took as a bad sign indeed. An ashen and tired face that was almost familiar smiled up at Selah, thin arms reached out to her through the water.

Selah wrapped her arms around the frail creature and pushed up off the ledge. She rose, but only a few feet. Beatrix, in her new body, was far heavier than she had ever been before. Selah began kicking, tried to beat her wings in the water. It was no good. They stayed where they were.

Beatrix put a hand on Selah's cheek, turned her head to face her. *Are you a good girl after all?* Beatrix mouthed the words. She was smiling, her eyes unreadable. *You should leave me.*

No, Selah replied. *I will not.* Even as she said it, Selah wondered if she would have a choice. The effort of moving both herself and the other woman up and through the water was depleting what little oxygen remained in her system.

She knew she would be forced to make a decision soon. But not yet.

Selah tried one last time, and in doing so she emptied her reservoir. She rose ten feet, twelve, and for a moment thought they both might have a chance. Then the weight and the water took hold, and they sank back down to the ledge.

Selah screamed in rage and frustration, and the sound was swallowed by the Fountain.

Useless girl. You forever disappoint me, the Beatrix thing mouthed. This time, Selah heard the words, or at least their message. It was suddenly, horribly clear. This beast was not Beatrix, not any longer.

It smiled, and then it lunged.

The creature lashed out and tore at Selah, at her wing. A ragged gash appeared down its center, the wing almost severed in two. Selah howled without sound in the void of the Fountain.

She shook the Beatrix thing off her. Fought and kicked and twisted one grasping hand hard enough she felt the beast's fingers break.

It was Beatrix's turn to howl. She released Selah, grasping her broken hand with her good one. As she did, she sank down to the ledge below.

Selah, left with just the one good wing, sank with her.

When they reached the ledge, Selah backed away from the precipice, and the Beatrix thing crawled toward her, her broken hand held protectively up against her chest.

When the thing was close enough, Selah charged her. She wrapped her arms around Beatrix and threw them both over the edge and into the abyss.

If I am to die, so are you.

And, falling into the midnight water, Selah knew she *would* die, but did not want to die cradling the creature.

So she let her go.

Heavier than Selah, she sank into the black beyond.

Selah closed her eyes, not wanting to see what came next.

Then, there were strong arms pulling her up, away from the black forever.

She opened her eyes to find Ava holding her, saving her.

In a few long moments, the two of them broke the surface of the Fountain. Countless strong hands pulled Selah up and out of the water.

There was a cacophony as some screamed to kill the creature, while others screamed louder, *No! It is Ava! She saved her!*

Selah reached for Ava, pulled with what strength she had left, wanting the others to see. To see this was no monster, this was Ava. Gabby and Miles rushed to them, turned to face the others, to explain.

Let them do it, then. Let them tell it. Selah collapsed. Her ruined wing crumpled beneath her, sang a song of high-pitched pain.

It would mend. Maybe.

Through the noise of her mangled wing, just before losing consciousness, Selah had the distinct thought she had never felt anything as wonderful as the hard, dry ground beneath her.

Chapter Seventy-Six

Gabby

Gabby was not the first to see Gideon approach. But she was the first to know who it was he carried with him.

"Simon . . ." The word was a moan.

She rushed to meet Gideon where he landed. With gentle, reverent hands, he laid the boy down on the soft grass in the clearing.

"Oh . . . no. No. *Simon.*"

"Gabrielle, we were too late . . ."

"No." An irrational resolve overtook her. "He is not dead. Not yet." She dropped to the grass, reached for her little brother's wings, to pull them back and show Gideon and everyone else that Simon was fine. Would be fine.

Gideon stopped her with a firm hand. "Gabrielle. He is gone. I carried him here. I am sure." *And I do not want you to see what is underneath his wings.*

"We could take him to the Fountain," she whispered. "If there is something in him that remains, it might live on . . ."

Gideon was kind but unbending. "And what, Gabrielle? Live on in the Fountain as a monster?"

Gabby's eyes pleaded with Gideon to do something. Anything. All she could manage was, "How?" Gabby forced herself to stand tall and straight even as grief wrapped cold, steel fingers around her rib cage.

"Creatures from the Fountain, or the lake, were at the Hatchery. The one that . . . it was seconds away from entering. If Simon had not arrived when he did and confronted the beast, it would have killed many of the Hatchery keepers. The little ones. There would have been nothing any of them could do to stop it. He is a hero, Gabrielle."

Gabby nodded. Her body thrummed with anguish. She vibrated with it. Gabby did not want Gideon to see her cry, but it was not her choice to make. "I am so . . . I cannot. I do not want him to go. He is . . . He is *my* Simon."

"I know, Gabrielle. There is nothing I can say that will make this any better for you. Know we will take care of him, now and after."

Miles joined them then. "Oh no," he moaned. "Oh no. Gabby, no. He was just a little kid. How?" Miles pushed his palms hard into his face.

Gabby had little room in her throat for words. "He is a hero. And everyone will know it."

She took a deep, trembling breath. "Gideon, when this is over, I am coming to find you. If there are more creatures on the island like the one that took my Simon, I am going to help you to kill them. And I will not go back to shepherding seekers to and from the Fountain like a trained dog. I am joining you to protect the island."

Gideon nodded, looked into her reddened eyes. "We would be glad to have you, Gabrielle. You will make a fine Groundskeeper. Your talents are wasted as a shepherd."

"And he will not be cremated." Here, Gabby's voice broke. When she pulled the shards back together there was a hint of the commanding presence she would become. "I do not care about custom. He will be buried in the cemetery under a tree. Simon loved that place very much. He found magic in it."

Gideon turned to her and met her eyes. "Yes. I promise."

Then, an afterthought, Miles asked, "Where is Ember?"

Chapter Seventy-Seven

Ember

Ember felt the heat and the hatred course through her.

In it, she tasted every awful and broken part of Sam, and every moment of pain that had honed him into the wicked, sharp thing he had become.

It coursed through her, but it did not fill her. The cool and calm were too ingrained now, twisted into her nerves and her tissue and filling the smallest gaps in her marrow. There was no room for the heat, so it built up until it exploded.

Ember pushed Sam off with a new kind of strength. She stood, towering over him as he scrambled to get up. He rushed her again, this time placing his hands on her chest, over her heart.

Ember did scream then. She screamed as her back tore open along the old scars. Those scars split apart at the seams and from them came all the heat and hatred, but it was soon burned off and replaced with a cool and white calm. Ember's back no longer hurt at all. It glowed with a sweet sort of numbness, a vibration, a rightness.

Sam retreated, awe spread over his face. Awe and something like bitter envy.

From Ember's scars, the cool and the calm became wings of white flame. They spread out behind her, ghost wings where her real ones should have been. The ghosts of the wings her father had removed so many years before. The wings he never spoke of but hated her for.

"What are you?" Sam asked.

Ember thought about it for a moment. "I don't know. What are *you*, Sam?"

Sam had an answer at the ready. "A curse. A weapon. A mistake."

"Me too, maybe." And she was upon him.

Ember pulled the knife from her tunic pocket. She lifted it high and drove it deep into the center of his right hand, so deep the hilt bit into his skin. So deep the blade pinned him to the strange soft ground.

Sam wailed like a creature caught in a mean-toothed trap. He struggled to pull the knife out, to pull his hand up, but the blade was fast. There was no blood. The metal so cold it burned and cauterized the wound.

As Sam wrenched and twisted and barred his teeth at her, Ember removed Ava's stone from her pocket. She rose into the air then, only a few feet but it was enough.

Sam couldn't look away.

She dove straight down, truly a weapon in that split second. She rammed Sam's chest with the stone and did not relent. She pushed down and something in Sam's ribs cracked.

She pressed harder.

It was not, it turned out, only Sam's rib cage that broke. It was also the very ground beneath him.

Ember continued to bear down, the stone between her hand and Sam's chest. As she pressed, the ground under him gave way and they both began to sink rapidly into a hole that had not been there before.

The hole grew deeper, wide enough to allow both them and Ember's great ghost wings. She was flying straight down, forcing Sam into what was becoming a deep, dry well. And with them came the bleak landscape, pulling like fabric into the hole.

As they sank, evenly set stones formed around the sides of the well. Black moss grew here and again in the mortar. The opening was a perfect grey circle above them. They sank very far indeed, until the landscape had no more fabric to give.

At the bottom, Sam was still pinned to the ground by the blade in his hand.

Ember breathed hard. She removed her hand from Sam's chest and, with it, the stone, which she returned to its place in her pocket. She pulled herself into the air, feet beyond Sam's reach.

"Are you going to leave me here?" He panted through the pain in his hand, the pain in his chest.

Ember nodded.

"You'll come back for me. Someone will find me. And then I'll find a way to kill you."

Ember considered this, shook her head. "I don't think so. After all, this place is all in your head."

And then she rose, up and up through the terrible well. Sam screaming threats at her as she went. By the time she reached the top, she could no longer hear him. Because he had stopped or was too far down to be heard, she wasn't sure.

Outside, the bleak landscape had been replaced with a watercolor forest. The well stood in the center of a small grove of trees. It was a replica of the one back on the farm, the place she'd first met Ava.

She knew this place, this space between the moments where trees and sky mingled and caressed one another. Sam might be trapped in his own mind, but he was also in a world that belonged to Ember. She knew how to leave this place, but she knew where to find it, too. Ember thought she might come back occasionally, just to be sure things were as they should be.

She walked for a time, savoring the wide and quiet spaces. And she thought about her last conversation with Alma. The woman had held her close and told her in a voice only Ember could hear, "You are made for this place, and it for you. Selah saw it when she found you. A light so bright it led her to you. You would make a magnificent Jury. But not if you do not want it. The choice is always, always yours."

Ember didn't know if Alma was right or not, but her words were said with love, and it was that love Ember would remember. She did not want it, wanted nothing so grand. A wooden building with dancing light and prayer songs and down-winged little ones called to her. She hoped she would be able to answer it.

Chapter Seventy-Eight

The Fountain

When the last parts of Beatrix died, somewhere in the unexplored deep of the Fountain, there was no one with her to bear witness. Nonetheless, all those at the Fountain knew.

The falls stopped running as if switched off from the source.

Out of the woods a beast, cracking and withered, slunk into the clearing. Gabby lifted her knife to attack, but Gideon stopped her. "We need to know what it will do."

The thing ignored them all, climbed over the edge of the Fountain and slipped noiselessly into the water. It was followed by another, and that creature did the same.

After that, they knew the beasts were done attacking. With Beatrix no longer at the helm, the creatures knew only to return to the Fountain to await their orders from the next Jury.

A third creature came from the woods. That one they slaughtered. And all the others to follow.

They would work late into the night, and pyres would burn.

Chapter Seventy-Nine

Miles

As Miles stood back and watched the chaos and tried to understand how the little red-haired boy with the giant green wings could be dead, Ember stepped out of nowhere and into the clearing. She was filthy and covered in what had to be crusted blood. *Simon's blood.* And for a fleeting moment he could have sworn she had wings, huge and bright. But then they were gone, and he forgot what it was he thought he'd seen.

Gabby approached and Miles did the only thing he could. He put his arms around her, held her close.

"He is a hero. And everyone will know it," she said into his chest.

All Miles could do was nod. He had no words for the dead boy and his brokenhearted sister.

After a time, "Gabby, does this mean it's over? In my *when*, too?"

She lifted her head. "I think so. The beasts are returning to the Fountain, and your strangers will return to the lake. Beatrix led them, and she is gone now. The next Jury . . . it will be different. It must."

"Then I have to go home. To my parents. My mom. I . . . I don't even know if she's still . . . and if she is I have to protect her." Miles thought of the blade he'd wielded and the blood he'd drawn and knew he could if he had to. "I don't want to be here. This place was Ava's real home, but it isn't mine. There's too much . . . there's just too much here."

Gabby smiled through her tears. "We will get you home, to your *when*. It is good you are going. Know you will always be remembered and will always be welcomed." Gabby took Miles's hands and looked into his reddened eyes. "But I do not think you will come back, will you?"

"No. No, I don't think so. I found what I needed. Thank you for that, Gabby. Thank you for helping me find Ava."

Gabby embraced Miles, wrapping her wings around him tight as she could. "Simon loved you, Miles. And so do I. I wish for you the happiest of lives and for you to be at home in your world. You do not need this place." Gabby held Miles closer for just a moment, let him go.

She left him then to check on Selah. When she turned and walked away from him, she walked toward her new life. She was a warrior, and Gideon was lucky to have her.

Miles knew he was losing Gabby as he watched her go, but he did not watch for long. She had her future to find, and he had his.

He was no longer lost.

Chapter Eighty

Ember

Miles and Ember sat together in the grass, as far away from the Fountain as the clearing would allow.

They watched as a dozen Groundskeepers took their places around its edge. They each had knives, or spears, or bows. Gabby stood with them, also armed.

Amid the chaos, Zebedee had disappeared. "We will find him." Gideon assured them. "The island is finite. Zebedee is a smart man, but he has a tendency toward cockiness. And the Groundskeepers do not miss much. He will be found."

They watched as Selah was taken away to the Infirmary. Ember would have to do the awful job of telling her about Alma soon enough, but not this night.

"What are you going to do?" Ember did not look at Miles as she spoke to him. She did not look at anything anyone else could see. Her eyes were focused on the middle distance, at a place that was only for her.

"I'm going home. I just . . . I don't know what I'll find when I get there."

Ember nodded, saying nothing, not giving voice to the part of herself that envied him having a home to return to.

Miles picked at the grass between his legs. "What are you going to do?"

Ember absently rubbed the handprint-shaped burn on her forearm and thought about how to answer him. She decided on the truth. "I hope I will stay here. I still have things to take care of. I hope they will let me. Stay, I mean. But I don't know. I think Selah would want me to."

Ember deliberated, and then decided the whole truth was in order. "I don't have a family anymore. My dad is . . . gone. And my mother hasn't been there for a long time. My brother killed himself last year, and everything . . . And I have . . . *had* this uncle . . . anyway. So, strange as it sounds, I think Selah is my family. Gabby, too. Not like my sisters exactly, but that's close enough. I hope they will help me convince the others to let me stay. I think I would like to work in the Hatchery, to take care of the babies. I think I would be good at it. I mean, I already know the song and everything." Ember smiled weakly at Miles.

"What was your brother's name?"

"Harrison. But we called him Hank."

"I'm sorry about Hank."

"Thanks, me too. He was my most special person. He was my whole family."

They allowed a short silence to sit between them.

Ember said in a sad, soft voice, "You remind me of him. Of Hank."

Miles was quiet for a moment as he wiped at his eyes. "Thank you." He wrapped his arm around her and pulled her close.

Ember smiled just a little. "I think I'm as lost as they come."

Miles was stern. "No. You're not lost at all. This place found you because it needed you. And you need it, too. You belong here, Ember. I know it."

Ember leaned her head on his shoulder, closed her eyes. *I hope you are right.*

"Do me a favor?" Miles had a question he seemed hesitant to ask.

"Probably." She smiled a little.

"Take care of Ava. I'm not . . . I'm not her son. Not really. Not anymore. But she needs to be a mom. She deserves it."

Ember's chest hitched. She sobbed as quietly as she could, but was sure Miles knew. All she could do was nod. She needed a mother as badly as Ava needed to be one.

Miles turned to Ember. "I'm going home. But, you know, there's a part of me that kind of wants to stay. I honestly just want to see what happens next here. How things turn out."

Ember nodded. "Me too." She leaned into him, her surrogate big brother. "And I guess, if you're needed, you'll come back?"

He waited a long time before nodding.

They sat that way together for a long while, watching the Fountain, and thinking of things lost and things found.

EPILOGUE

Found

Gabby

There was much for Gabby to learn.

She would need to know the plants of the island and what to do with them. Which to eat, which could heal, and which could poison and kill. She would need to know the wild animals and the menagerie. She would need to know the paths that existed between the trees and the streams, the paths that were not mapped and those that were not named.

Gabby would learn to hunt and stalk and hide. She would learn to defend herself, and others, and the many ways to take a life. She would learn to be alone most of the time, and part of the group when called.

In time, she would get stronger and faster.

Gideon told her, more than once, "Gabrielle, you cannot do this work if you are angry. Do this for Simon, because he would be proud. Do not do it to avenge him. The beast that killed him is already dead."

"Yes, Gideon."

But Gabby *was* angry. And the anger was hers to do with as she wished. She would embrace her anger and hone it. It would become a tool and a weapon.

She would honor Simon; she would make him proud. And, regardless of what she told Gideon, she would find a way to avenge her little brother.

Simon

Isabis entered the clearing at dawn.

She walked to the tree with the newest plaque. It read *Our Simon.* Isabis brushed off dust that was not there. It was still bright and golden, with no patina at its edges.

She sat on a low stone bench and opened a book. It was worn with time and with many readings. The name *Robert Frost* was engraved in the leather cover. The book once belonged to someone who visited this place. Now he was buried here, and she was the reader.

Isabis opened the book to a marked page and began to read to Simon, to all of them.

"Nature's first green is gold,

Her hardest hue to hold.

Her early leaf's a flower;

But only so an hour.

Then leaf subsides to leaf.

So Eden sank to grief,

So dawn goes down to day.

Nothing gold can stay."

Isabis read until the sun was higher, brighter in the sky. The plaques shone like stars where the light caught them. They slowly, slowly rose to meet the sky.

Miles

Because there was no Jury, there was no bridge to carry them across the lake, so they dragged a small boat to the water and took turns rowing.

At the shore, Miles climbed out and, feet back on ground he understood, turned to thank Gabby one last time.

She was gone. As was the lake and the island within.

Miles felt regret threaten to fill his chest. He knew he'd made the right decision, but that did not make it easy nor uncomplicated.

Miles ran home.

The day was blistering. Spring had become hot days of mid-summer in the time Miles had been gone.

The streets he ran and the neighborhoods he passed were oddly quiet.

Some houses looked abandoned, others fortified.

Birdbaths were overturned in some yards. Or smashed.

The people living in the big white house on the corner had filled their koi pond in with dirt and rocks.

Miles wondered just how bad things had gotten.

He ran faster.

At his front door he hesitated before ringing the bell. Wanting so badly to see who would be there waiting for him. So afraid to discover someone wasn't.

The door opened and, inside, his mother. She'd lost weight and was pale from days spent inside wandering the house, waiting.

Miles almost knocked her over with the force of his embrace.

She leaned her face against his shoulder, held him so hard he thought his ribs might crack.

They stood like that for a while.

And then, "Eighty-seven days, baby. I thought . . ." Her voice broke apart.

"I'll explain it all. I promise."

She pulled away and looked up at Miles, placed a hand against his face. He leaned into that hand, all the while thinking of another mother he'd held the very same way.

"Were they true? The stories Ava told?"

Miles didn't know how she knew.

He thought about lying.

He chose the truth. "Yes."

"Are you . . . staying?"

"I promise."

Fresh tears filled her eyes. She only nodded.

They went inside, Miles closing the door to his home behind them.

There were five locks to engage where before there had been just one.

Ember and Selah

Ember and Selah walked for a long time. Sometimes they spoke, but, mostly, they were silent. It was comfortable, the quiet between them.

It was nearing dusk when they reached a part of the island Ember had not visited before. It was a wild and rugged place with cliffs that dropped sharply to the water below.

From this vista, the lake was enormous. A small sea. Ember had not understood how huge it truly was. Far in the distance, jagged mountains cut into the sunset. Somewhere below them, objects too far away to identify glittered in the retreating sun like a thousand scattered jewels.

As she looked out upon a mountain range she could not name, a question returned to Ember, a question she had upon seeing the island for the first time in her daddy's wheat fields. She had forgotten about it until this moment.

"Selah, what is there? What is on the other side of the lake?"

Selah considered the question. The answer was complicated. She stood shoulder to shoulder with her friend, looking out across the water.

"For another time, Ember. For another time. I promise."

Zebedee

Zebedee stood on the shore of a land he never planned to visit.

The flight to the far side of the lake had been a long one, and dangerous, but staying on the island had not been an option, had it?

Zebedee was certain he had been spotted, and then tracked, long before he landed. It was only a matter of time before those condemned to live here approached.

Or attacked.

Zebedee was not concerned. He was sure he could, with minimal effort, demonstrate he was not a man to be challenged. He was not afraid to get a bit of dirt, or blood, on his hands.

Zebedee stood on the shore, looking across the vast lake toward the island he had fled.

Behind him, on the rocky beach, finally came the footsteps he anticipated.

A small group of men and women crept toward Zebedee, each armed with weapons, some crude and some sophisticated.

In the dying light of sunset, Zebedee turned to face them. He opened his wings wide and rose into the air. The small, bedraggled army never stood a chance.

When it was over, Zebedee rinsed his hands in the lake.

He stepped over the bodies now littering the shore, picking up the sharpest of the blades that had been dropped. This, he did not bother cleaning. *Let them see the blood.*

He made his way toward the sprawling encampment in the distance.

Here, with no one to follow, he thought perhaps he could rule instead.

Sam

Sam looked up from the bottom of a deep, dry well.

Far, far above him was a small circle of bright blue and white light. It was a watercolor sky. The smell of dry leaves and dirt, so arid it was powder, rose around him.

On the ground something glinted. Sam reached down and picked up a smooth, sharp chunk of what felt like warm glass. It shone pink and grey, softly illuminated from within. Dozens of similar crystals littered the space around him. They were important, he thought, part of something greater.

Sam picked up the pieces within his reach and placed them in his pockets and they *clink clink clinked* as he did. Their weight was comforting, grounding. Sam knew these things belonged to him and, he thought, completed him somehow.

He would not lose them again. Sam sat in the dirt in this place his mind had created and closed his eyes.

In the quiet there was the shadow of a sound.

Sam pressed his ear to the stone well wall. Somewhere behind it was the unmistakable sound of moving water.

Sam tried again to pull the knife out of his hand. He thought he felt it give. Not much, but he was almost sure it moved.

If he could get the knife out.

If he could chip away at the mortar between the stones.

If he could get to the water beyond the well.

If he could find the water, follow it to the source.

Sam might yet reach the Fountain.

He pulled again. And he was sure, this time, the blade moved.

Acknowledgments

One spring day, many (many . . .) years ago, I was out on a playground when a little boy brought me a pink plastic barrette and asked, "Miss Lora, where's the losting fountain?" He of course meant "lost and found," but that didn't matter. It was too late. The notion of a losting fountain was firmly planted in my mind. It took me years—too many years—to sort out what a place like that might be like, who would serve it and seek it, and what its real purpose might be. Over time the story itself became simpler but the world it took place in became darker and more complex and, I think, more human.

This book has been over twenty years in the making and for most of those I never thought my story would be more than an ever-changing file on my computer. Because of that, there have been countless people who have read bits and pieces, false starts and stilted endings. People who listened to me talk about it or encouraged me in ways big and small. To each of you I am grateful. The problem with musing over a project for this long is that I know I'm about to leave people out. For that I am sorry. This is me doing my best.

To my genius editor, Ardyce Alspach—thank you for understanding what this story could be, for having a vision for it, and for believing it was worth telling. Yours were the wise eyes and heart I needed to help me find the story's shape. This book is a thing in the world because of you and I am forever grateful.

To my friend and agent, Ali Herring—thank you for taking a risk on me all those years ago. You saw something in this story or me or both that no one else did. I'm proud to be building my career with you as my partner and am so grateful to you and for you.

To all the brilliant people I have yet to meet but owe so much to: Grace House, Renee Yewdaev, Amelia Mack, Rich Hazelton, Melissa Farris, Sandy Noman, Lisa Forde, and Tracey Keevan—thank you for turning my strange little story into a beautiful book. I appreciate you all.

To my dear friends and writing group, Jessica Conoley, Paula Gleeson, and Kellie McVeigh McQueen—you gave me fortitude when I couldn't find it for myself. Kellie, you'll always be with me and in my stories. I love you three a whole lot.

To the generous and talented author, Kurt Kirchmeier—thank you for reading an early-ish version of this story. Your writing inspires me and I trust your storytelling instincts completely. I am so glad to know you and call you a friend.

To some of my favorite people in the world: Anna Gamble, Courtney Morse, Georgia Oswald, Darlene Shinskie, Judy Senf, Stacy Shearer, and Bonnie Glantz—thank you for reading one of the many iterations of this tale. Thank you for your feedback and your encouragement and patience (so much patience). I love you all.

To my parents, Tom and Darlene Shinskie—thank you for teaching me the importance and power of words. I love you.

To my family—Miriam and Martin and Pete—thank you for going on this big, unpredictable journey with me. Every story I tell is as much yours as it is mine. I love you forever.

To the storytellers who taught me to love story for its own sake—there are too many of you to name but your words have shaped the way I tell my own stories to the world. Thank you.

And, reader—if you've made it this far—thank you. Ray Bradbury said, "Love is the answer to everything. It's the only reason to do anything. If you don't write stories you love, you'll never make it. If you don't write stories that other people love, you'll never make it." Sometimes it's all very simple—we tell stories for no reason other than we love them and hope that someone somewhere in the world will love them as well. I am grateful you let me tell this one to you.

About the Author

LORA SENF is a writer of dark and twisty stories for all ages. She is the author of *The Clackity*, Bram Stoker Award winner *The Nighthouse Keeper*, and *The Loneliest Place*. She credits her love of words to her parents and to the public library that was walking distance from her childhood home. Lora finds inspiration for her writing in that strange place between sleep and wakefulness, on road trips through Montana, and, once, while crossing a lake that was much larger than it appeared from shore. She lives in Eastern Washington with her husband and their twins. Their house may or may not be haunted.

Content warning
This book depicts animal death, gore, and themes related to suicide. Please take care.